THE SADNESS

BENJAMIN RYBECK

The Unnamed Press
Los Angeles, CA

For My Buddy (Ch-Ch, Ch-Ch)

Dear sir,

I write to you regarding my film, The Glazen Shelves, *so forgive me if I stumble—whenever one describes cinematic artistry of the highest order, words seem inadequate. Nevertheless, I must attempt to convey the nature of my film, the end result being that you, justifiably impressed, will provide the necessary support to finish it.*

To summarize the plot of The Glazen Shelves *proves difficult, for the film's greatness lies not in its story but rather its atmosphere, evoking the same decadence as Fellini, the same humanity as Renoir, the same dread as Haneke. It centers on a young man named Aaron, a resident of Portland, Maine. He goes to a high school where idiots surround him—wealthy idiots who imbibe spirits, ingest pharmaceuticals, and harass Aaron for not wanting anything to do with their foul preoccupations. Aaron, being intellectually beyond these people, desires some form of stronger connection—to be around somebody who respects him and wants to hear what he has to say, instead of being around his foolish peers, who don't appreciate his originality and genius. Enter Natalie, whom Aaron meets and befriends. She is the opposite of those cretins who cram the hallways of his high school, and she bonds with him through a shared love of cinema. The film is an ode to their beautiful, pure friendship.*

Now, as to the reason The Glazen Shelves *sits unfinished: I began it several years ago, when I was in high school. I played the role of Aaron, and my best friend, Evelyn, played the role of Natalie. We shot roughly half of the film before unforeseen circumstances tragically ended the production. I had given up on the project, until this past May, when I saw the news of Darren Stanford's success with* Land Without Water *at the Cannes Film Festival. Now that I have seen his film, I must reunite Evelyn and myself to finish* The Glazen Shelves *posthaste.*

I write to you because, in addition to being an Oscar-nominated filmmaker, you are a Maine dweller, and you will feel an instant connection to my material. Furthermore, I am aware that you helped Darren Stanford secure funds for Land Without Water; *clearly, you like to help Maine-based film-makers (Stanford and I are both from Portland, you know). Fairness dictates that you also help finance my film, which, I must add, is far superior to Stanford's.*

Seriously, how could you have lent your support to such a waste? I expect more from you, given your association with Kubrick. Surely you are able to understand the difference between artistry and hackery. Not every day does a filmmaker emerge from Portland, Maine, which is the reason it's especially important to choose the right one when the opportunity arises. You threw your support behind the wrong one. But worry not: I am here to redeem you. Helping me finish The Glazen Shelves *will go a long way toward rectifying your mistake.*

Now, as to what I require from you:

I require help securing funds somewhere in the ballpark of $4 million (we can sit down over a budget and discuss specifics).

I require 70mm cameras, sound recording equipment, and access to a first-rate editing/mixing studio.

I require a crew, although a skeleton crew will suffice. (Perhaps members of the crew you worked with on Little Children? *Or if you're still in touch with any of the people Kubrick used on* Eyes Wide Shut...)

I require a letter from you, sent to the people in positions of power at Focus Features and Sony Pictures Classics, vouching for the greatness of my film. Or, if you believe the film festival route better, I require you to submit the film, on my behalf, to Cannes, Sundance, Berlin, Venice, and all the others worthy of my achievement.

On all these points, I am unbending, so if you do not agree, we should sever our association immediately.

Please let me know when we can begin our work together to complete my masterpiece.

Sincerely,
Maxwell Enright
Writer/Director
The Glazen Shelves

THE
RECLUSIVE
GENIUS
RESPONSIBLE

DECEMBER 2012

Remember Kelly? This city holds thousands of her ghosts.

As she drives into Portland today, Kelly sees them everywhere. Ghosts in the gas station parking lots where she drank cheap coffee and smoked cloves when young and flailing and moody. Ghosts outside the pubs where Mom inflated her stomach with beer and then called her daughter for a ride. Ghosts on the sidewalks Kelly paced stoned in the months after Mom died when she didn't know how else to get the energy out. Even the snowbanks look like ghosts—the ghosts of storms she lived through as a teenager. Kelly left this town eleven years ago, but she remembers so much of it, so much of her life here.

And because of this, it kills her how little she remembers about her father.

Oh, there are some images, some feelings—sitting on his lap while he and Mom watched some artsy-fartsy black-and-white movie in which nothing happened, his fingers gliding across the underside of Kelly's arm while she closed her eyes and her lungs deflated—but she was only three or so back then and not much stuck. She does remember the word though: *Girly*—what he used to call Mom, and what he used to call his daughter. Once, when Kelly was fifteen, long after her father had left for good, she asked Mom, "Do you know where he is?" Mom jingled ice cubes against the side of her glass as she swirled cranberry juice with vodka. There was music in the other room; she was having a party. "He could be anywhere," she said.

Anywhere, indeed. Even years later, whenever Kelly jabbed her father's name, Miles Bennett, into Google, information was scarce. Despite the prominence of the Bennetts in Portland, Miles rarely came up in news stories—according to Mom, he had always been reclusive and uninvolved in the family business, Oakhurst Dairy—and until a week ago, Kelly had no reason to believe he still lived in Maine. But there's cash there, Kelly believes—no, *knows*, goddamn it: significant cash, a pregnant cloud of cash over his head, the sort of cash he drizzled from time to time on his estranged family after he'd scrammed. So a few days ago, Kelly scrounged online and scribbled down the names of every Bennett family member she could find involved with the dairy; then she scribbled down—seriously scribbled, her handwriting getting worse and worse, letters seeming to gather tangles of brambles on every curve—as many Bennett names as she could find in the White Pages that sounded even vaguely familiar to her, names that maybe Mom mentioned once or twice. She will visit these people—twenty-seven total—until one of them tells her where to find her father, who has to still live in Portland, *has* to. And when she finds him, what will he say? Maybe he will open his front door, maybe he will smile white teeth at her, maybe he'll look at her with those black-ringed eyes—almost beaten looking—and maybe he will say, "Girly—*finally*."

But first, Kelly needs her twin brother, Max, though she hates to admit it. Or, more bluntly, she needs a place to stay. So she takes a right, surprised to see a steep decline in front of her. Her wheels scrape rock salt. The car wobbles a bit. Eventually, the road flattens, and she takes a breath and wipes her eyes. Still crying. Cried the whole goddamned drive out here. She points herself toward the only place she knows to find Max: the crammed, beat-up apartment where Mom raised her two children amid faded movie posters and scuffed album covers and scratched records adorning the walls, bead curtains in every doorway, a kitchen filled not with food and plates and silverware but with empty Thai take-out containers. If her brother isn't there, he shouldn't be too hard to find, wandering the Old Port, visiting the movie theater or the video store—this, of course, assuming he still lives here at all. Kelly didn't exactly call ahead to check.

But then, where else would Max have gone?

Turns out she spots him well before she reaches the apartment. A quick glance out her car window as she passes a man with hunched shoulders and a torn peacoat that shows off patches of white fuzz underneath, and hey, there he is, wandering the Old Port, just as she expected. She can make out something in his hand—a book, maybe, clutched there, with paper sticking out the top like a bookmark. She keeps her eyes on him as she passes. His face looks so thin, and his curly hair tangles atop his head with no clear order—probably ages since a haircut. His mouth moves; talking to himself? He walks down the street in the slush, not even on the sidewalk. Maybe somebody needs to stop him, point to the relatively dry cement, and say, *Probably safer for you over there, sir.*

This is Commercial Street, where the tourists come—the most public part of the city, lined with shops with names like Nautical Treasures and Mainely Goods, selling moose hats and lobster claws you can wear on your hands. At least it's wintertime, and a particularly frigid day at that, so there aren't tourists gawking at Max. Still, summer will come—hard to believe, with the city encased in ice.

Kelly finds parking out front a Yankee Candle store, where a teenager in skinny jeans smokes a cigarette. She thinks about bumming one off him, but before she gets out of the car, he steps out his filter on the ground and heads back inside. After checking her face in the mirror once more, she unbuckles her seat belt. The cold outside feels like something physical, a mass of wind chimes hanging in the air that she has to climb through. She positions herself near her trunk. Should she hop onto it? Sure, she decides, why not? But when she tries to jump, her foot skids off the slick bumper; she plummets onto her ass. She regains her footing and reaches into her hoodie pocket, deciding to stand. Casual. *No, I'm not doing anything—just hanging out.*

"Very interesting," Max is muttering to himself as he approaches, eyes cast down. "A story of perseverance, you might say..."

"Hey there," Kelly says in the most ridiculous rendition of a New England accent she can muster. Max looks up, his head snapping back as though yanked from behind by a mugger, eyes landing, terrified, on his sister, like she's got a knife to his throat. "Sorry to interrupt," she says, "but can you tell me how to get to Bean's from here?"

Not an ideal opening line, she knows, this attempt at some good old-fashioned Maine humor—*barf*—but what else could she say after all these years? Something more meaningful? Give her a break—she has never done meaningful well.

"Oh," Max says. "You." And then nothing. Water streaks the lenses of his glasses, either from sweat or from passing beneath melting snow.

They stare at each other as if meeting for a blind date. She sees him completely for the first time in years, and he looks no different from before, still dressed like he used to in high school, in too-big dress slacks, sneakers, and an oversized button-down shirt and peacoat. All his clothes look like something a much fatter father handed down to his son.

"I can't really talk now," he says. "I'm busy."

"You're busy?"

"Yeah." He looks down at his muddied sneakers.

Kelly throws up her arms. "Too busy for me, a Christmas miracle?"

"Christmas isn't for another two weeks," Max says.

"So? I'm moonlighting as Santa. I brought you presents."

She expects at least a smirk—*something*. Instead, he mutters, "Dreadful timing, absolutely dreadful," a line so unexpectedly ornate Kelly imagines he must've nabbed it from a movie. With that, Max lifts his feet and gets back to his walking.

"Where are you going?" she asks. No answer. He heads down the street, veering farther into the road to get around a pickup truck hanging out of a parking spot muddied with rock salt; an oncoming car honks but does not swerve, passing perilously close to Max. This is stupid. "Can you stop for a second?" she calls after him.

He responds with more mindless marching—and probably more muttering too, as far as Kelly knows. So she cups her hands around her mouth. "Police!" she yells. "Apprehend that man! Get him out of the street!"

He looks back. "Why are you harassing me?"

"Because," she says, taking a step forward, speaking to him over the chasm of the pickup's bed, "it's nice to see you."

He stares at her, another drop of water falling down his glasses. Sweat. Now she knows. "It's nice to see you too," he says, so quietly she maybe imagines it.

She checks over her shoulder to make sure no car heads her way; then she walks into the street to get around the pickup. Face-to-face they stand. She curls her arms around him for a hug, but he doesn't move, making her feel like a straitjacket. When she unwraps him, his face is all red, but not in a teary way. His face is red like something else—

maybe the igniting match-head of his nasty temperature (one of Mom's old malapropisms, saying *temperature* instead of *temper*, and one Kelly has never been able to avoid). Whatever his redness, Max avoids her eyes. "Let's talk," she says, watching for something—a twitch even— but his face appears frozen. "I need to crash."

"No, no," he says, "that won't be possible. Not right now."

She nods, feeling her lips tighten. Behind Max, something jingles, and Kelly sees a man dressed smugly in a floral scarf and a beret entering a shop, the decorative Christmas bells knocking against the glass. She looks at the sunlight glinting off the closing door as an excuse to not look at her brother, even as she says, "Let me put it differently. I'm not *asking* if I can stay with you."

"But you *can't*," Max says. "It's my place."

"According to what? Mom left it to both of us."

"It's *our* place."

"That's right."

"No, not yours and mine. I mean, I have a roommate. There's no space."

"You have a roommate?" Kelly asks, her voice cracking a bit, if even just a hairline crack. Max has never had a roommate before in his life. He could barely live with his own sister and mom. "What's his name, your roommate?"

Max blinks. "Tobias," he says.

"You have a roommate named *Tobias*? Who the hell is *Tobias*?"

"My roommate," Max says flatly. "See, we're in a pickle. Plus, it's a bad time. I'm busy."

"With what?"

"Just... stuff." His eyes dart to the book he holds in his hand.

"What stuff? Being a bookworm?" She reaches for Max's book and, curling her fingers around it, tries to snatch it away—just as a tease, just to see what he'll do.

He pulls the book in the opposite direction, flinging his own body backward to keep his sister from what he holds. They struggle, feet sliding on the ground; the twins turn themselves around once, maybe twice. The book opens, and something slips out: a piece of newspaper, fluttering to the ground. "No," Max snaps, voice sharp in the cold air, and it startles her. So she lets go, and Max falls backward against the pickup truck's front mirror. He makes a farting sound with his lips that he probably didn't mean to make, and then he springs forward again—but he's too late: Kelly has already bent her knees, already picked up the strip of newspaper.

"It's wet," he says, reaching for it. "Lemme dry it."

She pulls it away. "It means so much you wanna tear it?"

He growls. "None of your business what I have, what I do. Give it back. Give it back. This is harassment, listen, I'll, uh, I'll call the police."

But Kelly already sees it. It's a newspaper column with jagged edges, appearing cut out in a frenzy by shaking hands. At the top, a black-and-white photograph of a sunken-cheeked young woman with large, almost oblong eyes and hair pulled back into a ponytail, her mouth open in a garish smile—the expression of a jubilant wax figure in the middle of melting. The headline reads "Search for Missing Local Girl Intensifies."

"Who is this?" Kelly says. But as soon as she says it, it clicks: the face of the girl, and the name, Evelyn Romanoff, even though when Kelly knew her before, the girl's face never drooped. "Shit, man. This is your friend, yeah? Evelyn? The one who was in your movie in high school?"

Max stops panting, gets quiet.

"What happened to her?" she asks.

"Give it back," Max mutters, reaching out again, his movement almost drunken.

She returns to the article, to the text. It's short, so she scans it quickly and gets the gist: apparently nobody has seen Evelyn since last Friday—so, almost a week ago—when she neglected to show for work and then for a weekly wine bar date with a friend. The work thing didn't raise any flags, really; according to the article, she'd been missing work a lot lately, was holding on to the job as a waitress at DiMillo's only because she'd had it for so long and it's always harder to fire somebody who has been around for a while. But missing the vino? Her friend (well, more like a guy she was casually sleeping with—so the article makes it sound like, anyhow) knew something was definitely wrong, so he went over to her apartment and found—well, *didn't* find her. That's the whole point. She was just gone.

From there, the article goes on to discuss the investigative efforts thus far, and how police have managed to assemble a vague timeline of her activities the day before. It was a rough afternoon for her: She went to go see a film at the Movies on Exchange—just around the corner from where Kelly and Max are right now—at noon. Then she paid a strange visit to Casco Bay Books, a coffee shop where she used to work. According to an employee, Evelyn used the bathroom and then claimed a table, where she opened a notebook and scribbled for thirty minutes without looking up, after which she tore out the pages, hit the parking lot, and burned them. Then, around four in the afternoon, witnesses saw her walking down Commercial Street, crying—

At this, Kelly looks up from the article, looks around at Commercial Street, with its shops and slushy roads, a smattering of winter people wandering in their heavy coats, window-shopping, pointing at cute trinkets inside stores and sighing—then she looks at her brother, who stares right back at her. "Is this what you're doing out here?" Kelly asks. "Trying to find her?"

Max turns and rests his head against the pickup's door. Is he about to cry? How the fuck could she possibly deal with that? She still feels on the verge of tears herself, and watching her brother lose it would trigger what happens when one little kid sees another little kid start to wail: all hell would break loose.

Then, his face pressed to the glass, she hears him mutter something she doesn't quite catch.

"Hmm?"

He lifts his head from the pickup. "You've interfered with my schedule. My timing is all off now. So we might as well eat."

Only when Max walks away from the pickup, leading the way to God knows where else, does Kelly notice a young boy inside, staring out at them behind tinted windows—a boy who was there all along, watching the foolishness of grown-ups with a smirk on his face.

The mirror in the pub's bathroom reveals how awful Kelly looks. Not just awful, but—and this word has rattled in her head ever since Max used it on the street—*dreadful*. Eyes, lips, hair—everything droops, like Evelyn in the photograph. If Kelly were an idiot, she might also claim that her *soul* droops, but she's not an idiot, or at least not that type of idiot. She opens her purse and removes blush and eyeliner and lipstick, then applies each medicine quickly. Not knowing what to do about her hair, she collects it into a ponytail. For the grand finale, she pulls off a square of toilet paper and dabs at her fresh pomegranate lipstick.

When she exits the bathroom, the darkness of the bar steals her eyesight for a second. She feels her way along the wall, down the hallway, until she turns the corner into what a sign calls THE TAP ROOM, though that sounds too grand for this neighborhood dive, full of middle-aged men who live a block away. Maybe she knows a couple of them from her days frequenting Portland dives, back when bouncers and gobbledygook like *legal drinking age* were no match for a fake ID in the hand of a girl who knew how to smile. But a decade later, Kelly has put on weight, and... well, her appearance has changed in other ways she prefers not to talk about (skin blemishes, looser backside; *just don't talk about it, don't*). Forget whether she might recognize anyone; would anyone recognize her? Or *care* to?

Max sits at a table in the corner, his back, as he insisted, against the wall; he wants a view of everything. Kelly joins him at the table, which now wears two baskets of food. "Yum." She tries to sound pleased, picking up a cold mozzarella stick and taking a bite; the cheese inside has already congealed. "You're missing out."

Max keeps his eyes on the table. He refused to order anything except ice water with lemon. Kelly was starving and badly in need of a drink, so she ordered a Shipyard (she already forgets which style), mozzarella sticks, and chicken fingers—a fairly standard meal. Hopefully Max will pay for this crap—his idea to come here, after all—although he's likely as poor as she is. (She hasn't yet dared bring up the subject of what, if anything, he does for a living.) She returns the mozzarella stick, half eaten, to the basket and works on her beer instead. She gulps it, nothing but warm fizz, then sets it down loudly, hoping to rouse her brother. But he doesn't budge. So she snaps her fingers. "Earth to Max."

He looks up and squints.

"What's up with you?"

"With regard to what?"

"I dunno. Just, what's up with whatever. What's going on? Do you still have that job?"

"What job?"

"The movie theater job? Weren't you working at the Nickelodeon?"

"No."

"You sure? I think you told me that in an e-mail, maybe..." She turns her mouth on its side and narrows her eyes into a face that suggests she's counting years in her head (*how long ago was it?*), but really, she has no goddamned clue whether anything she's saying is true—nor can she even remember when last she spoke to Max, via e-mail or otherwise. "Maybe," she decides, "four years ago?"

"You came all this way to see me and ask me whether I still have a job that I never had and never told you I had?"

Kelly shakes her head. "Like you know anything about me or what I'm doing."

"So tell me something then. Tell me about *your* job. Do *you* have a job?"

Kelly stares at him for a moment. "Duh," she says, unsure of how else to answer.

"Where do you work?"

She can't tell him the truth: that she lost her job three months ago—followed by her apartment a few days ago—prompting this trip out here to Maine, because without work or housing, she had no real reason to stay in the Southwest, especially when Dad may be here, still in Maine, living in opulence. "I'm a manager," she says. "At a Safeway." A lie, yes, but also a *sort of* truth, since until a few months ago, this was the job she had—well, not a manager, a *cashier*, but still.

"You mean you run the whole Safeway?" Max asks.

"No, I manage the front. But it's a lot of money."

"Yeah?" Max stares at her; can he tell? "Well," he says, "I work at Hugo's. The tips are great. I'm doing very well for myself."

Kelly has never eaten at Hugo's—has never really known anyone who ate at Hugo's, in fact. Six-course meals, servers in tuxedos, no check under, like, $500. She can't even begin to imagine her brother working in a place like that, interacting with that clientele, squelching the more cantankerous aspects of his personality. Obviously it's bullshit, even worse than her lie. Nevertheless, she grunts, "Hmm, well, great, great," and clicks her tongue. Oh, such awkward politeness from both of them; at the very least, they're even.

She tries to think of something else to talk to her brother about—something safe that won't lead to a stalemate of dishonesty—but nothing other than movies has ever interested him. He was always so single-minded, certain he would become a famous director one day, never preparing for the eventuality that he would fail. Now look at him. Thirty, she supposes, hits the Enrights like a gunshot.

"So," she says, trying, "did you see *Dark Knight Returns*?"

"*Rises*." Max closes his eyes; he can't bear to look. "He rises in this one. He *returned* in 1992."

"Huh." Kelly shrugs and drinks more beer. The liquid fills her. She might not need to bother with the chicken fingers. "Well, did you see it?"

"Of course I saw it."

"It was cool. Kind of long, though. Awful, what happened in Colo—"

"Christopher Nolan exists only to make idiots think they have good taste."

"Huh. Well, I thought it was good." She fights to keep her voice friendly.

"I try to explain that to people," Max mutters. "About Nolan." At some point he'd grabbed on to his fork, and Kelly notices that he now squeezes the utensil. "People need to listen to me."

"Oh. Sorry, I guess. If I could unsee it, I would."

Max mutters something else, but she misses it. She keeps an eye on the fork squeezed in his fist. If he jutted it in her direction, could she dive out of the way in time? Not that he would do this, though; Max inflicts harm upon inanimate objects, not people. But her brother has always had a temperature. Whenever he got mad in the old days—someone around him not adequately appreciating his genius—he would lock his door and beat his bedroom to death. He'd reemerge into the world with splinters in his hair.

"So," Kelly says, "do you want to tell me about Evelyn? Do you still hang out?"

"Every day," he mutters.

"Have the cops asked you questions?"

He shakes his head. "I don't know what happened to her."

"Not really what I asked, but okay." Kelly eyes the book sitting between them on the table. "It's awful anyway. Her, Dad: people around us just... disappear, I guess."

"Dad didn't disappear. Someone knows where he is."

Kelly bites her lip. Not time to bring up Dad yet. She can't guess how Max would react if she told him about the phone call she got a week ago.

"So," she says, "your plan is just to walk around, trying to find Evelyn?"

"I'm going to the places she went," he says.

"You can get time off from Hugo's to wander around?" A bit of a cruel poke, yes, and a violation of their liars' détente. She must take greater care to avoid a fight.

"I just told you," he says, eyes on his fork. "I'm not *wandering*. I know where she went. They have it right there in the paper. So that's what I'm doing: going where she went, when she went there. According to the paper."

"For how many days now?"

"This is my second day."

"What happened yesterday?"

"I fell. On some ice. I hurt my ankle and couldn't walk. I had to call a cab to take me home. But today my ankle felt better, so I went out to try again."

"And that's when I found you?"

"That's when you *interfered*," Max says. "The timing needs to be perfect."

"Perfect for what? You think she's going to magically appear somehow?"

"Because the *timing*," he says, then closes his eyes and exhales in frustration, an actor blowing a line and starting again. "Because the timing is important. Timing is *always* important. Nothing bad happened to her, I'm sure. She just *went* somewhere. So if I go to the places where she went, then maybe I'll figure out what particular things *happened* to her the day that she disappeared that led to her going wherever she went."

"Because every day happens exactly the same?" Kelly says, raising an eyebrow—and, yes, maybe even smirking, goading him just a tad.

To answer her attitude, Max widens his eyes into a quick, unhinged look that suggests her worst fork-related fears might come true. But then he shakes his head and issues a shallow snort. "Magically appear, yes.

You're right. You were right the first time." He rolls his eyes and makes a *get-a-load-of-this* gesture with his thumb, performing for nobody in particular.

Hearing him talk like this, Kelly isn't sure how she should feel—angry that he almost blew off his sister today for this wandering nonsense? Of course, it's possible Evelyn could be in some real trouble. But Kelly remembers her well enough: a little flighty, a little mysterious, the kind of girl who gets labeled odd all through childhood. Sometimes people need to disappear for a little while. Sometimes it's nothing to worry about.

"Well, what do I know?" Kelly says. "I mean, I guess you knew her better than anyone if you hung out every day. Maybe if you go out looking, you can find something the cops missed."

No answer—just eyes tipping like a capsized boat as he glances down at his book, still on the table between them.

"Can I see this?" Kelly asks, tapping the cover.

"I don't know," Max says. "Can you?"

She sighs. "You were always such a wit."

Max pauses for a second as the jukebox music—that whiny Neil Young song about being an old man, which always sounded to Kelly like a feeble-minded fellow in a nursing home wrote it between bouts of yelling at the grass outside his window—fills the air. Somewhere, somebody bangs glasses—a sound from behind the bar, not a noise made by one of the two or three other patrons here, all of whom are old men in overalls. After a second, Max nudges the book toward her, granting her permission to look by scraping the cover against the patina of sticky beer mess on the table. "It's about a film," Max says. "What do you care about that anyway? You don't like films."

She picks up the book before her brother changes his mind. "Maybe not compared to you. But in my defense, I don't think anyone watches movies the way you do."

"Mom did," Max says. "And Evelyn."

"Well," Kelly says, opening the book, "I stand corrected."

The book feels awful in her hands, flimsy, the paper poor quality, and she can tell immediately, even with her limited knowledge of publishing, that this book wasn't made professionally; instead, it feels like the sort of thing somebody paid to publish—maybe even ran off the copies at Kinkos. The book, called *Land Without Stanford: A Cult Film and the Reclusive Genius Responsible*, claims (according to the cover anyway) to tell the true story about *Land Without Water*, a little indie film Kelly has never had the patience to watch all the way through, but about which she still knows three things: First, it was filmed in Portland a few years after she and Max graduated high school. Second, the very fact of the film, which Max loathes, reminds her brother of his own—um, what's the polite way to put it?—*unfulfilled ambitions*. (Years ago, after seeing it for the first time, he phoned her and ranted for an hour without asking a single question about her life. After that, she made a point of being too busy to take his calls.) And as for the third thing Kelly knows about the film? Let's not mention the third thing, because Kelly would prefer not to think about it right now.

As for the book, though, the author is a guy named Ford Hunter, and as Kelly flips through the pages, she picks up a bit here and there: Hunter was an actor in *Land Without Water*, apparently, and the book is full of jazzy bits of reminiscences, a lot of stuff about a guy named Darren, who seems to be the film's director. "Is this even a real book?" she asks.

"The guy self-published it a few weeks ago," Max says, "but you can buy it in bookstores here. Just in time for Day Without Water."

"What's Day Without Water?"

He rolls his eyes at her. "What kind of a Mainer are you?"

"Oh come on, I haven't lived here in ten years."

"Eleven," he says—and it startles her that he knows well enough to correct her. "It's a winter arts festival they do each year. They do screenings down on the pier. People sell things. Next one's on Sunday."

"And it's all about *Land Without Water*?"

"No," Max says. "More like inspired. Just an excuse to have a festival."

Kelly looks back down at the book and glimpses one passage: *And Darren didn't believe me, but I told him, "Man, after we make this film, we'll get all the girls we want."* Kelly grimaces. "God, I thought you said this movie sucks."

"I don't like the film, no. But it's more complicated," Max says. "I sent you something I wrote about it once, remember?"

She was wondering if this would come up. For years after she left home, Max had sent her things—mostly movie reviews that he typed up and mailed to her with notes that said things like *Keep an eye out for this one in the* Phoenix (as if she still got copies of the *Portland Phoenix* all the way out in Tucson)—but she shrugged at them and put them in a box. Of course, she can't tell him this. So she says, "Oh, right, maybe I remember that one. You sent me a lot of stuff, though. Then you stopped. I was bummed."

"Sure," Max grumbles. "I'm sure you really miss getting them. I'm sure they were the highlight of your life. Especially after you changed your address and forgot to tell me."

She scrunches her nose, narrows her eyes, rattles her head a bit—one of those expressions (in this case, meaning *fuck off*) that somehow people recognize, even though its individual components seem absurd. Flipping through the book again, she notes underlined passages, at first just a couple, then more and more:

...a loft on Congress Street...

We got takeout from Tandoor, right across from where Darren was living at the time.

...in Tommy's Park, where a group of our friends gathered to watch.

Everything underlined has to do with some geographical location where they did something or other with the filming; the kind of notes a fan would make, wanting to visit Portland to find all the behind-the-scenes locations related to his favorite obscure movie. "I really don't get you sometimes," she says, closing the book and putting it back on the table.

Without hesitation, Max reaches forward and snatches the book, stowing it on the chair next to him, away from Kelly's grasp. "I'm looking for Evelyn, and I'll do whatever I can to find her."

Often it's best to ignore her brother's edges, like a mess of broken glass you try to clean up without hurting yourself—but this remark breaks the skin of their conversation, draws a dab of blood. "Evelyn?" Kelly says, drawing her voice out a bit, perhaps to prolong saying the rest of what she needs to say. "I don't understand. She was in your movie, not *Land Without Water...*"

Max shakes his head, mouths, *No, no,* but makes no sound, like a TV on mute.

THE SADNESS • 15

"Are you okay? You seem a little confused, or something—"

Max cuts her off with a wave of his hand. Eyes still slits, he glances around the bar. "Nobody knows what I'm about to tell you, and I don't *want* anybody to know, okay?"

"Okay," Kelly says, the word drained of energy by the time it leaves her mouth. "You can tell me. I won't blab."

Max's eyes settle on a man in bright red overalls sitting at the bar, alone, sipping a beer.

"It's probably safe to talk," Kelly says. "That guy has his overalls turned up too loud to hear you."

Max turns back to his sister, his face a mask of seriousness, and he leans across the table. "Okay," he says, practically at a whisper, leaving Kelly no choice but to lean forward too, her exposed elbows sticking to the patches of dried beer on the table. "The other day, I went to see *Land Without Water*. They're playing it at the Movies on Exchange again. They always play it the week before Day Without Water. Anyway, I stayed afterward and watched the credits roll. I watched them closely as they went through all the acknowledgments, thanking the locals here in Portland. It was mostly the director's family, businesses, things like that. But then, near the very end, I saw it: Evelyn Anderson." He widens his eyes and jabs his head toward her a bit, as though ready to respond to her shock by saying, *I know! Crazy, right?*

But no shock comes; Kelly feels decidedly *un*shocked. "How does that—did I miss something?"

"That's her," Max says, "thanked at the end of the film."

"But her last name was Romanoff, right?"

Max nods. "Yes, but Anderson was her stage name. Her artistic name. She always went by Anderson. Evelyn Anderson. And her name was there. She was there. Thanked."

Kelly notices that Max is still clenching that fork, though it seems suddenly less likely that he means to jab out his sister's eye with it and more likely that he plans to jab out his own. "Anderson isn't exactly the world's least common name," Kelly says. "Isn't it possible there's another Evelyn in Portland—or, hell, *anywhere*—that had something to do with the movie?"

"No." Max shakes his head like a boss shooting down a poor suggestion. "It's her."

"Is she mentioned in that book you're reading?"

"No," Max says. "I've read it three and a half times now, trying to find some mention—even something oblique—but I can't find anything."

"So then?"

"So nothing. That doesn't mean anything. Just because she isn't mentioned in the book doesn't mean I'm wrong about her being involved."

"But if you guys hung out every day and yakked about movies all the time, wouldn't she have said something?"

Max shrugs. "All I know is, she had something to do with *Land Without Water*. I don't know what yet. But this is what the cops aren't thinking about. They don't know this yet. And I'm going to figure it out." Max's voice accelerates; Kelly hasn't heard him say so much in one go since she left home. "Because if she was involved in the film, and then she just happens to go missing right before Day Without Water, right when the Movies on Exchange is playing *Land Without Water* again, right after she goes to see it, right when Penelope Hayward is back in town— that's just too much. You're going to tell me it's a coincidence?"

"Wait." At the sound of Penelope Hayward's name, Kelly feels a rush of air against her face, against her exposed wrists lying flat on the table; each hair on her skin rises as though preparing to ask a question. "Penelope's here?" The physical sensation of this surprises her, makes something flail in her abdomen, makes her sort of want to jump up right here, right now, and go find her. Even the beer-smell in this joint—nauseatingly sweet and hanging like humid air—vanishes, leaving for Kelly only a name: *Penelope Hayward*.

See, this is the third thing Kelly knows about *Land Without Water*: that it stars her best friend from high school, who even back then acted the part of prim prima donna so well that Kelly just knew, even though she never would've admitted it years ago, that her friend was going to charm her way into some venal industry. Not that their teenage years weren't fun in many ways, and when Kelly drove into town earlier today, as she saw her ghosts everywhere, she saw as many ghosts of Penelope as she did of her brother or her mother. (Didn't she even drive by the North Street apartment of Mrs. Hodgkins, the Deering High School English teacher into whose lawn Kelly and Penelope once drove a hundred plastic forks after receiving a paltry C-plus on their *White*

Noise presentation?) But since Penelope got famous—not A-list famous, mind you, because she's a *minor* movie star, the colead in half a dozen soul-crushing rom coms but not necessarily bankrolling stuff on her own, not yet at that point of true success, and maybe will never get there if she keeps making the kinds of moronic movies she makes, just fucking batting her fucking eyelashes and pouting for the camera and whatever the hell else—where was Kelly's mind again? Oh yes, ever since Penelope got famous, Kelly hasn't mentioned her old friend much—in fact, she never talked about her in Arizona—but back in Portland, their broken friendship feels like an inescapable fact of Kelly's life, a scar down her face that she hopes nobody asks her about. Yet somehow, the notion that Penelope might be back in town had never occurred to Kelly, not even as a fantasy on her long drive out here; why would it have?

"Penelope," Kelly says. "Like, she's *here* here?"

"She comes every year for Day Without Water," Max tells her.

"So she's in town right now?" On the last two words, Kelly pokes her index finger into the tabletop.

"She's here. And you know what?" Max leans forward. "I would *love* to talk to her. And you can make it happen."

"Um. No. I'm not really sure I can make anything happen—"

"No, no, it's perfect. Tomorrow morning, she's doing a breakfast thing for charity. You and me, we can show up, we can go, you can talk to her. I only want a couple minutes, okay? I just want to ask her a few questions about Evelyn and *Land Without Water*."

Kelly shakes her head. It sounds like a disaster. Kelly and Max just showing up and hoping that somebody in Penelope-the-(minor)-star's entourage—because God knows she's going to have one—will grant them access to her? A long shot at best. She opens her mouth and feels the warmth from the bar's heater on her teeth, smells all the dust burning in the vents—a smell that exists nowhere in Arizona like it exists here.

What an embarrassment that would be, seeing Penelope again, towing along her drooling brother, desperation thick on his skin the way dogs and salesmen can smell. Watching how her brother leans forward, his eyes wide, his cheeks red, the blood in him finally boiling over, she understands that he has hit his final punch line—the reason he wanted to eat with her, the opportunity he began taking advantage of as soon as he saw his sister back in town. Turns out Max wants something from Kelly too.

"Is this why you wanted to have dinner with me?" Kelly folds her arms across her chest. "To ask me about Penelope?"

Max shrugs. "Not the *only* reason. But we could go tomorrow. Will you go with me tomorrow?"

"Can I stay at the apartment tonight?"

"*Tonight?*" He grimaces.

"Yes, the apartment I grew up in. That I technically have every right to still be in." Then, to milk it a bit, she says: "So we can get up early. And see *Penelope.*"

Max regards her with the unease of a man who has discovered a letter from his wife's lover, as if one night with his sister will cleave his life into two epochs: before and after.

"I don't care about—" What ridiculous roommate name did Max give her? Thadeus? Tobias? Whatever the name, Kelly forgets, so instead of asking, she waves her hand in the air. "Whatever, I don't need my room. Do you have a couch? Something else?"

"Okay, okay," he says. Sighs. "Yes, you can stay. But we have to go. Penelope's event starts at eleven. We need to be there early."

"Fine."

"Good." He leans back. "And I'll get to talk to her. I'll get to ask her my questions. Because there's no way this is all a coincidence. No way, no way, no way."

Kelly looks at him—at his curls matted from sweat, at his pupils wide and fearless, as though staring at something bright, daring himself to keep his eyes open as long as he can. Fuck, he's gone. Is it possible? Lost his mind?

"It's fine," Max says, as if answering the question she didn't ask. Already, he's looking away from his sister, snapping his fingers to gain the attention of the nonexistent bartender—unless the bartender is one of the men in lumberjack uniform. He wants the check. Then, with his voice low, almost the sound of a cell phone vibrating in a neighboring diner's pocket, he says to his sister, "Are you fine with a sleeping bag?"

"That's a joke, right?"

Max snaps his fingers at his sister now—a fluid movement from the bar to her face. "No, you know what? I'll put you on the futon. We still have the futon."

The futon, where Mom stretched her legs, exhaled her poison breath after nights out, and closed her eyes—still here, as Max promised, along with so much else. Her brother has discarded little of what Mom used to have in this apartment; all her posters and bead curtains still hang where they hung a decade ago, the rooms preserved perfectly in her image, preserved as the place where Max, years ago, settled in to watch thousands of films, to write his screenplays, and to believe himself a genius, back before sadness gripped his throat and reality came to matter. And Kelly, now a part of this preservation again, only this time as some version of Mom, here on the futon, where she slept each night, leaving the two upstairs bedrooms to her children; after all, Miles Bennett bought this apartment for her when she thought she was pregnant with only *one* child, not twins.

When Max pulls the futon out, it vomits dust, likely having avoided any and all snoring bodies since Mom's death. The cushion is torn, the fabric shredded and stuffing coming out like congealed orange goo. Evidence of cats, maybe—though when has Max ever shown any interest in cats? He disappears into the closet where Mom used to keep nothing much beyond an inexplicable pile of sleeping bags and produces, yes, a sleeping bag, which he tosses atop the futon, now yawning open in front of them. Kelly can't say why exactly, but she knows that sleeping bags are not something an indoorsy man who lives alone should own. If this were a date, and she came back to the dude's apartment to find sleeping bags? No way.

Still, it's not a date, and it could be worse. She puts down her glass of murky tap water (handed to her automatically upon entrance), and she climbs inside the sleeping bag on the futon, wondering as she stretches out if it'll feel funny, lying like this, if she'll feel suddenly—even though she must've slept here once or twice while growing up—if she'll feel suddenly, *today*, like Mom. But no, when her body goes horizontal and she feels the foam under her all misshapen and bent—no, she feels nothing like Mom and feels only *homeless*. Besides, she does something Mom never would've done: she looks at Max and chides him. "Aren't you going to ask if I need anything else?" she sneers good-naturedly (or so she hopes). "Man, what kind of host are you?"

"You going to sleep already?" Max asks.

It's not even nine yet, though the blanket of winter darkness makes it feel past midnight. "I'm exhausted," Kelly says. "I just want to lie down for a minute." Really, what she wants is to lie down on his bed upstairs, to—fuck it—just share her brother's bed tonight, or, at least, she wants him to offer this as a possibility so if the futon becomes too backbreaking, she can make a move. But he hasn't offered—hasn't offered her anything, in fact, other than the glass of murky tap water, which she reaches toward the floor to fetch.

"Anything I should know about your roomie?" Kelly asks. "Heavy cougher? Allergic to women? Ax murderer who stands over your guests in the night?" She takes the water into her mouth, cringing at the taste, like breaking an ink pen open between your teeth.

"You won't even see him," Max says. "He's out of town."

The sip crams in her throat like salt water from the ocean, and she chokes on it before spitting it back into the glass, no less discolored now than it was straight out of the tap. "What, for how long?"

"Death in his family."

"When's the funeral?"

"Someone's dying," Max says, voice flat. "Don't know how long it'll be."

"I'm not diseased, you know. I could sleep in his bed and just, I dunno, wash the sheets?"

Max shakes his head. "He's very private. Even has his door locked when he leaves so I can't get in. It would concern my roommate greatly."

"Your roommate," Kelly says, "whose name again is ...?"

Max's eyes head toward the ceiling for a second and he mutters, "Tobias." Then, stronger, "Tobias. I told you already."

"Sure," she says, then sets the glass down on the floor again. Looking down into it from this aerial view, she can see all kinds of scuzz around the top rim that she hadn't noticed before; it looks almost like streaks of milk, dried. Kelly licks her lips, which taste suddenly bitter. "How often do you guys have visitors?" she asks, before changing her mind: "No, never mind, forget it." The condition of the glass answers the question well enough.

On her back again, she looks up at Max, who has his hands in his pockets. It would seem polite, or at least *normal*, to comment on the condition of this place. An apology would be too much to hope for from Max, of course—*sorry for the mess*, that sort of thing—but wouldn't most people acknowledge that the place had gone to hell? In her adult life, Kelly has found herself in the apartments of countless young men, often way past midnight, often when the beer waterlogging her brain made acknowledgment of uncleanliness mostly unnecessary, but even in those cases, the majority of young men would at least look a little ashamed for a second—ashamed at having someone else see the pile of unwashed dishes in the sink, or at having to brush the dirty boxers off the bed and onto the floor—and vaguely apologize: *Sorry I didn't clean, didn't know anyone was coming over tonight*, etc. This crass duplex was bad before, with its drooping eyes of windows; its sun-paled blue skin, the worn-away patches of paint looking like bruises; its roof, the entire thing at a forty-five-degree angle, some odd sloping haircut that was maybe trendy decades ago. But inside? Dishes clog the sink, packages of opened and partially eaten ramen tower on the kitchen counters, bananas blacken on various surfaces, grime makes jam on the unmopped floors, the living room looks torn apart and in the midst of a deep reorganization— well, shouldn't Max shrug and apologize, however meekly, for not taking care of the place? Shouldn't he at least look ashamed? And what does all this trash—both the garbage in the kitchen and the retro Mom-junk on the walls—say about Max's supposed roommate?

But before she can ask anything else, she spots something dark moving on the floor—something scurrying then darting between some piles of DVDs. "Christ," Kelly says, sitting up, "was that a Satan bug?"

Max nods solemnly—the saddest he has looked over this whole mess. House centipedes, which the siblings used to call *Satan bugs*, have always been a problem here. After Mom died, Kelly had to go into the basement to get her stuff out of storage in preparation for her westward move, and when she flicked on the exposed bulb, she watched the centipedes, with their thousands of legs and their slithery bodies, scatter from all over her boxes of clothes. Most of that stuff she left behind.

"Wanna know what I hate in Tucson?" she says.

"What?"

"Palo Verde beetles. Google them; they're disgusting. I can't even stand to look at pictures." She shudders, though mostly for dramatic effect, since she actually got used to the beetles fairly quickly, accepting them as one of the many unpleasant realities of a Sonoran summer. "They hang out in the trees. Sometimes, during sunset, you see them flying around. They look like birds, until they hit you in the face. Just like big, nasty cockroaches—ones with wings."

"Huh." Max scratches at the stubble on his face. "That's unfair."

"What's unfair?"

"I don't know." Her brother stares at her. "Okay, well, good night." He turns and starts toward the stairs.

"Is that it? You don't want to talk a bit?"

"You look like you want to sleep."

She does—that's clear enough to her. Even now, she feels the world around her strobe a bit, going black then back to light again as her eyes flutter shut and snap open. She presses her fingers to her eyelids. Truth is, she should talk to Max, should tell him about their father, about the phone call, about the actual reason she's here. She'll *have* to tell him, she knows—and what's more, she sort of *wants* to. They may not be terribly close, Max and Kelly, but that doesn't mean they don't share a father, and just that little bit makes her feel like the two of them are tethered at the ankles by the world's longest rubber band, and no matter how far away from each other they drift, they will eventually snap back into place. She wants to talk to him, yes, even if it scares her a bit, even if she's unsure how he will react. And really, she suspects he wants to talk to her too; why else would he have told her so much about Evelyn with so little prompting?

"I have tomorrow off," he says, half under his breath. "Early in the morning. Penelope. Okay?"

"Yes."

"*Early.*"

She rolls her eyes and nods. Yes, yes, she knows.

"Okay," he says, then stands there for a minute.

She squints. "Good night?" she says with hesitation, as though an acting coach feeding him his next line.

"Okay," he says again. "Sleep well."

It sounds like a friendly wish, sure—so why, when Max turns to look at his sister one last time, do his eyes narrow like two coins lying flat, viewed from the side? And then he leaves her, heading upstairs to his room, the stairs sounding so creaky that she worries his footsteps will one day bring them down.

She turns off the light—rather, a desk lamp Max put on the floor next to her—and tries to get comfortable on the futon. First, she tries her back. Then she tries her side. How the fuck did Mom sleep on this thing? Of course, booze, yes—but what would Max have to drink around here? Probably nothing. Besides, it'll be fine, she knows; if she can stay still for a minute or so, she'll fall asleep. It'll be easy. Yes, easy.

In the darkness, she pulls the sleeping bag over her ears but can't avoid the sound—Jesus, she hears it right now, she *swears* she does—of another house centipede, or maybe the same one, or maybe something else, scurrying on the floor across the room. She feels like a kid at some dreadful (that word again), forced sleepover—one to make an unloved youngster happy for an evening. But then, what the hell *is* this exactly, a sleepover poised to last God knows how many nights? And which of them, Max or Kelly, is the unloved youngster?

On the fabric next to her ear, she hears something like a finger dragging across the surface; then something hits her face, her forehead, wobbling there for a second before dismounting. She sits up and reaches for the lamp, her hand walloping it, knocking it to the floor, where the overturned light casts grotesque shadows on all the walls. Off the futon, she picks up the lamp and uses it as a flashlight, pointing it at the floor, trying to find what crawled on her. She felt something—no doubt about it. But she finds nothing.

So she sets the lamp back down and untangles herself from the sleeping bag. Earlier, she saw the centipede hustle toward the corner, right? It rustled something there—the stack of papers, probably. She looks down at this stack, at the top page: *The Glazen Shelves, Draft 61*. Then a date, just from this past summer. She picks it up. Held together by a paper fastener, the document feels thick. She flips to the last page, number eighty-nine. He's still working on this, all these years later? She opens to a spot at random:

```
INT. COFFEE SHOP - EVENING

Max and Evelyn sit across from each other. Max looks
tired, his eye blackened, bulging. He has his hand
out on the table, begging Evelyn to take it. But she
doesn't—not yet. Instead, she stares at him, hair fall-
en in front of her eyes. Still wearing her scarf and
her summer dress from the event, she looks beautiful.
Under the table, her legs are slightly exposed—pale,
hairless, and lovely.

                    EVELYN
     So you were coming here all this time?

                     MAX
                     Yes.

                    EVELYN
                     Why?

                     MAX
     I didn't know where else to go. I didn't
          know where to find you.

BEAT. Evelyn stares at him, sniffs slightly.

                    EVELYN
               Well, hear I am.
```

It seems to be a big moment in the film, but Kelly struggles to forgive the typo. Say what you will about Max's artistic drive, but he was never too careful—he never paid attention in school. Kelly knew little about *The Glazen Shelves*, but she knew it well enough to know that it was never explicitly about Max himself. But now, after a decade of working on it, it almost seems like a self-fulfilling prophecy: Max has turned into the central character, a man romantically battered and pursuing his love.

Stacked here, there are probably ten more drafts of *The Glazen Shelves*, judging from the height of the pile. She bends to return the copy she holds to its place—and then, snakelike, the house centipede reemerges, slithering out from behind the pages, its body a mess of legs and fur. Kelly drops the screenplay on the floor and jumps back. Fuck this. She's not sleeping down here. No way to treat your sister.

Darkness crowds the peak of the staircase, but Kelly knows Max isn't asleep yet; she can hear noises up there, the sound of him muttering. So she climbs and, at the top, looks to her right: her old room, the door shut. As a teenager, she never hung anything on this surface, but seeing it now, she kind of wishes she had. This face, blank, that her brother and her mom saw each day when coming up here for whatever reason: Shouldn't she have found a little something more to tell them about herself? She can't resist squeaking the floor and getting closer to her old door, against which she presses her ear, listening. When Mom or Max used to do this—assuming they did this from time to time—what did they hear? Dinosaur Jr.? Snickering phone conversations with Penelope? Muffled tears into a pillow because, with Mom always drunk or away, and Max's eyes on a screen all day, Kelly so often felt alone? (On these occasions, she has to confess, she always hoped somebody was listening in; she always sort of loved the feeling of misery, but only when she imagined somebody being right there, ready to stop it.) Despite Max's warning, she wraps her hand around the doorknob and tries to turn it—but as her brother said, *locked.*

To her left, Max's bedroom door rests open a crack. She peeks inside. Nothing on the walls and no furniture, except for a nightstand, a bed— upon which Max lies—and a bureau in the corner, holding the same boxy television with a built-in VHS player that he had as a teenager. More books and paper stacks clutter the corners on the floor—additional screenplays, maybe. In bed, Max stares ahead at the screen, the light flickering on his face. But the television is muted; instead, Max fills the room with his own voice, which sounds formal, a few decibels lower than usual: "Now, Mr. Enright, *The Glazen Shelves* premiered at Cannes in May to amazing reviews. Now you're only thirty, so—"

"I'm actually twenty-nine," Max says back to himself, in his normal tone.

"Even more impressive!" Max responds, formal and deep-voiced again.

In high school, Max often used to talk to himself: one of his favorite things to do was to "give interviews"—Mom always used to say, "Leave the guy alone, he's giving an interview"—in which he would play Maxwell Enright, the great filmmaker, sitting down with an interviewer, whom he also played, and answering questions about his latest film. Kelly would lurk outside his bedroom door and listen—sometimes with Penelope, the two of them tittering, hands over mouths. But today, she feels creepy standing here, eavesdropping. As soon as she puts her palm against his door, planning to push it open the rest of the way and take the plunge into Max's space, she hears him say, in the deeper voice, "So tell me about your relationship with Evelyn."

Okay—maybe Kelly can listen for just another second or two.

"Evelyn plays my colead and helped develop the screenplay," Max says. "Also, she's my best friend. I wouldn't have made this film without her. And it's one of those crazy stories, right? We worked on it, on and off, for ten years. Life intervened for both of us in a number of ways, and sometimes, the feeling was bleak, like we would never finish the film. But we had to, you know? After a while, what can you say, other than that obsession takes over?"

"And now," the interviewer says, "all this acclaim. What does that feel like?"

"Marvelous," the great filmmaker responds. "But even if the film had never been finished, it would've been worth it to spend so much time with somebody I love so—"

Kelly, palm to the door, misjudges her force, and the door squeaks open a bit, hinges crying out. Max goes quiet, rustles the sheets, pretending he'd been asleep the whole time.

"Max?" she says. "Who you talking to?"

He grabs the television remote and hits a button, killing the light. "Nothing," he says after a hiccup. "I was asleep."

"Can I come in?" Kelly asks. Max doesn't answer. She opens the door. He lies on the bed on his back. "Scoot over."

"Why?"

"Now."

He presses himself against the wall. The bed opens its arms wide enough for them both, and she lies down next to her brother. He faces the wall and lies there, stiff. She can see his bare shoulder; he's probably naked under the covers.

"I need to tell you something," she says, figuring now's as good a time as any. She feels more or less awake—or at least unlikely to sleep any time soon.

"What?"

"It's about Dad."

"What," he says, though the question mark at the word's end has vanished.

She takes a deep breath, then tells him—tells him about the surprise call a week ago, tells him about the woman with the sonorous voice of a high school music teacher who had found Kelly's phone number in her husband's things, who said, "Stay the fuck away from Miles." Before Kelly could say anything, the woman hung up. Kelly looked at the caller ID on her cell phone: the number began with 207—the Maine area code. Kelly kept trying it back, wanting to tell the woman that she had no idea what she was talking about, that she wasn't—what, the *mistress to a Mainer*? Kelly had never bothered to discard her own 207 number, had not been able to bring herself to do it, in fact; so it wasn't beyond the realm of possibility that, simply going by her phone number, she could be confused for someone still living (and cheating) in Maine.

"And so you think it was Dad's wife, or girlfriend, or whatever? Because the guy's name happened to be Miles?"

"Come on, It's got to be him." But Max remains silent. Staring at his back, she asks: "I mean, does she even know about *us*, that her new husband has twin adult kids living in the same town?"

"Well," Max grumbles, "*one* adult twin living in town."

"If he's still here, don't you want to find him? Don't you want to meet him?"

"It's a mistake to do that. It won't help anyone."

Eyes still on her brother's back, she wonders: Was his skin always so scaly, giving off this easy-to-peel vibe? She saw skin like this in the desert, but rarely in Maine. "You can come with me, you know, to see him," she says. "He owes us."

"Owes us what? Money? Is that what you want?"

"I want—"

"Why don't you try working? Mom worked."

"Oh my God," she says, "don't start this *Mom-was-a-fucking-saint* bullshit with me right now. I really, really can't handle it."

"It's a mistake," Max says. He clears his throat and stirs, but he still faces away from her. The blanket falls a bit, revealing more of Max's shoulder. Kelly focuses on it—focuses on one long hair that reaches out from his skin.

"I met him," Max says.

Kelly notices for the first time a tower fan in the corner, making a low hum, rattling. For a moment this sound confuses her and almost puts her in a trance. But then it hits: "You met him?"

"He knocked on the door here one afternoon," Max says, "and handed me a business card. He had scribbled his address on the back. Told me to stop by."

Her face heats up. "You never told me?"

Max shakes his head against the pillow.

Kelly exhales and realizes that her anger toward her brother is already fading—if it existed at all. Frankly, she understands: their line of communication has always—or at least since Mom's death—been a clogged artery.

"Okay," she says after a moment. "So where does he live?"

"Now? I don't know. When I got to his house, I saw boxes everywhere. He told me he was in the middle of moving. I don't know to where. He asked me if I wanted anything to eat. I said no. So he made me a drink instead. Something red, I remember. We sat across from each other in the living room. It felt like we were waiting for someone else to show up. He started to ask me questions about myself. He asked me if I went to school and where I worked. He kept saying, 'I want to know about my son,' like we were talking about someone who wasn't there. I didn't ask him anything. I didn't want to know anything. I answered his questions until it got dark. He kept giving me drinks. I never drink. I don't know why I drank there. 'Do you have any of your mother's things?' he asked me finally. It was the first time we talked about her. First time he said anything about her. I told him that I had some of Mom's things in boxes. 'Well,' he said, 'I'm looking for something in particular. Something I gave her.' So he described it to me: the gold necklace with the locket and the engraving."

Kelly remembers this necklace, of course—remembers that Mom kept it stowed in a drawer. Sometimes she took it out and fastened it around her neck. One morning, she told Kelly, "This was the first thing Miles ever gave me. This was from his family. See the engraving?" Kelly peered at the locket and saw the initials, K.B. "Those are his grandmother's initials," Mom said, "Katherine Bennett." But they weren't Mom's initials—not even close. So why did he give it to her? "Sentimental value," she said. "He gave it to me so I could give it to you." "But those aren't my initials either," Kelly Enright said. "Sure," Mom said, "but they were *supposed* to be. And then after he left, he asked for it back. Can you believe that?" Mom stubbed her cigarette out in the ashtray. "I told him I threw it out with all his other bullshit. But I didn't. No." Mom looked at herself in the mirror and caressed the gold locket with the blue-polished nail of her index finger. "No, this necklace the Bennett family is *never* getting back." Mom clasped it—K.B.—around Kelly's neck, and she caught sight of herself in the mirror; the gold seemed to make her entire face shimmer. She felt her father hanging around her neck. It was a lovely, glinting piece of work; Kelly missed this necklace once Mom had laid it back in the drawer. Years later, when Mom died, Kelly rummaged through the dresser, hunting for this piece of jewelry: *I'll take this one thing*, she thought, *just this one thing*. But she couldn't find K.B.

Max continues his story: "He wanted the necklace back, but I told him I didn't know where it was. Some of Mom's stuff just vanished, and I don't know to where. So he told me to spend the night. I was in no condition to go anywhere. So I agreed. In the morning, I went downstairs, and I heard voices in the kitchen. So I peeked around the corner. I saw them, heard them there, Dad and a woman, much younger than him, probably in her twenties. Dad was telling her something about me. He was telling her that I was there, but you know what he called me? He called me *his nephew*. I watched them for a minute—I watched the way she watched him as he talked, with her eyes big, with her whole face orange like he was a light shining on her, with her smile so fast and easy it seemed almost elastic. So what then? What then, what then—" Max takes a breath here. "She stood up, crossed the table, kissed him on the cheek, her stomach huge. Another one. 'Go wake your nephew up,' she said, 'I want to meet him,' and then off she walked, carrying inside her—what? Another *nephew* for him to introduce to some future wife?" Max sighs. "So I left. That's it. I left. All he wanted was that heirloom, that necklace, for his new family. Sentimentality afflicts even the nastiest among us, I suppose."

Kelly doesn't quite know where to start, but one thing is obvious: "When his wife called me, she said she found my number in his things."

"*If* his wife called you."

"He must have looked at your phone. While you were passed out. Must've scribbled down my number."

"Sure," Max says, "but he probably saved you in his phone as *niece*."

"So all that time," Kelly says, "he never called me. He talked to you, but he never talked to me."

"He's a monster, leaving Mom, reappearing in my life, just for a necklace."

"And you definitely don't know where he is? I mean, like, zero idea?" For a moment, the fan in the corner fills in for Max's voice as her brother goes silent. "Why aren't you answering?" Kelly asks after a pause.

"I don't know where he is." And in his voice, what does she hear? The same goddamn tone from earlier, when he told Kelly he works at Hugo's, or about his roommate *Tobias*—a little too clear, a little too forceful, coming from a guy who has never been clear or forceful in his life.

"If you know," Kelly says, "then you need to tell—"

"I never want to hear about him again," Max sniffs, and shivers. "You have no idea how it felt to be treated that way."

And here, the crying? Finally, the crying? Christ. Kelly hears her mother's voice reminding her: *Take care of your brother*. She almost sees her mother hovering there, whispering urgently: *Take care of your brother*. It was quite possibly the only expectation her mother ever had of her—and how unfair was that shit? Still, Kelly knows she should do something comforting; yes, she knows she should—but what? She decides to put her fingers in his hair. Yeah, that ought to work. But as soon as she touches her brother, he flinches. That's okay, Kelly didn't want to touch him anyway. She snaps her hand away and feels the grime from his unwashed hair on her fingertips. Max doesn't move, doesn't answer. She wipes the grime onto his pillowcase.

"Hey," she says. "Can I stay here tonight? Do I have to go back downstairs?"

"I'm asleep," Max says, then makes a ridiculous snoring sound.

So she decides to sleep here too—not downstairs with the house centipedes.

M om was young when she fell in love with Miles Bennett, a member of one of Portland's oldest and wealthiest families, owners and founders of Oakhurst Dairy. Mom was nineteen when she met him, twenty when Miles bought for her a two-bedroom apartment in a decent part of town, twenty-one when Max and Kelly were born. For three years, Miles hung around, never moving in but coming over a couple times a week for fun with Mom and paternal indifference elsewhere, but then, when Mom was twenty-four, Miles left her for another woman, someone a little richer (a grad student at Boston College) and someone the Bennetts approved of (more than they approved of dingy, wild Mom, anyway); every week an envelope of cash arrived in Mom's mailbox, the return address a lawyer's office in Hartford. It was hush money, *stay-out-of-my-life-and-I'll-make-it-worth-your-while* money, that sort of thing—just enough so Mom never worked anything more than the occasional part-time job, but not so much that they could ever live in a better house, or take trips, or own more than a couple pairs of shoes. And what did Mom care? She was barely around, preferring to spend money on herself than on her children. But didn't she have a duty as a mother? Please. That hardly stopped her from leaving town for several weekends each year. She would knock on a neighbor's door— or call a coworker, during her rare periods of employment—and, eyes leaking, Mom would lie about a sick family member or close friend, and then once this almost-stranger had agreed to watch her children, she would drive to wherever: some friend's apartment in Burlington, or a music festival near UMass. When Kelly turned ten, babysitters became unnecessary. "You're old enough to look after your brother," Mom told her daughter. Mom lived a throwback fantasy, pining for a lifestyle, to belong to something that no longer existed. She fancied herself some kind of wild child—an artist, although she never considered working at it. As a result of this immaturity, the house wound up resembling a bohemian college girl's dorm room, decorated with bead curtains, posters for esoteric films from the '60s and '70s, record covers pinned to the walls, hookahs—pretty much the same way it looks now, under Max's care. Most nights, Mom fed her children Thai takeout served on paper plates. Mom acted like a friend or, at best, a rebellious older sister, which made Kelly feel like she was always waiting for her real mom to show up, instead of this child playing dress-up. But Max? Hell, Max loved it. Why wouldn't he have? When he started writing scripts, Mom encouraged him as any good parent would: *follow your dreams, be true to yourself,* that kind of shit. When teachers tried to make Max do schoolwork, he became combative, but whenever a counselor called home to voice concern, Mom acted polite on the phone only to later tell her son, "Don't listen to those idiots. They don't know genius when they see it." By senior year, it had become so much worse. Sometimes Mom became so high on the idea of artistic expression that she would write notes excusing Max from school whenever he preferred to stay home and work on his "art." His grades suffered, but what did he care? He got to watch movies all day and write his screenplays. Kelly could tell that something had changed for Mom too.

Then, with the March sunlight starting to melt the snow and thaw the ground, Mom left for one of her trips, telling Kelly, "Look after your brother. I'll be gone for the weekend." Because Mom always said to look after Max, Kelly barely took it seriously, going about her usual business of watching bad television and hanging out with the increasingly dramatic Penelope Hayward, whose early acceptance into Columbia—about which she wouldn't shut the fuck up—had not slowed her acquisition of an insane number of extracurricular activities, including dull stuff like editor in chief of the video yearbook. Kelly, on the other hand, had been accepted into the considerably less impressive University of Arizona, but whatever: she couldn't wait to get out of Maine and into the sun, so she bided her time doing the minimum of what was expected of her.

The first indication that something had gone awry—that Mom's latest trip wasn't just another trip—came when one of Mom's friends knocked on the door Sunday afternoon, claiming to have lost contact with Mom, who had recently been rambling on about some guy she met—Rafael, maybe? "You never met him?" the friend asked. Then, frowning, the friend—was her name Melanie?—added, "Neither have I." Kelly tried calling, but Mom never answered, and Kelly refused to leave dumb, desperate messages. Monday morning arrived, then Tuesday, then Wednesday, and finally, on Thursday, Max asked what was going on, whether Kelly had heard from Mom or anything, and Kelly said, "She, uh, had to go on a job interview in Mass. Apparently it's going well and they need her to stick around." Was this what Mom always meant when she told Kelly to look after her brother? Maybe Mom really meant for Kelly to just lie.

On Friday afternoon, the weekly envelope arrived, stuffed with $400, and Kelly put it in her pocket and slid on a cardigan to walk the few blocks to TD Banknorth. While outside the bank, finishing her cigarette in the cold sunlight of early spring, perched on the edge of the curb, her cell phone vibrated: Mom, wondering whether the money had arrived like usual. "Where are you?" Kelly asked. "I'm fine," Mom said, "but, uh"—Kelly could hear laughter in the background, and Mom's voice sounded more musical than usual—"but, uh, things are pretty crazy here. I just want to make sure you remember to deposit the money." "Why?" Kelly asked, lighting another cigarette. "Because," Mom said, "it's important that you don't leave cash lying around. That's all. That's all," clipped, rhythmic. Kelly's hand shook. "When are you coming home?" "I'll be home soon," Mom said, "things just got crazy. It's just a thing with a friend. But you'll remember to deposit the money before the bank closes today?" "Yes," Kelly said, "I will." "Okay, I love you," Mom said. Kelly swallowed and said, "Okay." Inside the bank, she asked the teller for the account balance: $1.34, the last transaction being a withdrawal of $240 from an ATM in Bedford, New Hampshire. Kelly thanked the teller and walked home with the cash still in her pocket.

The bank closed at 6 P.M., and twenty minutes later, Kelly's phone shrieked again. "I'm just wondering," Mom said, "if you, uh, deposited the cash and everything, like we talked about." "Mom," Kelly said, locked in the darkness of her bedroom, sitting on the floor in the corner, "I need to know when you're coming home." "Listen," Mom said, her voice even stranger than before, like she was an actor playing Mom, "listen, I'll be honest with you: Remember my friend Melanie? Well, Melanie's having some trouble, so I'm here trying to help. I just need—" "Melanie came to the house," Kelly said, "and she's worried too. She doesn't know where you are." There was a pause. "If I give you an address," Mom said, "can you mail me that money overnight?" "If you don't come home," Kelly said, "I'm calling the police." "Okay, I'll, um, I'll come home tomorrow." Mom cleared her throat. "But, uh, can you put Max on the phone real quick?" "No, I can't. I won't put Max on the phone." "Kelly Jennifer Enright, put Max on the phone right now." "No," Kelly repeated. *"Now,"* Mom said. But Kelly stayed strong: "You want me to let Max talk to you when you sound like this? No, I won't do it. And I'll take his phone away too so you can't call him." Kelly was trying not to cry; Mom was silent. "You need to come home," Kelly said. "Please. Max won't go to school. Not for the last week. He won't go." "He doesn't need to go." "Yes, he needs to go." "He's smarter than that." "Yeah? You want him to be a fuckup like you?"

The silence on the other end of the phone made it clear to Kelly that she shouldn't have said this. But she felt unable to control herself anymore. And Kelly, in that moment, didn't care. She knew she should apologize, but she didn't apologize. Maybe, compared with all the other things ever said by teenagers to their parents, this wasn't too bad— no different, really, from *I hate you, Mom,* followed by the slamming of a bedroom door. "Kelly..." Mom said finally, her voice weak. Kelly snapped her phone shut and threw it across the room. Now, she wishes that Mom were the one who hung up in anger. But it wasn't like that; it was Kelly who couldn't take another second, so she threw her mother across the room—snapped her mother's head off against the wall.

Kelly never called the police; instead, a week later, they called her. There had been an accident. It was April by then. When Max found out that Kelly had lied to him about the circumstances surrounding Mom's death—that there was no job interview, that Kelly had spent time on the phone with her, that all Mom wanted was money—he took it surprisingly well, nodding and shuffling to his bedroom, whose door he didn't even bother to slam. Kelly had felt too stunned to cry or get angry about the death, and perhaps Max felt the same way. Or maybe the funeral and the reality of being orphaned adults who happened to still linger in high school fused the siblings together. Maybe Max accepted Kelly's dishonesty simply because he had nobody else.

In May, Max asked her to be in his movie, *The Glazen Shelves*. A few days passed, and she heard nothing further about the movie or her part. She asked him when she was going to become a movie star and flipped her hair back, affecting a glamorous pose—the sort of silliness that usually would have amused him, but all humor had drained from her brother. Soon, Kelly discovered what the part was; she'd been playing it for a week. She woke in the middle of the night and saw Max at the end of her bed, a video camera glued to his hand. Kelly told him to get the fuck out of her room, then locked the door. She slept with the covers over her head and the blinds drawn. It wasn't anger, really. It was fear. He terrified her, and she avoided him, instead spending her time with all the willing kids around town, drinking and doing drugs and other stupid things teenagers do, but doing them with the desperation of somebody who understood genuine pain. She gained a reputation as the person who never wanted to stop, begging people not to leave her, to stay up with her all night. Maybe Kelly could have helped Max, but she was scared, drained; she had nothing to say to him, no way left to look after him. And now, some nights as sleep washes up around her body, Kelly hates herself for hiding and running from Max, instead of trying to help. So, should she have stayed here in Portland? Should she have tried to look after her brother, the way that Mom asked? Then again, who the hell ever tried to help her?

The answers to these questions, and to all her other questions, lurk somewhere in the darkness. Sometimes she brushes her fingertips against an answer as she reaches out, but she never grabs it, because sleep always comes and pulls her into blackness, and then the morning sun blares, evaporating what came before.

EXTRA, EXTRA!
A HOLLYWOOD
NEWS EXCLUSIVE!

Already the December morning—with the clouds and muted ambience more befitting a city approaching twilight—has begun extracting the sunlight from the sky. Kelly can't remember: Has nighttime always seemed to come just a couple hours after the day begins?

Running through downtown Portland, Congress is a thin stretch of road, not like the multilane city streets in the Southwest, so of course traffic is backed up and parking is nonexistent. What a mess. Kelly used to love driving this street, especially after midnight. Up late some weekends, either Kelly or Penelope would turn to the other and say, "Crime patrol?" Usually it was two in the morning, after the bars had closed. The girls would hop in a car and drive up and down Congress Street. They weren't actually looking for anything—just an excuse to get out of the house, really, and drive deserted streets, the lampposts and moonlight meant only for them. Occasionally they'd see drunk drivers and call them in. Once, a young woman, clothes torn, hair crazy, ran in front of the car. They stopped, and the woman screamed at them about somebody named Billy Joe. "Billy Joel?" Kelly said, and Penelope began laughing hysterically. The woman walked away from them, still yelling.

This morning, Kelly finds parking several blocks down, off Congress, in a residential neighborhood. After turning her car off, she looks around for a second, making sure that no valuables lie out in the open. Then she scoffs: What valuables?

Max has already scrammed from the car; he can't wait to get there.

Kelly moves down Clark Street, past the Cumberland Farms, past the gay bar Blackstone's—she notices several upscale-looking restaurants in this formerly run-down area—and when she approaches Congress Street, she looks at the traffic jammed around Longfellow Square, where the statue of that poet stands, defaced with red graffiti. She catches up to Max just in time for him to point out several closer parking spots, now empty, while the cold spits in her face, drenching her in the sort of unpleasant freeze that wiggles its way through layers of clothes, finds her skin through the spaces between stitches. She steps on some gum, which she feels snapping underfoot. "Watch the gum," Max says pointlessly.

On Congress Street, people duck under awnings to smoke cigarettes, and others shuffle down the sidewalks clutching plastic bags with shop logos on them, packed with rustic toys. Each window seems to blaze with Christmas lights, as do the trees, some with ropes of green and red threaded through the branches, others decorated with purple domes, lit up like Kelly never remembers from the past. Max hustles ahead of her. Accustomed to the slippery bricks, his feet fly, whereas she finds herself walking with her head down for every step, eyeballing the ice, well aware her Converse sneakers, good for desert, match poorly with Maine. Encased in one icy patch, she spots remnants of warmer days: receipts, cigarette butts, lollipop sticks.

As they pass a brick wall, something catches her eye, and she raises her head. "Whoa," she says. "Cool."

"What?" Max says, stopping so suddenly on ice his soles must be salted.

Spray-painted onto the brick, an image: on one side, a black-and-white circular table, men in uniform sitting around it; elsewhere, Mary Poppins holding an umbrella, floating through the sky. More images blend together and pop with color, the whole piece of art at least six by six feet. "That's awesome," she says, reaching out to touch the paint, but finding against her fingertips nothing more than cracked brick. "Who did this?"

"Some guys," Max says. "Graffiti artists. They do paintings of movies around town." Then, quieter, "They never take my advice."

Kelly's fingers land on an image of a man with sunglasses and a Mohawk, dressed in army greens. "Hey," she says, tapping the brick, "that's, um, that's from *The Taxi Driver*, right?" She has seen this man on posters before.

"*Taxi Driver*. No article," Max mutters as he moves onward toward Penelope.

A man and a woman stand near the entrance to Nosh on Congress Street, a new upscale restaurant whose name—for Kelly at least—conjures the image of someone on all fours, chomping asphalt. The man smokes, shuffling feet on the slick sidewalk around the A-frame sign announcing the Penelope Hayward appearance: EXCLUSIVE!!! HOLLY-WOOD COMES TO PORTLAND!!! MEET PENELOPE HAYWARD TODAY!!!

The man is ugly, with long hair and rimless glasses. In just a T-shirt, his arms look ridged, the hairs erect, goose-pimpled from the cold, and like all Mainers, his skin is pale from months of winter marooning him indoors. But the woman who stands next to him—dressed like a real grown-up in a blazer and slacks, with a heavy-duty scarf around her neck and sunglasses perched atop her head—has skin so vibrant and tan that she must have accompanied Penelope from Hollywood. She gestures at the Mainer as she speaks—often with her index finger extended toward his face—breaking eye contact with her iPhone only long enough to check that the man still listens, before continuing to dart her thumb across its screen. The Mainer nods, dragging away on his cigarette.

"Just stay here," Kelly hisses to her brother as he starts to cross the street. "Let me talk, all right?"

"I'm coming," Max says.

"No," Kelly says, eyeballing her brother's splotched face, his wild hair, his tattered peacoat. Kelly looks a little more together—though admittedly, not by much. Were it early autumn, leaves just starting to change colors, the chilly breeze merely a nibble on her skin, her hoodie might make more sense—but not so much now. She looks across the street again, sees the faintly lit windows of Nosh, candles flickering inside. Classy, classy. "Just stay here," she tells Max. "I'll be right back."

"We're not doing that. You can't tell people we're doing that," the woman from Hollywood is saying as Kelly makes her approach.

"Oh yeah," the Mainer replies, "well, I just thought—"

"No, you thought nothing. The staff can't meet with her after lunch. *You* can't meet with her after lunch. I don't care if you help out here. All she's doing after lunch is half an hour to sign some stuff for the ticket holders, but that's it. And she'll need a bottle of purified water for the signing and a bowl of lemon wedges."

"I'll get her another glass of water, of course—"

"Not a glass. A bottle. She doesn't want to sign stuff, knock things around the table, spill a glass of water on herself. God. It needs to be a bottle with a cap. We explained that before. A bottle of purified water. And a bowl of lemon wedges."

Kelly cracks an acorn under her left shoe. "Excuse me," she says, shivering.

The woman from Hollywood pulls away from her as though alarmed. Must be the way Kelly is dressed; she hasn't had much time in the last few days to track down a Laundromat. The woman from Hollywood looks around for a second, maybe to flag a security officer who can escort this homeless woman away from the event.

"Hey there," the Mainer says, friendly, like he knows Kelly—and maybe he does, though she doesn't have time for him right now.

"Ye-es?" The woman from Hollywood elongates this into two syllables.

"I'm here to see Penelope."

The woman from Hollywood swats some incoming cigarette smoke away from her face before taking a step toward Kelly. "You're participating in the brunch?"

Kelly shakes her head.

"Then who are you?"

"Kelly Enright."

"What does that mean?"

"That's my name."

"Huh," the woman says. She gives a little cough to scare off the smoke.

"Are you Penelope's friend from Hollywood?" Kelly asks.

"Yes," the woman says flatly. "*Best.*"

"Cool, cool." Ugh, Kelly can't imagine what she sounds like. She shifts her weight onto her right foot to lean toward the window; when she peers through the frost, she sees only crowded tables full of people laughing and eating and raising glasses of polished-looking liquid to their lips—no sign of the movie star. "I went to high school with her," Kelly says.

The *friend* looks at her iPhone again and fondles the screen a little more. "Neat-o," she drones.

Kelly fights the urge to swat the phone from this bitch's hand and crack the screen on the cobblestone. "Seriously, if you could tell Penelope I'm here, she'd want to see me."

The friend looks up, dead-eyed. "What do you want exactly?" she asks.

"Well," Kelly says—and then cotton stuffs her mouth. She has no idea how to answer this question. Standing here seems suddenly absurd. "I'd just like to say hi."

"Okay," the friend says. "I'll give her the message." Then, turning to the Mainer, "No Poland Spring, okay? Purified. *Purified.*" She annunciates this like a foreign language teacher. Then the friend leaves Kelly and the Mainer without saying good-bye.

So that's that, Kelly supposes—and really, she can't say she's too surprised; she's not an idiot, after all. It's not so easy anymore as it was in high school, showing up at Penelope's house, knocking on her door, knowing she'd be around and drop everything to do something inane like hit the Wendy's drive-through for Frosties or bother the lacrosse team boys who worked part-time at Amato's. Success allows people to insulate themselves from their memories. Penelope probably wouldn't have recognized Kelly anyway.

The Mainer left at the door stares at Kelly with the cigarette between his lips, so she feels fine putting her hand out. "Can I bum one?"

He cocks his head at her—cocks it so much he seems to disjoint it completely and lay it on its side. "You don't recognize me?"

Does she? Prompted, she squints. At first, there's only a groggy flicker of recognition, followed by something brighter; she feels like a person emerging from unconsciousness, watching the world cohere once more into recognizable shapes.

Oh, Christ. "Garrett," she says. Can she keep her face from cringing?

It makes total sense to run into Garrett Labrecque. Portland, after all, is an epically small town; many people from her graduating class still haunt these streets. (Say what you will about Kelly's choices, at least she didn't get stuck here straight after high school graduation; it took her a decade of failure in *other* places to drag her back to failure at home.)

"You look terrific," he says—one of those things people always say whether it's true or not. But Kelly can't bring herself to say it back to him. It's not that he looks terrible exactly, but in her memory, he's a thirteen-year-old boy, cute enough, if overweight, with scraggly hair and glasses—a boy whose geometry homework Kelly once wanted to copy. So what did she do? She danced her fingertips along his neck and in a vibrating voice said, "Please?" He relented. The next day, Garrett slipped an affectionate note into her locker and started telling people that he and Kelly were an item (where he got such an old-fashioned-sounding word she couldn't imagine), so she waited until later in the day, when he approached her outside after school in the area where everyone waited for the bus, and in front of as many people as possible, she screamed, "Your hair looks like a cat that died in the rain. Fuck off, creep." She watched him for a second, watched his face go white, watched whatever he'd made for her (something out of colorful construction paper, but she didn't get close enough to see) droop at his side. Did he cry? Yes, she's ashamed now to admit, he cried—and not mere mist in his eyes, but a wail, and tears like someone had poked two holes into his head to let the liquid flow unabated, sort of like when someone gets shot in a movie and blood comes in spurts. Around them, people laughed. It was a pathetic moment, Kelly first's experiment with cruelty—made her feel tall and sick at once, like she had grown to frightening dimensions in her actions, but had torn her organs and stomach lining in the process, ensuring that nothing inside would fit together again.

Of course, Kelly would prefer to avoid that subject altogether and hopes Garrett neglects to bring it up.

"Do you work here?" she asks, motioning to the frosted glass, the warm rich people within eating their food while the poor kids stand out here, drawing smoke into their lungs.

"Not really," he says, "but I'm part of the team taking care of Penelope today. My dad knows the owner of this place, so he got me in."

"Cool," Kelly says blandly. "Sounded like that lady was pretty mad at you."

"Oh, Chelle? Nah, she's cool. Penelope's assistant. Fun to work with. We were just sort of joking, you know? See, I'm writing this piece about Penelope for the *Portland Phoenix*—remember the *Phoenix*?"

Yes, Kelly remembers the free weekly, a ramshackle publication of pretentious cultural criticism, with political beliefs so left-leaning they're nearly fascistic. This paper her brother always imagined himself writing movie reviews for one day. "Yeah," she says, "how could I ever forget?"

"So I'm writing this story about Penelope's visit for the *Phoenix*. A Hollywood news exclusive, right here in Portland! That's all Chelle and I were talking about. I was just trying to get an interview today, but it's cool, no worries, I can wait until tomorrow. But forget all that. What's up with you? What's going on? Been ages."

Kelly presses her fingers to her forehead, feeling for a second like she just inhaled something very cold. "Wait. *What* are you doing tomorrow?"

"Interviewing her. It's amazing, really. Even with all her success, she's never forgotten her roots."

Kelly laughs. Can't help it.

"It's true," Garrett says, defending his religion.

"I know. I was just—never mind."

"Oh." He shrugs. Smiles. Then he points at her with his cigarette. "Hey, you two hung out in high school, right? Knew each other a bit?"

"Uh," Kelly says, "yeah. *A bit.*"

Does the tone of her voice register as sarcasm with him? She can't be sure, because he ignores it and takes out, of all things, a business card. "If you want to talk to me at all for my piece, give me a ring. It'd be great to catch up in general."

"Okay," Kelly says, holding the business card as far away from her as she can without looking unnatural, wondering which pocket of her hoodie will make it easiest to forget about this encounter entirely. "Maybe I'll give you a call. Meanwhile, what would it take to get in here?"

"The brunch? The tickets are, like, three hundred dollars."

Wind comes through, hits her ears, and she feels them redden. "For real?"

"Yeah, but they're sold out anyway, so I dunno, maybe a hefty bribe, or a quick BJ?" He laughs awkwardly; this joke was tough for him to spit out.

She narrows her eyes. "I hate jokes like that. Seriously."

He keeps laughing and shrugging and stomping erratically, as though a robot with wiring wet and malfunctioning. "I know, I know, I was just—hey, look," he says, changing the subject, "you have a busy schedule in the next few days?"

"I dunno. Mostly I'm hanging with my brother."

"Oh yeah? He lives here still?"

"Yeah," Kelly says, turning to look across the street, "he's—" She stops. Where is he? A man in a suit with a handlebar mustache has taken his place. "I gotta go," she says, turning back to Garrett. "But I've got your number." She holds out the business card to remind him. "If I get a chance, I'll call."

"Sure thing," Garrett says. "I'll look forward to it."

But his voice is already faint as she walks away from him and jogs across the street, into traffic, a couple honks coming her way. Her cigarette is done; she was barely able to enjoy it. She throws it to the road and, on the opposing sidewalk, looks around.

Where'd Max go?

Of course, she knows where he went, because this morning, before they left, she took another gander at the newspaper article about Evelyn's disappearance. Now, glancing at the time, she sees it's nearly noon—the time that Evelyn saw *Land Without Water* at the Movies on Exchange. A five-minute walk, if that, from Nosh, so Kelly works herself up into a bit of a jog—which is nice; keeps her warm—and finds her brother, sure enough, walking down Exchange Street toward the theater. She skids to a stop next to him, her feet scraping the slushy salt on the sidewalk. Huffing now, red-faced and out of breath—a feeling of dense warmth in her lungs—she says, "The fuck'd you go?"

"It was obvious you weren't getting in," he says, barely picking his feet off the ground, shuffling noisily on the bricks.

"You didn't tell me that shit cost three hundred dollars. Of course I didn't get in."

"You didn't try. You just got all chatty with those people. I had more important things to do than wait for you."

"Really? Like what?" They've arrived out front the theater, and she points up at the marquee, where the title LAND WITHOUT WATER is emblazoned. "*This* insanity? We're going to see this shit now?"

Instead of bothering to look up, he bows his head even deeper. "You can do whatever."

"Do you want me to help you or not?" Kelly says, craning her neck and bending her knees to place herself in her brother's eyeline. "Hey. Help? Yes or no."

He sniffs, the cold getting to him; she notices his cheeks have reddened too. "Yes," he mutters.

"Then don't fucking walk off on me again," she says. "Ever." If he's going to act like a crazy person and pursue this ridiculous fantasy of tracing Evelyn's footsteps, the least he can do is make himself easy to find.

On the day Evelyn Romanoff disappeared, she spent most of her time wandering barefoot. The papers have reported this with, depending on the nature of the publication, glee or solemnity; either way, it's the detail that most media have glommed on to the quickest, as evidence of some kind of psychosis—or maybe just an out-of-body experience. "Drugs," Max tells Kelly inside the theater. "People leap to the drugs. But she never did drugs."

"What was wrong with her then?" Kelly asks.

"My guess?" Max wipes his face with his sleeve. His nose keeps running in the cold; they seem to have the air-conditioning flowing in here, despite the winter. "She was distraught. She also took medication. Maybe there was a problem with that."

"But she cared about this movie?" Kelly gestures to the screen, though the movie hasn't started yet; most movie theaters show something before the trailers—commercials for other movies or television shows, or, in the old days, movie trivia—but this theater does nothing of the sort. No music even. "Did she care about this movie?" Kelly asks again, since Max neglected to answer. "Did you guys talk about it? Did she invite you to come see it that day, since you guys hung out all the—"

"Be quiet," Max says. "The film's going to start." Even though, still, the blank screen.

A heavy man leans forward to scratch his ankle, making the entire row of seats squeak. Kelly's feet stick and snap on the soda-splattered ground. Expecting something glamorous? Tough luck. Welcome to the Movies on Exchange, the run-down art house theater where Evelyn and Max used to see films during high school. And when Max sits here in the dark, what is he trying to conjure in his mind: an image of Evelyn at his side, accidentally nudging his elbow while, say, trying to hog the armrest?

Whatever he's thinking, of course he's thinking about her—thinking, *She came to this place.* He sits accordingly, his hands folded over his lap, his eyes on the screen. Serious. Like at a wake. It's half past noon. Evelyn was here a week ago exactly, and Max treats this space like something solemn, even though there's nothing solemn about it—not about the smell of popcorn butter in the air; nor about the signed movie posters (including, yes, *Land Without Water*) hanging on the walls above the seats, visible only when the lights are up; nor about the car horns honking outside, the door behind them exiting directly onto the street and, therefore, holding back zero sound. Nobody else in here, really— how does this place stay in business? A few other people—older people, age-shriveled—are scattered throughout like ashes, but Kelly cannot make out their faces. Are these hoary people enough to keep the doors open? The filmgoers have tracked snow up and down the aisle; it will melt soon, and the floor will be slick on the way out.

Finally the interior lights begin to blacken. Kelly dreads this movie, dreads sitting here in the dark next to her brother for two hours, dreads watching Penelope on screen, especially after the embarrassment of this morning.

There are some movie trailers—that ubiquitous nod to commerce not even this art theater can jettison—but compared with the normal trailers, with explosions and women removing clothes and getting flipped over in bed by men, the sheets clinging magically to their breasts—compared with those trailers, these ones are nothing. The movies previewed have names like *The Kid with a Bike* and *Amour* and seem to be about people staring at each other and not saying anything for long periods of time, and during every trailer, Max says something, whether "the greatest filmmakers alive" (after *The Kid with a Bike*) or "the mise-en-scène remains the same, but the concerns are unnecessarily melodramatic" (after *Amour*). Kelly nods and grunts in response, while shuffling in her hoodie, the fabric bunched around her body. It's cold in here, and she isn't about to remove the sweatshirt. Max shoots her a glare and puts his index finger to his lips, shushing her and her bunched fabric. Kelly sees her feet, stretched out onto the seat in front of her, silhouetted against the screen, the tips of her Chucks dripping water. Max can probably hear that too.

After just three or four trailers, the movie starts with a logo for Focus Features, which Kelly has seen at the beginning of other movies, though she can't remember which ones. Then a black screen, no music, except for a hum in the background and a ticking that gets louder and louder. Then the words, big on screen, white against black: LAND WITHOUT WATER. The ticking, louder, one last tick, then—a house on fire? What? It was a long time ago that Kelly tried watching this movie, bored out of her mind (the only Penelope movie she never finished), and she had forgotten this beginning. The ticking is gone, overtaken by the sound of the flames, wood cracking, some bystanders shouting, though none of those people is on screen. And after a few moments, the scene cuts to a close-up of a woman in bed: Penelope. Her hair is brown. She's asleep, without makeup, crusted knobs under her eyes. A man hovers over her, gets close to her ear, mutters, "The house at the end of the street burned," to which she responds, "Let me sleep," her lips drooping on the pillow, her nose clogged and breathing labored.

"They never explain the house fire," Max whispers into Kelly's ear. "Total rip-off of Antonioni, to work with disconnected images and then refuse to explain them."

"Totally," Kelly says drily, pretty sure her brother just said the word *pepperoni*.

In *Land Without Water*, Penelope Hayward plays two characters: one a brunette (Erica), one a blonde (Angela). The brunette Penelope is frumpy, plain, the girlfriend of the main character, their relationship as drab as the colorless house they wander through. The blond Penelope is the brunette's sister, an exciting woman from the past returning to upend both of their lives. In the first hour of the movie, the blond Penelope Hayward rears her head only in hazy sunlit shots, the wind blowing her hair, an idealized image stored somewhere in the recesses of the main dude's mind. In those glimpses, Penelope looks different from how she looks now. She looks like a memory—the main dude's memory, yes, but also Kelly's memory of an eighteen-year-old Penelope, before she mutated into a movie star. (This fact—how little Penelope looks like a star and how much she looks like Kelly's old friend—might have also contributed to Kelly's inability to make it through the movie.)

The blond Penelope Hayward becomes more prominent in the second half; her hair is natural and dirty, not bleached or polished like in later movies, and her body looks round and sensual, but not airbrushed. A little blush, which appears to have been self-applied, haphazardly, marks her face; apart from that, the makeup is unobtrusive. Whenever a close shot of Penelope pops up, Kelly can see a few stray hairs above her lip. Penelope always used to have such a hard time remembering to pluck those hairs, so one night, in high school, Kelly took a pair of tweezers and plucked Penelope, who cried from the pain.

Late in the movie, the characters come upon—really? A burning house? So it comes full circle, but what does it mean? Kelly has no idea: she hasn't understood a second of this garbage. Might've even dozed off somewhere in the middle. "Is that the same house from the beginning?" Kelly whispers to her brother, who shrugs and says, "They never explain it. Just like in the *pepperoni* film." And as the house burns, blond Penelope and the main dude do little to stop it. For a while, they try to find water—but after a while, they just watch. Then they get back into the car and drive away, down a long road, the car getting smaller and smaller as the camera looks downward until the flames eventually block the view, until the flames of the house seem to eat the camera itself. Cut to black. Surely the movie is over, right? Kelly waits for the credits to start, the music to blast, something. But no—there's just another shot of the house burning. Then another cut to black. Then a closer shot of flames. Kelly feels disoriented, blinded, angry. This movie is just fucking around now, isn't it? And then the last shot, which comes after another cut to black: a body of water, the ocean, near some rocks, under what looks like a bridge (a giant post seems to hold something up). The water ripples against the rocks, the edges of the waves elastic. The camera moves to show more of the water, to drift away from the rocks, until it reveals a person floating there—a woman. The camera gets closer, doing that thing where one shot becomes the next one slowly, with the previous image superimposed over the new one for a few seconds—what's that called? A fade? A dissolve? (As Max Enright's sister, Kelly has no excuse not to know.) Anyway, the camera gets closer, closer, until there, the face of the girl floating: it's Penelope. Is she the blond one or the brunette one? Hard to tell with her hair wet. But the character doesn't appear to be dead; instead, she smiles—faintly, but it's definitely a smile. Even Kelly knows this is the film's most famous image, the one that appears on the posters and in Google image searches. The camera finally pulls away from her, moves up, and shows a cluster of buildings on the shore. They're all on fire. Portland is burning.

Here, the movie cuts to black, and then huge letters on the screen:

WRITTEN AND DIRECTED BY

DARREN STANFORD

"What the fuck," Kelly moans.

Max stares at the screen. "You've never actually seen your friend's film before?"

"Not all the way through, no."

"The only significant piece of cinema to come out of Portland."

"So *now* it's significant." Kelly nudges him. "Ready?" Something in her hoodie pocket crumples like tinfoil.

"Hang on," Max says, eyes still on the screen. "This is the only important part."

The few people scattered throughout now make their way toward the door in the back—the door that exits directly onto Exchange Street. But Max stays put, staring at the credits.

After a minute, Max hits Kelly on the shoulder. "Okay, watch, are you watching?" It startles Kelly. This isn't her brother: this is Mom, the way she used to hit people on the arm when something supposedly magical was about to happen—sometimes in a movie, but sometimes at a party, when a drunk woman was about to recite a speech on something, or when a blustery man was about to strum a song on a guitar. "Are you watching?" Max says, hitting her again, pointing at the screen. "There."

On screen, the SPECIAL THANKS section appears, a dense block of names scrolling upward. Kelly watches as mostly local businesses and vendors are thanked (Coffee by Design, Material Objects, Silly's, Norm Jabar)—but then, there, she sees it. She has to squint, but still she sees it: EVELYN ANDERSSON.

A typo? "Shouldn't it be one *S*?" she asks her brother.

Max shakes his head. "Her stage name. From Harriet Andersson, spelled with two S's. One of Bergman's actresses in Evelyn's favorite film, *Cries and Whispers.*"

"I don't know," she says. But with the name spelled *that* way? Well, when Kelly imagined the name spelled the normal way, it was a different matter, there were probably thousands of people named Evelyn Anderson. Is it possible that Max actually has a point about all of this—that it might, indeed, be the same person?

Before Kelly can sort anything out, Max is on his feet. "Come on," he says, reaching for his sister—the first time in years, maybe ever, that he has held out a hand to her. But before she can take it, he pulls it away, turning from her, heading toward the back of the theater, toward the sunlight. Kelly's own hand hangs there a moment, before drifting alongside her body as she follows Max outside, where it now snows, where the snow has already begun to gather on the ground, her brother nowhere near her fingertips.

After her trip to the theater to watch *Land Without Water*, Evelyn walked up the cobblestone street, underneath the purple bulbs, geodesic almost, hanging from the trees as Christmas decorations, and past the brick buildings with their doors opening into restaurants, the steam from the diners' collective breath hitting the air like a smoke bomb. Evelyn trudged toward Casco Bay Books, the coffee shop and used-book store where she briefly worked. According to reports, Evelyn entered Casco Bay Books at 2:57 P.M. As Kelly and Max head up the incline of the street on their way to the coffee shop, the hourly church bell audible throughout the city dings three times, meaning the siblings have made good time, only three minutes late. Once in Casco Bay Books, Evelyn sat there for thirty or so minutes, in the corner, scribbling something in a notebook that, later, she walked to the parking lot and burned, eyes vacant, body moving like a somnambulist. "She loved this old film," Max says at the door to the building housing the coffee shop, "called *The Cabinet of Dr. Caligari*, all about sleepwalking. Robert Wiene directed it. It's a masterpiece of German expressionism."

"Huh," Kelly says, not sure how this connects with anything. She reaches for the door handle, which chills her palm. "After you," she says, the door whining open.

The building is two stories: on the bottom live Videoport, Bull Moose record store, and a pizza place called Anthony's, a fixture at which used to be a dude named Leon who played in ska bands all around town and whom Kelly was always pleased to find flirting with her and Penelope, until she realized he flirted with everyone—even the boys. The lighting in this building feels familiar to Kelly, garish and yellow—yellow like mineral piss, like piss after a strong vitamin—and the various businesses, a nexus of hip Portland, create a particular scent, balanced between pizza, cigarette smoke, body odor, and the dust covering old VHS cartridges. This smell always used to attach itself to the plastic white Videoport logo bags provided with your rental; Max carried this smell home, filled the house with it.

"She always used to draw these pictures inspired by *Caligari*," Max says, headed up the stairs toward Casco Bay Books. It takes Kelly a second to remember he'd been talking about this—whatever the fuck it is—before. The rubber mat walkway is slick, melted snow and rock salt stuck in its crevices. Feet squeak here. "She used to imagine remodeling her bedroom to look like a *Caligari* set, all sharp angles, Gothic lighting."

Casco Bay Books always seemed too cool for Kelly—though, to be clear, it was in no way a kind of cool she aspired to. The patrons were mostly high school and college kids (and a handful of mildly creepy older bohemians). They wore jeans and T-shirts so tight it was a wonder they could move at all, and they sipped coffee while talking about movies and art, each kid trying to one-up the others with his or her eccentricity and esoteric knowledge. As Kelly's and Max's feet squeak and pound down the hallway, the echoes armylike, she glances through the coffee shop's window and sees that nothing has changed, except maybe for fewer books, more clothes for sale, and additional wall space for black-and-white photographs of fruit and empty swing sets. A handful of people cluster around tables as youthfully as they can muster, none of them looking even half as morose and run-down as Max. How has he ever fit in here?

Well, the way he enters, maybe he never has. He avoids eye contact with everyone, hurrying to the window in the corner, next to the corkboard advertising bands and art openings—and, yes, also advertising the face of Evelyn, the word *missing* covered up, making it look like any other flyer, something advertising an exhibit you'd go to a grungy gallery to see. Max stands there, next to Evelyn's face. In the heavy air of the place, drooping with heat and coffee fumes, Kelly has no idea what to do—stand with her brother, sit at a table, order a coffee, what? How long will he want to stand here motionless with that haunted look in his eyes?

A barista stands behind the counter, shoulders hunched, a mug under a machine that produces a frothing noise, rattling so hard the screws might fly off. After a moment, he sprinkles the resulting foam with cinnamon and walks the concoction to a table, where a gentleman with gray dreadlocks thanks him. When the barista turns Kelly's way, she catches the familiar sight of his red crew cut. Kelly recognizes this man... not that she went to high school with him, but from somewhere, right? But something is off. His features are familiar, but not the pudge around his abdomen and the way it sneaks out over the top of his jeans, nor the scowl on his face—nor, most alarmingly, those two exclamation point tattoos, one on either side of his neck; whoever this guy is, he didn't have *those* before.

"Hey, you," the barista grunts, approaching Max, eyes locked on him—and not in a pleasant way. "What have I—"

"Chad." Kelly puts out her hand. "Remember me?"

See, it hits her, all of a sudden: one night, senior year, Kelly smoked pot with Chad and some of his other friends, all lacrosse stars at the nearby Portland High School. They all met up after some random party—the sort where teenagers become electric and spend hours bumping against each other, trying to shake the static off—and the lacrosse players pushed Chad and Kelly together and started chanting "Kiss, kiss, kiss." So they put their dry lips together, and then each drank a gallon of water and fell asleep. A night like many—one that Kelly remembers only because, the next morning, Chad left a note pinned to her cell phone that said *Sorry*, and instead of his name, it looked like he had signed *Chud*. Never again did they speak, or even see each other, but once in a while she would spot his name in a newspaper after winning something or other. Now, pudgy and tattooed and angry looking—*this is what happened to the poor devil?*

When Kelly says his name, his eyes widen in recognition, but in a vague way that demonstrates no urge to do anything about it. "This is your friend?" he grumbles, throwing a thumb at Max.

Kelly watches the fine hairs atop Chad's lip. When Chad speaks, those hairs, they wave hello. "My brother," Kelly says.

"Huh." Chad shrugs. "Well, your brother can't be here anymore." His eyes dart to Max, an exhausted fury blackening them out; he looks like a boss ready to fire somebody, emotionally drained after years of worthless discipline. "And he *knows* he can't be here anymore."

"Why?"

"Because I have a rule about him. It's really simple. He can't be here." The exclamation points on his neck make everything he says sound louder.

"Listen, can we talk?" Kelly raises her eyebrows. She puts her hands out to show she poses no threat. "Please?" Then she juts her head to the left, proposing a location for a chat out of Max's earshot, though she doubts he cares or notices one way or another.

After a deep breath, Chad shrugs. "What?"

"My brother," Kelly whispers, once they've taken a few steps away from Max, "is going through a hard time. I'm sure whatever he did to piss you off is totally legit, but can you cut him a break? Just for today?"

Chad stares back. Kelly can't stand it; as she waits for an answer, she cranes her neck and looks up to the ceiling, at the panels of pastel color above them—a soft-hued ceiling better suited for a mental ward than a trendy café.

"Are you two close?" Chad asks.

Kelly scoffs—buying time, really, since she has no idea how to answer the question. "That's none of your business."

"Didn't think so. But I'll tell you what's my business: this place." Chad points his index finger at Max. "And I've only ever thrown one person out."

"Yeah? Let me guess."

"One person," Chad reiterates, counting to one on his hand and holding up the proof.

"Fine, and after today, keep him out. He's a fucking weirdo. I don't blame you. But for today, let him stand here for a few minutes. He's looking for a friend. This girl who went missing. Used to work here, actually."

"Who, Evelyn?" Chad sneers the name.

"You know her?"

"You bet I know her. I *hired* her, eight years ago. Then she worked here for seven months."

The precision startles her, so Kelly tries out the math in her head: eight years ago he *hired* her... so did Chad start working here after college? Or did he start working here straight out of high school? She wants to ask him what he prefers: winning lacrosse trophies or working—as a manager, it seems—in a coffee shop that must be in danger of closing its doors. Hard to believe his change in appearance, anyway. Of course, it's possible he's mulling over the same thoughts about her—minus the job part, of course.

Thinking about all this, she misses part of what he says, but then snaps back in when he goes, "And your charming brother—know what he did? He used to follow her. Used to sit here every goddamn day. Used to stare at her. When she was working."

"They were best friends," Kelly says.

"Best friends?" Chad laughs. "She didn't want anything to do with him."

"Well, maybe since then," Kelly says, but her voice lacks energy.

"Since then, I dunno, I don't care," Chad says. "I would've kicked him out without question, but she said not to, leave him alone, all that. She pitied him. But after she quit, he kept coming here, same table, like he was waiting for her, looking for her, something. Did this for years, a couple times a week, but what could I do? Guy just sat there. After a while, though, he started bothering customers. Hovered near their tables. Tried to talk to people, butt in on private conversations. A few years ago, he got into an argument with one of my best regulars. Something about a movie they were playing down on Exchange. So I threw him the hell out. Now he walks by the window all the time, real slow, looking inside. But I can't do anything about that. I don't own the building." Chad blinks. "Yet."

Over Chad's shoulder, Kelly sees the guy with the dreadlocks, rainbow scarf around his neck drooping into a smile down his back, standing at the counter, awaiting assistance—but Kelly has no plans to tell Chad this. Instead, with her fingertips and nose feeling numb (the cold, hopefully), she says, "Well, I didn't know any of that."

Chad shrugs. "Your relationship with him isn't my business. But him getting the fuck out of here is." Those exclamation points. Kelly almost covers her ears.

The dreadlocked man, sick of waiting, goes behind the counter and fishes a spoon out of a drying rack resting on a towel near the sink. Like a cat hearing a noise in the night, Chad spins around and points at him. "Eli. Drop the spoon. Wait a goddamned second." When Chad turns back to Kelly, his face tightens. "Get him out of here. I mean it. I *will* call the police. Your brother really freaks people the fuck out, okay?" Chad looks Kelly up and down, holding his gaze the longest on her white Chucks, now stained with brown snow. "Good to see you again," Chad says, spinning away like the athlete he once was to intercept Eli at the counter.

"Fine, fine, fine," Kelly mutters under her breath, staccato, but unsure the reason for this muttering (not a habit of hers, normally). She turns toward Max, who still stands there, a dead man on his feet, neither muscles nor nerve endings working. Completely motionless. If an industrial fan were pointed at him, no doubt he'd find a way to keep his clothing from rustling.

"We need to go," Kelly says.

"Wait."

"Right fucking now." She grabs his wrist and yanks him from his standstill; it feels like pulling from a garden a particularly stubborn weed. She drags him from the warmth of the coffee shop, ejecting them back into the snow and what sun still remains, mere threads of light poking through the clouds.

"Five years ago. That was the last time I saw Evelyn, okay?" Max waves his hand in the air. "Can you not blow that shit on me?"

Kelly flicks her ash onto the snow; she'd bummed the smoke from a protester, one of a cluster of people holding poorly written signs in the park. "Why did you lie?" she asks—but it's obvious, isn't it? The same reason Max lied about having a job. Probably lied about having a roommate, friends. Because here he is, nearly thirty, and what has he made of himself? He's nowhere—not even close. Kelly knows the answer to her question as soon as it leaves her mouth—and Max, knowing that his sister knows the answer, refrains from answering at all. "Well, you should've said something," Kelly says, bringing the cigarette to her lips for another drag. "I looked like an idiot in there." The smoke hits her lungs, then flees.

Max coughs, waves his arm again, and stands up. "It's disgusting. I hate it."

"I can't help it," Kelly says.

"Yes, you can. You can not smoke." Max stands in front of her, bouncing back and forth, maybe to keep warm, though maybe also trying to avoid the wisps of smoke lifting off the tip of her cigarette. "Mom never smoked. I don't know where you got it from."

Kelly feels pressure in her chest, like a hand on her rib cage. "What? Are you fucking kidding me? Mom never smoked?"

Max looks away from his sister, looks across the park.

"All Mom did was smoke. Filled the whole fucking house with it."

No response; instead, Max narrows his eyes at the cluster of people across the way, the ones with the signs. Then he looks at the sky, then the other direction across the park, toward the street. He's an actor who's about to perform a stunt and is judging the dimensions of the stage.

"Could you really not smell it? The way it got in everything? I smelled it on my fucking textbooks at school, for God's sake."

Max shrugs. "I figured that was you."

"That was me? When I was six? When I was a baby even?"

Her brother dances again, dodging a dart of smoke. "How would I remember what you smelled like as a baby?"

Few people hang in the park on such a cold, snowy afternoon, the white accumulating maybe two or three inches; approaching Friday night, most people would rather sit in restaurants and bars, filling their stomachs. On the southwest boulders of Post Office Park, the protesters—whatever they're protesting—hold signs that say things like THE MAYANS WERE RIGHT and NEWTOWN WAS GOD'S WORK and THE END IS COMING. In the back of the park, the snowdrifts whiten the unoccupied benches; today, people warm themselves in Sonny's—the spiffy restaurant just beyond the trees—and look through frosted glass upon the park, but nobody sits on the outside benches—too cold and snowy. In the southeast part of the park, some people Kelly remembers from a decade ago are out, sitting on frozen stone, the deadbeats who have nothing better to do, will never have anywhere else to go: Devlin and Oliver—but no Cat Dancer. Where's Cat Dancer? Kelly always liked him, the wiry man who wore a spandex jumpsuit and cat ears and used to jump from rock to rock, twirling ribbons in his hands—none of this in a manner even *vaguely* well coordinated. Nevertheless, today, Devlin strums his guitar, and Oliver pounds his bongos, and they both wear heavy trench coats, and they pass something back and forth, something small and burning, and they smile at each other, temporarily pausing the playing of music to color their lungs with smoke. They put on a show for the protesters only, as nobody else hangs out in the park today—none of the high schoolers these musicians usually seek to impress, none of the dreadlocked girls with tattoos and nose rings and big dogs on choke collars. But in spite of this, Devlin and Oliver sing.

Kelly watches the two men so intently for a moment that it really surprises her when Max says, "I'm not a fool, you know."

She turns to her brother, who stares at her. "I know," she says, taking another drag, the nicotine wobbling her vision, making the park feel like a boat ride.

"See," he says, hands in the air, but not to wave away smoke, "see, if this were a film, if the scene were just starting, if I were directing it, know what I'd do?"

Kelly can't keep up with his changes in temperature anymore, so she rolls her eyes and says, "I really don't give a—"

"The camera would begin overhead, like the view of the plaza that begins *The Conversation*, to provide spatial coherence for the spectator." He shifts his feet back and forth, looking skyward as he says all of this, making a box with his hands. "The camera would start up high, while the snow falls around it, downward mostly, though sometimes gusting across the lens to momentarily blind the spectator—for reference, see the opening shot of *The Umbrellas of Cherbourg* and imagine snow instead of rain—but the camera would hang there nevertheless, providing a view of the setting."

Kelly glances around the park quickly, wanting to make sure nobody watches him, snickers at him, the way he stands, eyes to the sky, hands in the air.

"And the spectator would watch the scene for a moment," Max continues, "kind of like one watches the wide shots closely—although for very different reasons—in films by John Ford and Sergio Leone and Michael Haneke. The spectator would watch, trying to figure out where his eye should fall—until there! See? Something has changed. Someone has entered the frame." Max lowers his hands and points toward the back of the park, where the empty benches are. "And so, leaning forward, the spectator would see. On the north side of the park—so the upper part of the frame—where those snow-covered benches lie unoccupied, a figure would enter. And the spectator would want to see this figure—*you*"—his finger extended toward Kelly now, entering her headspace—"would want to see this figure, so badly that you would lean forward in your seat to try and get a better look through the snow gauze. But you can't get a better look, so the camera would help you. The camera would begin its descent, craning downward. You would float into the dream of the film."

"Marvelous," Kelly says, throwing the cigarette to the ground. "I left my Oscar at home. Otherwise, it'd be yours."

Max laughs. "Who'd want an Oscar? None of the best directors ever won. You want to know what happened the last time I saw Evelyn?"

The way he packages these thoughts together, Kelly almost doesn't notice the shift: at first, she thinks his mention of Evelyn is just more movie nonsense, and she watches Devlin across the way cough as he passes the joint back to Oliver, their singing ceased.

But then Max's words hit her, and she looks up at him. "Yeah, what happened?" Kelly sits up straight and then tries to loosen her joints, not wanting to seem overeager. Where does that leave her? Looking something like a marionette, probably, with wooden arms flopping against the bench.

"It was five years ago, like I said at the beginning of this scene," Max says.
"Beginning of the scene?"

"The scene of this film opened on me saying, 'Five years.'"

"I thought it opened with the camera overhead."

"Five years ago," Max says. "It was December..."

By calling in to a radio contest, Max tells Kelly, and answering correctly
its trivia question ("In which Alfred Hitchcock film has a killer, at the beginning, recently fled the police in Portland, Maine? Do you know? Any
idea? It's *Shadow of a Doubt*. An easy question. Almost childish..."), he won
two tickets to a special screening of *Land Without Water* at the Portland
Museum of Art, which would be followed by a discussion/Q&A with
Darren Stanford himself. The film had been playing at Nickelodeon for
a few weeks and was receiving national acclaim, but Max had already
seen it and his negative opinions had begun their gestation. Nevertheless,
being the thorough critic he was—"And still am," he assures Kelly—he
decided to take another look. After all, he'd also hated *Cries and Whispers*—"Evelyn's favorite film, whose final monologue she used to recite
with regularity, almost like a mantra"—the first time.

So that night, he gave his extra ticket to a brown-eyed girl outside (who,
upon receiving it, kissed a nearby guy in skinny jeans and hustled inside
the museum without another glace at her benefactor) and then crowded
into the small screening room—smaller even than the theater at the Movies on Exchange, but cleaner—and he watched *Land Without Water* for a
second time, feeling his "attention slip like smooth wet glass" from his
fingertips.

"Did you just think of that," Kelly asks, "or have you been rehearsing
this?"

"I couldn't focus on the film," Max says. "I was too busy thinking about
The Glazen Shelves"—specifically, he tells Kelly, about the thirty hours of
footage he shot for it, about how angelic Evelyn looked sitting on that
dock with wind and sun in her hair, about new ways to handle the ending,
"which had always given me trouble, the question of whether the two
leads should stay together. God, I've done draft after draft, yet I've never
figured it out."

Anyway, after the screening (so Max tells her), one of the museum
employees came onstage to announce that Darren Stanford was running

late but would emerge in a few minutes to discuss the film ("Such an appearance would turn out to be a rarity, given the complete lack of publicity he did following *Land Without Water*"). But how could Max sit still and listen to Darren Stanford pontificate about *Land Without Water*, his puddle of art film puke? Max was the one destined to become the next great Portland filmmaker, and he should have been on that stage instead; it should have been *The Glazen Shelves* at the museum that frozen December night.

"I wasn't bitter about it, though," he says. "I just knew it. Like one knows a fact."

So, after the screening, Max climbed over some long-legged people in his row, then made his way up the aisle and out of the screening room and exited the museum. He saw others standing outside—young people, lighting cigarettes, flicking collars skyward for shelter from the breeze. Max flew his hands to his own collar to pop it—to warm his neck—but unhappily remembered he wore a sweater instead of a jacket. So with no collar to pop, and no cigarette to light, and no companion with whom to speak (he's digging for sympathy now, Kelly knows, and she wants to crank her hand in the air, *hurry up, get to the point*), he started off home, going around the side of the museum to head south down High Street, looking upon the Portland bay spread out before him, seeing all the lights and streets snaking together into ramshackle circuitry, lit up and electric... (*Now, definitely, you really must please get to the point*, Kelly thinks.)

As he hiked down High Street, he heard something up ahead and then saw two silhouettes standing at the back museum entrance: a bulky man and a slim woman. He planned to pass without eye contact, so "I turned my attention to the brick houses around me, then frontward to the dark water—upon the surface of which city lights shivered—at the bottom of the hill." (How can Kelly take him seriously when he talks like this? All of this, she knows, she can see him, rehearsing this whole speech in the mirror, memorizing it like a script.)

But then the woman spoke, Max tells Kelly. And what did she say, this woman? *Please, I need to see him. Please.* It was Evelyn. The back of his throat went dry, and he quickened his pace to meet them.

No entry this way. You need to go to the front and show your ticket.

I don't have a ticket, I told you.

Then no entry period.

Max's feet felt like feathers as he glided on the ground, sighing her name, *Evelyn, Evelyn.* She and the man looked at Max, who sighed, sighed, *It's me, I'm here. Where have you been?*

Closer, Max saw them clearly. The man wore a shirt with STAFF splayed across his substantial chest. Moisture glistened on Evelyn's red-splotched cheeks, and she sniffed something back—something so thick it sounded clogged in her throat. Max came to a stop.

Evelyn stared at him and opened her mouth, startled to see him. She huffed, then sharply drew air. Her shoulders quaked, and it seemed like she was seeing how long she could hold her breath. Then she looked Max in the eye and shook her head, and a fresh drip rolled down her cheek. She turned from both men and hurried across High Street, neglecting to check for oncoming traffic, then dove into a parking lot. The light held her for a moment, but Evelyn hustled into darkness, and Max lost her.

"This was not the response I'd desired," Max says.

"Obviously," Kelly says.

So Max called her name. He made a megaphone of his hands and called her name once more. Then he launched himself after her, and a couple cars honked, "but what did I care? Across the street I flew, calling her name again—again. I ran into the darkened lot and couldn't see anything. Where was she? I'd completely and utterly lost her, but this didn't stop me. I ran, shouting her name into the darkness, through the residential parts of Portland, shouting her name into trees, into bushes, shouting her name at houses lit dimly as though by candlelight, their gentle glows illuminating miniature portions of the road. I shouted her name, and for half an hour, I ran around my city, until I was lost and confused in Portland for the first time in my life. But still I called to her, 'Evelyn, Evelyn—'" He stops, takes a breath. "So that was that."

"Bravo." Kelly claps weakly, shaking her head. "Bravo."

Max narrows his eyes. "What? You asked. That's what happened."

"I didn't ask, you just started talking."

Max's eyes, still narrowed, not understanding.

"Forget it," Kelly says, "I was just thinking I might get a little honesty here—you know, something real—but I should have know it would be just *another fucking performance.*"

She scans the park. Anyone she can bum another smoke from? She can't spot the protester who loaned her the last one. *Hey,* she should tell Max, *get back into character and use all that speechifying to rustle me up a pack of Camel Lights.* Meanwhile, Devlin puts down his guitar and stands, trench coat falling to his ankles; the way it flutters open reveals, for a second, bare legs, and Kelly wonders whether, underneath the garment, he wears only his boxers. Devlin clears his throat, turns to the protesters, and begins to recite... a poem, it sounds like, though nothing Kelly recognizes:

Leaning from the platform, waiting for a glimmer
to braid the rails

the eyes of the action hero cut from the poster

all that concrete pressing down

"I'm going to find her," Max says. "I'm not messing this up, you understand? Last time, five years ago, she got away, disappeared into darkness. But now..." He shakes his head. "Tell me the time."

Kelly fishes her cell phone out of her pocket. "It's half past three."

"Half past three." Max nods, biting his lip. "She would've been leaving Casco Bay Books right about now. Burning those pages in the parking lot. So let's go."

"You have to refresh my memory," Kelly says. "Where did she go next?"

"She walked down Commercial Street," Max says—which is where Kelly found him at around this time yesterday. "And then she went across the Casco Bay Bridge."

"Then where?"

"That's it," Max says. "Then nowhere."

And Devlin, the poet, concludes his poem:

A candle could keep you alive
the engine of your lungs

will heat the air around you, someone will
miss you, they will send out dogs

You must be somewhere, right?

A new shot of the park, but Max and Kelly? Gone. Only the bench left behind, bare from when she brushed off the snow.

Within an hour, the storm has fizzled out, the light has vanished, and the twins have reached the clunker of Casco Bay Bridge, which flies outward from the banks of the Portland shore and lands in the city of South Portland. Kelly rarely came down here when growing up; she never had much use for South Portland, with its Blockbusters and community colleges and apartment complexes for elderly people. Now, they cross the bridge, the twins, shuffling along the walkway as traffic slides by.

"You know what happened here, right?"

"Happened where?"

"They filmed the end of *Land Without Water* underneath this bridge. That's where they filmed it. The scene when Penelope floats on the water. That's *under* the bridge."

"Okay." Kelly throws up her hands. "So?"

"That's where Evelyn went."

"Or maybe she went somewhere else." Kelly gestures ahead, where she can see the faint glow of a golden McDonald's sign. "Maybe she needed some gristle nuggets."

"If she came here," Max says, "she went under the bridge. It's the film. The reason she's thanked at the end. The reason she wanted to get into the museum so badly the night of the screening."

A passing truck splashes Kelly with wind, and she slips a bit on a patch of unsalted walkway; while steadying herself, she dislodges a smidgen of packed snow and kicks it off the bridge. Max stares at this clump falling straight down. Didn't even help his sister, didn't even reach out. Kelly brushes herself off, even though there isn't anything to brush off; this is just her automatic response to falling.

"Careful," Max warns.

"Like five minutes later you say that. Tell you what? I need to take a trip to Bean's," she mutters. "Get me some snow boots." Then, remembering

Mom, Kelly raises her pitch to something cartoonishly high and says, "Ooh, I'm an out-of-towner. I like to go to Bean's and walk around real fast and bump into people!"

When they were kids, their mother always tried to do impressions of people, but the impressions never made any sense, like some kind of absurdist stand-up routine. One day, Mom was watching the news, and Joe Cupo said, "Looks like we'll have snow for the weekend," and Mom said, "Ooh, I'm Joe Cupo and I wish I were made of snow," jazz-handing. For whatever reason, Max and Kelly curled into balls of laughter. (Mom laughed too, though probably for the wrong reasons.) The siblings adopted this as a sure way of cracking each other up. Max would utter, "Ooh, I'm Kelly and I like to wear French fries for earrings," and Kelly would retort, "Ooh, I'm Max and I think snow shovels should be used to shovel snow." It was funny. At least for them. At least back then.

But now, Max keeps his head lowered, keeps moving onward. Too serious for such games now.

"You kicked that snow off the bridge," Max says after a moment.

"Yeah? So?"

"I watched it fall."

"I know. Did you watch *me* fall?"

"I couldn't even see when it hit the water."

"It was a little snowball. Barely that. A clump."

Max stops. They have almost reached where the bridge arrives at South Portland and tapers off. "Do you think Evelyn went over the edge?" he asks.

Kelly feels a lump start up in her throat. She hasn't thought much about what happened to Evelyn, hasn't thought that something bad really has happened to her. But it seems likely, right? Of course something bad has happened. If Evelyn was fucked up on something—and really, Kelly knows, she *had* to have been fucked up on something, the way she was acting that last night, walking barefoot, scribbling in journals, burning paper—then it wouldn't have taken much to send her small body plummeting.

She doesn't say anything and goes to the edge, to the railing, and leans out to look into the water. She lifts her feet, then balances them on the second horizontal bar of the railing, so that the top bar crosses right under her breasts. She doesn't mean to be reckless, but if a strong wind came through, or if somebody gave her a little push, would she fall like that clump of snow? The wind blows, and Kelly's hair darts around, covering her eyes. The wind seems stronger than ever. Kelly looks over her shoulder at Max and shrugs. "It's hard to go over the edge," she says. "Hard to have an accident here."

The wind becomes so strong that she can hear the traffic no longer, unless the wind and the traffic have merged into one monolith of sound. Kelly leans farther out over the water and looks down. The wind keeps pounding on her, and she fidgets, repositioning her hands and legs to hold fast in the face of the winter onslaught. The metal bar she holds feels so cold. The water looks pissed, waves contorting like angry faces as they hit against the shore, lit mostly by the streetlamps lining the surface streets near the water's edge.

Of course, Kelly thinks, maybe it was no accident, whatever happened to Evelyn.

Wind comes powerfully—a shove. Kelly wobbles, and Max grabs her shoulder, steadying her. She didn't know he'd moved so close behind.

"We don't need to go down there," she says.

Max yanks his hand away from her and listens. To what? Kelly hears nothing apart from the traffic, whooshing behind them in a steady stream.

"The cars," Max says, looking at the smear of headlights. "Sounds like a film projector whirring to life, doesn't it?"

"I don't know what that sounds like," Kelly says, knowing that no matter what, they're going underneath this bridge tonight, in the dark. Not a goddamned thing can stop Max now.

Kelly and Max step over snowbanks and approach the base of the bridge. This terrain proves treacherous, so they make wings of their arms to improve their balance as they cross snow-dusted rocks. Kelly takes her time, her shoes inadequate, her balance rickety. Max shares none of his sister's hesitation. More agile than Kelly has ever seen him in his life, he spirits ahead, from rock to rock, like he does this every day, like this is his usual path to work. He gets several feet ahead of her; if he keeps leaving her behind, eventually he'll disappear into the dark. Only the distant streetlamps on the bridge overhead light this path across the rocks. Nevertheless, Kelly can see something, toward which her brother heads: some thin beams of light playing near the water—and, yes, voices, laughter, profanity, the familiar sound of spray paint cans shaking, the hissing sound of the colors being expunged, and the other grunts of the young. On one step toward the light, Max's foot slips. He stumbles but corrects himself. "Hey," Kelly says, "not so fast," but Max pays no attention and continues, eventually turning a corner, out of Kelly's vision.

As she scrambles forward, there is silence; the youthful noises stop. And then she hears her brother say, "What the hell is that?"

Kelly knows this will be bad, even before anything bad has happened.

When she turns the corner, she sees what Max sees, what the flashlights show her. Down here, under the bridge, among broken bottles and cigarette butts and plastic bags, Kelly sees two young men in the shadows, one of them on a ladder leaned against the bridge's pillar, putting the finishing touches on an image Kelly can faintly make out: a humungous painting of Penelope Hayward's face—a nearly photographic representation of the final shot of *Land Without Water*, the eerie smirk warping Penelope's lips. This is where they filmed the last shot of the movie? Well, there that very shot is, painted in this spot. And Max raises his arms as though Penelope's face is a flyer he can tear down. Again, he groans, "What the hell is that?" He seems posed, and Kelly wonders whether her brother is mimicking a film.

"Hey, man." The guy on the ground says this. The second guy on the ladder, painting away, barely pays attention. Both men wear black, rendering them almost invisible except for their heads, pale like two Kleenexes glimpsed in a darkened theater. "Need something?"

"This guy," the guy on the ladder says, exasperated. "Forget it."

"Her face can't be here," Max says. "No, no."

"Yeah?" The guy on the ground laughs. "It's been here for weeks, man. We're just touching it up."

"Don't talk to him." The guy on the ladder comes down, the metal legs wobbling on the rocks. Will he fall? No—he makes it to the ground and turns toward Max. Neither guy has seen Kelly yet. Perhaps even

Max has forgotten his sister lingering behind. "This dude's been following us around," the guy with the paint says, "and I'm sick of it."

The other guy looks Max up and down. "You're not following us,
right?"

"That's terrible," Max says, still looking at the portrait of Penelope. "To
memorialize that film?" He shakes his head. "You have terrible taste."

Kelly remembers the painting she saw earlier, on the way to Nosh—
all those colorful movie images, churned together like a pop culture fe-
ver dream—whose artists Max complained never listen to him. "Do you
know these guys?" she asks him, closer now.

"Never seen them before," Max shoots back at her over his shoulder,
before moving ahead and widening the gap between them once more.

A truck flies overhead, rumbling the entire bridge, making a rushing
noise so brutal that, for a second, Kelly thinks the steel and concrete
might crumble.

The guy with the spray paint comes toward Max, rattling the can with
menace. "Terrible taste? Us?" He points at Max with the can. "What do
you know about our taste? All you do is follow us around and rant at us
about movies, like you're the world's greatest fucking film scholar. I'm
sick of it."

"Easy there, Adrian," the other guy says, closer to Max.

So where were we, before our interview got interrupted?
You wanted to use **The Glazen Shelves** *as a way of applying to film schools, but
you didn't finish it in time.*
Ah, yes. That's correct. Life gets in the way, you know?
*Well, life, of course, always life. But eleven years is a substantial diversion.
Especially when compared to the relatively short length of time these films
often take. Darren Stanford shot* **Land Without Water** *in a couple months. Yes,
you can say that the screenplay had a long gestation period, but he was making other short films during the gestation. He was working jobs, making contacts.
Yet it seems, to my mind, that you have done absolutely nothing for the past
ten years of your life.*
Well... I don't quite know what to say. "Nothing" is in the eye of the beholder,
perhaps.
Perhaps. But Darren Stanford's path was quite different. He finished **Land Without Water** *at age twenty-five (four years younger than you are right now) and
released the film to rapturous acclaim.*
What's your question?

"You easy there, *Leo*," Adrian says. Kelly wonders why these two guys are calling each other by name in this way, as if characters in a movie trying awkwardly to let the audience know who they are. But then again, at least Kelly knows their names now, for whatever that's worth.

"He's just messing around," Leo says, then raises an eyebrow at Max. "Right, man?"

Max shakes his head. "No."

Goddamn, Max—he could've gotten out of this!

Adrian has reached Leo now, stands next to him, a few feet away from Max. He shakes the spray paint can, still. Rattle, rattle. Between the can and the traffic overhead, nothing but rattling. Both of these men are attractive in a boyish sort of way; closer now, Kelly can tell they're much younger than she and Max—probably twenty or so. These guys have the same hips, oddly feminine and curved. They wear warm-looking L.L. Bean fleeces, which hug their bodies and accentuate their shapes.

Adrian spits on the ground. "Fuck him anyway. He doesn't know shit about movies."

"They're not called *movies*," Max says, stepping forward, a small rock tumbling under his foot, rolling a little ways down the slight incline. "They're called *films*. You're a philistine, and you'd be lucky to learn from me."

Well, you began work on The Glazen Shelves *when you were eighteen, and then you abruptly stopped. In effect, you failed, didn't you? You failed at the film.*

It's not a failure...

Oh, but think of it from the outside. How it looks to people. In high school, you took advantage of Evelyn's friendship by putting her through the ordeal of working on this film—

No, no, no, it was her film too.

What I heard was it became an ordeal for her. That you dragged her to see all those films at Movies on Exchange in the name of "research," that you awkwardly knocked your elbow against hers, that you tried to hold her hand—

No, she wanted to see those films.

She put so much effort into making that film, working on it with you throughout that year, putting up with your insecurities and obsessions. And then, after your mom died—

I don't want to talk about Mom.

After your mom died, Evelyn couldn't take it anymore, could she? She couldn't put up with your possessiveness. She couldn't put up with your insanities. For

"I'm going to NYU, man," Adrian says, prodding his own chest with his index finger. "Next year. Tisch. What the fuck do *you* know?"

"You couldn't even think of directors who employ rapid montage."

"What?"

"You said the other day. I heard you talking to those girls."

"See?" Adrian nudges Leo. "Following me."

Kelly has no idea what Max means, or when he heard Adrian say this about whatever kind of montage, but she wonders whether Adrian's right.

"You said that to those girls," Max says, "when you were describing the film you wanted to cast them in."

"I said no other directors do what I'm doing," Adrian says, "which of course they do! All filmmaking is copying! But I wanted to impress them."

"The directors?"

"The girls, you moron!"

"A likely story," Max says, crossing his arms.

"You *really* think I can't think of directors who employ rapid montage?"

"Name one."

"Name one? How 'bout Eisenstein."

"Oh, Eisenstein. Oh, of course, Eisenstein! What an obscure director to name! Vertov's contributions to the development of montage were far

---

her own well-being and sense of safety—sense of a future—she had to leave your film. Isn't that right? And now, it's all meaningless. You'll never finish it.
Our work wasn't meaningless. Evelyn was my friend. I'll finish the film.
She wasn't your friend, Max. She was a girl who was being nice to you. Because she felt sorry for you. Until, of course, she reached her breaking point. Am I wrong?
[No response]
Your relationship meant far more to you than it ever did to her.
She came to Mom's funeral.
Of course she did. Mom died during the making of the film, when Evelyn was spending a lot of time around you. She wasn't evil. Of course she went to the funeral. What was she going to do? Say no? Not go?
But she sat up front with me...
You made her sit up front.
[No response]
And after she saw how possessive you were—how obsessed you were with her—she couldn't take it anymore. She couldn't stand to be around you

more aesthetically accomplished, but you probably don't know much about Vertov, do you, so you go with Eisenstein instead."

"Vertov?" Adrian throws his hands in the air. "No, of course not. I don't know anything about *Man with a Movie Camera*. And I certainly don't think that Vertov was nothing more than a second-rate Dovzhenko."

Max scoffs.

"Dovzhenko? You scoff?" Adrian smiles. "You clearly don't know him. Haven't you seen *Arsenal*, the greatest Soviet film ever made?"

As Max stares at Adrian, Kelly feels the situation tilt ever so slightly; can it be that Max is stumped?

"*Arsenal*? No? Even though its modernist symbolism was a clear influence on Parajanov? Or, let me think of somebody even *you* would have heard of... Tarkovsky, perhaps?"

Max squeezes his fists even tighter, and his shoulders begin to shake, and his face reddens. His temperature, frying. Then his hand flies, points at Penelope. "Get that goddamn picture down from there!" Max's jaw stays clenched.

---

because you were obsessed with her. Because you thought she was going to save your life, save your film. You scared her, Max. She couldn't take it. And why would she have wanted to be around you, the way you acted during the filming? She hated you. She felt bad for you and you trapped her. And she finally escaped. And now you cling to this idea of reuniting the two of you to finish the film? Give it up. If you wanted to be a filmmaker, you should have made another film, instead of waiting around for her.

[No response]

See, Darren Stanford made Land Without Water *because he worked hard at it. He didn't give up. He didn't think he was inherently some genius to whom the world owed something. You've gone through your entire life thinking that people who don't recognize your genius are fools. But when have you worked for anything? This dream of making films, when did you work for it after Mom died? The Glazen Shelves. That's the dream, isn't it? That's it. That's all you had. That's all you ever had. And now, you're almost thirty. Understand that? You're almost thirty, Max. You know what most people are doing when they're thirty? Tell me, what was Truffaut doing? Fassbinder? Welles? Godard? Scorsese? Countless others? I don't need to tell you this. You know the odds for you at this point in your life. Almost thirty and you haven't even set one foot into the world of filmmaking as an adult. So what are the odds you'll ever make anything of yourself?*

I don't want to talk to you anymore.

"Go fucking die," Adrian says. "Worthless."

"Stop, now, leave my brother alone." Kelly *thinks* she says this with some volume, but she only whispers it, so nobody hears. But what can she do? Her brother has lost control. And as proof, he picks up a rock and pitches it at Penelope's face. It hits with a flinty snap.

"Hey," Adrian says, "what the fuck?"

Kelly takes a step backward. Leo and Adrian stand a few feet from Max, who picks up another rock, yells, "Cretins!"

Maybe Kelly shouldn't do anything—shouldn't stop her brother or involve herself at all. Maybe Max just needs to learn. He can't yell at people. He needs to sober up from the psychological drunkenness of his life, needs to understand that the world doesn't work like this.

"Evelyn was here." Max squeezes the rock like a head he wants to crush. "Don't you understand what that means?" He cranks back his arm again.

"Who?" Leo asks.

Well, that's unfortunate because I'm the only person left for you to talk to. Unless... unless you want to talk to your sister instead?

[No response]

No. I didn't think so. Not after what she did to Mom, right? Not after how she abandoned Mom and abandoned you.

[No response]

You like to blame Kelly for what's become of you.

If she'd told me about Mom. If she'd told me Mom was missing, then I—

Then you would've done nothing. Not a thing. Nothing would have changed. Mom would still be dead, one way or another. She was born to die, understand?

[No response]

You're to blame for what's become of you. You're the only one to blame for the failure of your life.

[No response]

So go ahead and tell me some more bullshit about **The Glazen Shelves.** *About how you watch it every night before you go to bed. About how you dream of finishing the film. About how you still believe that one day Evelyn will come back into your life, begging you to finish the film. Go ahead, Max, and tell me some more bullshit about* **The Glazen Shelves,** *which wasn't even that good in the first place, which never would have amounted to anything even had you finished it, even had Mom lived, even had she seen it. Tell me about your plan, whatever this plan is to try to find Evelyn or whatever it*

Overhead another truck rattles the concrete and makes its deafening noise. It's weird to hear something so poundingly without being able to see it. But as this sound destroys the air around them, Kelly watches Adrian leap forward and try to knock the rock from Max's hand. But Adrian misses the target and slams Max's shoulder instead. Max's feet leave the ground; he seems to go horizontal for a moment. Then his head hits the stones.

Kelly should rush forward and see if she can help; she knows she should do this. But she doesn't do this. Without feeling her body step backward, she steps backward, putting more distance between her and her brother. She isn't trying to get away from this scene; it's just that one moment she's in one place, and the next moment she's in another.

She does not think, *My brother is hurt and I'm doing nothing to help.*

Overhead another sound roars—endless, these noises, endless—but not a truck this time; Kelly knows it's a plow, and she hears the shriek of the shovel against the pavement, and sparks shower over the bridge's edge like a molten waterfall.

For Max, this sound works as an alarm. He sputters, gasps, contorts.

"Whoa, are you okay, man?" Leo steps forward and extends his hand in an offer of assistance. "We didn't mean to hurt you."

"Speak for yourself," Adrian murmurs.

But Max refuses Leo's hand and flattens his own palms against the

---

is exactly that you want to do (if you even know what you want to do). You want to find her? Or now you just want to find out why she was thanked at the end of Land Without Water. Or I don't even know what you want to do. Maybe you're just bored, just lonely. Maybe you want to feel like you have some kind of purpose, however insignificant. Maybe you just want to have something to do instead of talking to yourself all day. So go ahead, Max, tell me, what is your plan? Everyone else has a plan. Even your sister, who has amounted to as little as you've amounted to, even your brain-dead sister has a plan. She's here to find your father. She wants some $$$. Even your sister has a plan, Max. So what's your plan, huh? WHAT THE FUCK IS YOUR PLAN?
[Unintelligible]
But you already know all of this, don't you? You're ashamed of yourself. You've spent your life locked away. You've spent your life in a dream world. You're a failure, Max. And you've never even heard of Dovzhenko.

rocks, pushing his rickety body up like an awakened drunk. Once standing, he turns to Leo and Adrian and straightens his shoulders—seems to fortify himself in the hope of avoiding another fall. Leo and Adrian take worried steps back, and then Kelly sees why: her brother holds another, slightly larger rock—a weapon—at his side. Then Max raises that hand in the air. Leo and Adrian flinch, crumble up into slouched, defensive positions. But the rock isn't meant for them.

The rock is meant for Max. He hits himself in the face with it, again and again and again, each impact looking brutal enough to knock an eyeball from its socket. He doubles over, howling, pounding the rock into his face. Even in the dim light, Kelly sees some of her brother splatter onto the rocks. At least she *hears* her brother splatter. Right? Or does she imagine it?

Unable to tell, Kelly just closes her eyes. When she opens her mouth, it's not to holler; instead, she imagines something new: a ribbon of smoke escaping her body as her stomach burns.

Whenever the Casco Bay Bridge prepares to separate, to raise its two sides upward to allow a ship to pass underneath, the horn blares so loudly you can hear it all over Portland. Like a foghorn, but not quite— closer to a school bell bringing to close a class, though lower-pitched than that. So not exactly like anything, really; Kelly never could quite figure out a proper comparison to the sound, but she'd know it anywhere, and she knows it now as it goes off. She looks out to the water but can't see the ship. This noise, disturbance, for what? To prepare for something still invisible?

Leo and Adrian are gone—ran off as soon as Max hit the ground— and now Kelly stands over him as he tries to sit up. Blood drips down his face, making his eyelids flutter. He looks beyond his sister, looks to the painting of Penelope. But Kelly has seen it already, doesn't need to turn around. "What the fuck's wrong with you?" she says. "Why'd you do that?"

Nothing. He stares. The blood wiggles down his chin onto his coat. She needs to get him to a hospital, she knows—the pulsing of her heart tells her so—but she feels too angry to bring him anywhere. God, does part of her want to pick up another rock. God, does part of her want to finish the fucking job. But *look after your brother*, Mom's ghost whispers into her ear.

The bridge keeps wailing—and beeping now too—as it separates and lifts. The cars are jammed above, Kelly knows. In those cars, people are angry, no doubt, beating fists against steering wheels, punching upward toward roofs.

And Max, still bloody. Every time Kelly blinks, she hopes the blood will vanish, and there he'll be, standing before her, seventeen again. Salvageable.

"Can you hear me? Answer." She doesn't want to touch him, but she does crouch. "Get up. Let me help you up. Let me help you."

He looks away from the painting—looks right at her. The blood separates at his nose, one stream trickling to the right of it, the other stream to the left. He opens his mouth and licks at his lips, a bit of blood getting on his tongue. Then he says something—something she can't hear. "What?" Did he say anything at all? Or did he mouth words?

And then silent goes the air as the bridge racket stops, making the space around them feel lighter. A small rock has snuck into Kelly's shoe, between her toes; for a moment, this is all she can think about. No more racket, and no more brother—just the rock between her—

"Do you want to meet Dad?" Max asks.

Kelly flinches. "What?"

"Remember how I told you that I don't know where he is? That he was moving when I went over to his house?"

"You lied to me?"

"I know where to find him. And I'll tell you. But only if you do something for me."

To steady herself, she presses her hand to the ground. Then, without meaning to, she curls her fingers around a stone. It fits into her palm with grace. "What?" she says.

"Bring me the head of Penelope Hayward."

A WOMAN
WITHOUT
QUALITIES

N obody has ever called Kelly *likable*—not even people who have liked her.

But *like* seems an inadequate word to describe Garrett's feelings toward Penelope Hayward, whom he watches on television as she plays a clumsy, girl-next-door-type lawyer in the romantic comedy *Approach the Bench*, which came out in February 2011, during a time in Penelope's life when she was buying a home in the Hollywood Hills, getting millions of dollars to endorse Baked Lays, and, in general, being *likable*.

What was Kelly doing during that time? Don't ask.

In this scene, the handsome male lawyer questions the buxom blonde on the stand. "So, Ms. Lawford, please describe what you're looking for in a man."

"Objection," shouts Penelope Hayward, the opposing lawyer, "flirting with the witness!"

Garrett snorts, his laughter almost like food on which he chokes. A glob of spit escapes his mouth, darkening his tan khakis—his khakis, clean and pressed, even though vegging out before the TV seems his only activity on this Friday night, something Kelly can't understand since Garrett lives downtown, in the Old Port, and could easily go see a movie, or meet some people at a bar, or see a band, or whatever. In fact, he looks dressed to go out; when he opened the door to let Kelly in, his appearance threw her. She expected to see him in gym shorts or something that would make her own shlubbiness forgivable; instead, he stood there, clean-shaven, trim in a sweater and pressed-looking khakis—dressed for a night spent sinking into the world of Penelope Hayward, alone.

On TV, Penelope drops some folders in the courthouse hallway—it's a new scene—and the love interest helps collect the spilled files.

"Makes you wonder how she made it through law school," Kelly says, laughing *at* the movie, not *with* it.

Garrett puts a finger to his lips. "Shh. Remember. My grammy." He points at the floor, gesturing toward downstairs, where his grandmother lives.

"Oops," Kelly says, hushed, trying not to laugh again. She looks around at his living room—clean, like a grown-up's house, scrubbed and dusted—while Garrett turns back to the screen, watching his girl clean up paper.

"So what's the plan for tomorrow?" Kelly asks once the urge to laugh has subsided. "Are you interviewing her before the event? After the event?"

The event being: tomorrow, Deering High School, their alma mater, will commemorate its newest addition, the Penelope Hayward Auditorium, at which the star herself will make remarks—the second part of her three-part trip (her final engagement being a visit to Day Without Water on Sunday). Earlier today, when Garrett spoke to Kelly outside Nosh, he told her he had arrangements to interview Penelope at the grand opening—had a scheduled audience with the movie star, something that Kelly, Penelope's old friend, couldn't get.

Garrett shrugs, not taking his eyes off the television. "Not sure," he mutters, sedated. "We'll see when I get there."

This sounds strange, a touch unprofessional, to just *show up* at an event like tomorrow's and figure shit out on the fly, but then again, what does Kelly know? She has never interviewed anyone; maybe it often works this way, and only a know-nothing would think otherwise. "So you have a ticket," Kelly says—not quite a question, but close enough.

"Mm-hmm."

"So, can the *Phoenix* get a lot of tickets? Like, for your friends or whatever?"

"Oh, I don't know. I don't think so. They had one press pass. It's a smallish auditorium, so I don't think a ton of press were invited."

"So they gave you the press pass to go—"

"Oh no, not to me. No. They gave the press pass to some other reporter who's gonna go and write some coverage of the event."

Kelly shakes her head. "So, then, the *Phoenix* bought another ticket so you could go interview Penelope for the paper?"

"They didn't buy me a ticket, no. I bought my own. But that's okay."

"And how much was the ticket?"

"Uh, like, a thousand."

"*Dollars?*" Kelly sputters.

"Sure," Garrett says, "but I did some landscaping work for my grammy, so, you know, that helped with the cost and everything."

"Okay... but you *are* doing an interview, right? That's what you said before."

"Well"—Garrett smiles—"knock on wood."

"Knock on wood?"

"I don't exactly have an interview planned yet."

"*Yet?*"

"No, they decided not to do interviews, her publicity people. They're real mean about it too. It's all nonsense." Garrett waves his hand in the air. "But, you know, I'm just gonna go and see what happens. I mean, Chelle likes me."

"Who's Chelle?"

"Her assistant."

"The one who was yelling at you?"

"That was just kidding around."

Kelly makes her mouth into the shape of the word *wow*, but she doesn't say it. She can't get over how pathetic this sounds. When Kelly showed up here tonight, she thought that Garrett was a journalist who had a press pass to Penelope's event and was going to be conducting an interview with her. The best plan Kelly could come up with was to charm Garrett—as she charmed him before, years ago—so that maybe he would bring her along tomorrow, and maybe she could convince Penelope, her old friend, to spend a little time with Max. But apparently this was never even an option. Kelly glances toward the door, already thinking about how quickly she can excuse herself without appearing unforgivably rude.

"So," Kelly says, just to double-check, "you spent a fortune of your own money to go to the event not as a member of the press but just as a fan to try to conduct an interview with Penelope at some point, even though you aren't scheduled to and they don't want to do any interviews?"

He nods, looking proud, like she just mentioned something that was self-evidently complimentary—his big muscles, or a flashy car. But she doesn't tell Garrett how this actually sounds. Imagine going to a U2 concert with a general admission ticket and expecting—no, *depending* on the fact that you'd be able to just grab Bono for a quick chat, you know, just one-on-one, shooting the shit, without security or publicity people noticing.

"I don't mean to be negative," Kelly says, "but that plan sounds a little... difficult. Won't there be hundreds of people trying to get her attention?"

"Uh, maybe. But I'm gonna have a pretty powerful edge."

Kelly tightens her face. "What's that edge exactly?"

"I used to know Penelope. We were... involved."

"You were *involved*?" This time, Kelly can't hide her incredulity.

"Yeah."

Kelly shakes her head. "No, you weren't."

"Yes, we were."

"I knew everything about her all throughout high school. You two were not involved."

"Maybe you don't know everything."

"Look, success changes people, okay? I just don't want you to be disappointed." Kelly softens her voice as though speaking to a child.

"Well," Garrett says, "I think she'd remember."

"Okay... then maybe, I don't know, maybe you misinterpreted something."

Garrett stares at her. "What does that mean?"

Come on, is he really going to make her say this out loud? *You have a history of misinterpreting the signals that girls give you.* But watching the redness seep into his cheeks, and looking at his index finger twitching in Morse code at his side, she cannot bring herself to be so explicit and cruel, to reference their own shared history.

"Nothing." Kelly smiles. "I'm sure it'll be great. Tell her hi for me, okay?"

He locks on to her for a second, frozen mid-wince, trying to size her up. Then he clears his throat and dusts pointlessly at his knees before standing. "I need to use the restroom. Maybe when I come back I can get you on record? Get some quotes and memories and stuff for my article?"

"Oh, uh, yeah." Kelly had forgotten the stated reason for her visit. "Sounds great. Lemme think of something juicy."

In a moment, it's just Kelly and the TV, Penelope on the screen kissing her male costar, some budget Hugh Grant, on the cheek. How wholesome! Remind Kelly to barf later.

Hollywood views Penelope Hayward as a sex symbol. She participates in photo shoots for men's magazines, airbrushed, scantily clad. In interviews, she bats her eyelashes, flirts with the hosts—but she never gets dirty. All her love scenes are of the tasteful PG-13 variety; she makes romantic comedies, after all. Of all the bullshit male myths about women, this one drives Kelly the craziest: that women who act sexually forward don't actually have much sex. Men want a woman who acts game for whatever but isn't a slut. They want a sexy woman to straddle them, to seduce them—they want a woman to do all the work—and then, after it's over, they want this same woman to whisper, "That was my first time," or something equally cute. As if.

Kelly spots Garrett's Camels on the couch and, craving a cigarette, she snatches one from the pack. Then she snatches another. In his kitchen, she roots around for matches, opening some drawers, looking inside some decorative teapots, but coming up empty. Then her eyes settle on the fridge. A magnet of a cat shrugging—even though Garrett doesn't seem to own a cat—holds something in place: one ticket for Penelope's event tomorrow. She stares at it, head cocked. Sure, the plan Garrett just sketched out—simply showing up at the event and hoping to win Penelope's attention—sounds crazy. But does Kelly have a better one?

The toilet flushes behind the bathroom door, and she plucks the ticket from the fridge. With the stolen ticket—her second act of cruelty toward Garrett—feeling like a hand in the back pocket of her jeans, she makes for the front door.

Friday night in the Old Port, the part of downtown where all the boutique shops and cobblestone streets, toured by frequent horse-drawn carriages, exist side by side with the ancient bars and the seedy new dance clubs that look like they'd rather be in New York City. Trying to forget about the stolen ticket in her pocket, Kelly sets out into the crowd, leaving her car where she parked it a few blocks away from Garrett's apartment. Yes, she thinks about Max, how earlier he seemed to be okay, but she should check on him soon. Get back to the house. And yet, she knows this area—and she knows, just around the corner, is the Armory. She wants to see it again, wants to sit on the bench out front and smoke a cigarette, if she can find someone to loan her a lighter. Later, Max will still be where she left him, so for now, she wants to see the Armory, the place where, thirteen years ago, she went to find her father—the last time she ever searched for him.

Kelly eyeballs the people crossing the road from bar to bar regardless of oncoming traffic, the cars that pilot this area creeping, wheels grinding in slow-motion against the rock salt. Some beefy guys go "wooooo," but their frat-boy drunkenness feels incongruous when manifested in front of a store with Christmas villages and Jamie Wyeth prints on sale in the windows. The streetlamps cast generous globes of light on the brick buildings and snow-covered benches, while one of the bar-exiters, a young man in a scarf and mittens, kneels on the sidewalk and vomits at the foot of a tree strung up in Christmas lights whose reds and greens seem to dance around the branches. The vomiter uses his scarf to wipe his mouth before standing and politely shaking hands with one of the bare branches. Maine: the way life should be, where even the debauchery is sort of quaint. Except for her brother. There's nothing quaint about her brother.

Why can't Max just be sincere—just help his sister out—without all this other bullshit? Besides, Kelly can't imagine what good could possibly emerge from uniting Max and Penelope so late in their lives, now that the movie star has likely detached entirely from normal human existence, while Kelly's brother has become the sort of person who bashes himself in the face with a rock to make a point. But that's what he wants: to talk to Penelope. "I need to ask her about *Land Without Water*. About Evelyn." He said this with the makeshift ice pack—crushed ice cubes encased in Ziploc—pressed to his face. So they made a deal: if Kelly got Max together with Penelope for a few minutes—alone, so they could talk—then Max would tell Kelly where to find Dad. And about the lie, when Max said before that he didn't know where their father was? What-the-fuck-ever. Kelly was beyond anger; she just felt numb and unsurprised.

Now, it's half past ten, and Kelly trudges through the Old Port. It's a little disappointing to see how similar this area is to any town anywhere. With the exception of the spiked winter air and the brick buildings, she could be standing on Fourth Avenue in Tucson—or, actually, the Old Port kind of reminds her of Flagstaff, where she lived for a year. These young men and women do the same things in Portland that they would do in Tucson, or Flagstaff, or wherever; their lives are depressingly easy to transpose onto any city. For the last eleven years, living throughout the Southwest, Kelly has remembered New England—Portland specifically—as a special place, and she has told all her friends so, drawing sharp distinctions between not only the aesthetics of the two regions, but also the atmosphere and behavior. Were those distinctions only imaginary? She keeps thinking she can burrow inside the core of Portland—the core of any place, really—and find the aspects that make it uniquely itself, but that seems increasingly unlikely. Of the locations she has lived, her favorite was actually Las Vegas. That city's nothing but facsimile. In a way, what makes Las Vegas unique—from the New York–New York "skyline," to the rodeo-themed station casinos, to the Beverly Hills–lite shopping strips in Summerlin—is how badly it wants to be like a million other places. No qualities of its own.

When Kelly was a freshman at the University of Arizona—it feels like such a long time ago now—she visited her composition instructor, a literature grad student, Mr. DeJong, in his cubicle during office hours. As they spoke, she eyed the book on his desk: *The Man Without Qualities*, it was called—something DeJong was reading for his own studies, he told her. The title lodged itself in her mind. What did it mean to be without qualities? And what, exactly, were qualities anyway? Dad, Mom, Max—they all had qualities, didn't they? Negative qualities, perhaps, but qualities all the same. But what about Kelly? If asked to describe her, what would her friends say? *Oh, Kelly? Well, Kelly... let's just say she's a woman without qualities.*

On Fore Street, Kelly passes an underdressed girl who reeks of vodka and has her high heel stuck between two cobblestones and who, when she falls forward, flashes the gang of people behind her an up-skirt glimpse. Kelly absents herself from the laughter. This is not her Portland. She walks away from the Old Port commotion, down Fore Street toward the roundabout. The lights aren't so bright down here, and the air feels colder; her hoodie does nothing faced with these temperatures, and Kelly shivers and rubs her body like somebody performing the feeling of being cold—but then again, walking through the old neighborhood is such a cliché, its own kind of performance, Kelly performing the idea of memory, the idea of nostalgia, the idea that she feels some investment in this place. When she drove into the city yesterday, she thought she saw her ghosts. But a ghost haunts you. A ghost refuses to leave you alone. And now, it shocks Kelly how easily she feels herself letting go of Portland. In each doorway, under each awning, on each bench, she sees something, some image of her past, some memory, but none of these memories compels her to stand in the doorway, or under the awning, or sit on the bench—none of these memories draws her away from her path. She hopes this will be different when she reaches the Armory, but Jesus, walking through the old city: what a fucking cliché. Kelly had been looking forward to this, but now she feels stupid. But at least she has a minute's breather from Max.

Her brother needs help. She needs to take him to the hospital. Not for the head injury, necessarily, but maybe for that too. She needs to—she doesn't know exactly. Where do people go for psychiatric help? But of course he's not the only one who needs help. Kelly will turn thirty next February, yet so many facts of adulthood still hide from her. How can she even begin to help her brother when she can't even bring herself to register her car? Or learn how many different sizes curtains come in? Or how often she should get a physical? Of course, when she finds Dad, when she has his money, she'll be able to help her brother. Then she'll find something that interests her, somewhere to settle down, some qualities with which to decorate her life. Then she'll be an adult.

Around the corner from the Armory Hotel now—or at least she thinks so anyway. The word *Armory* reminds her of Armory Park, in Tucson, across the street from which she lived up until last week, when her landlord evicted her for neglecting to pay rent, three months after she'd lost her job at Safeway—the culmination, in many ways, of ten post–University of Arizona years flitting from job to job, interest to interest, which she still obsessively catalogs in her mind with brief capsule descriptions:

College Student

That time she tried out higher education at the University of Arizona; ended when, after three semesters of a crushing work-study job on top of failing grades, a form letter arrived in her mailbox asking her politely to leave.

Skate Shop

That time she and Alan moved to Flagstaff to work in Alan's friend's skateboard shop; ended when an audit revealed Alan's friend had spent most of the money on heroin and the shop was promptly closed.

Cross-Country

That time she and Pam decided to drive across the country to settle down in New York City, where they could start their lives anew; ended when Pam ditched her in Hoboken and, almost broke, Kelly had to catch a train back to Tucson without ever setting foot in the so-called Big Apple.

Animal Rescue

That time when she, after successfully getting a stray alley cat to trust her, became very passionate about the idea of animal rescue; ended one evening when she called the stray cat for dinner and, as the cat came flying across the road, so came flying a minivan on an interception course, flattening the stray cat, whom she had named Jolly.

Las Vegas High Roller

That time when she stuck around in Las Vegas following an acquaintance's wedding and, after learning and winning Texas Hold'em at the bachelorette party, decided that her true calling was poker; ended when she played her first hand ever—at the Palms, for what it's worth—and, upon going all in pre-flop with 3-9 unsuited, busted to a partying frat guy's Q-Q, losing $300 in roughly forty-five seconds while the frat guy's friends cheered wildly for their bro's success and then tried to get Kelly to spend the night with them in their suite.

Disney Mascot

That time when she got a job working for Disney, dressing up as Minnie Mouse—head and everything—to pose with families on the Strip and to, for novelty purposes, pretend to be drunk and passed out against the side of the Bellagio, her face hidden behind a wedding veil, a jilted bride; ended when she was chased away from the Bellagio by LVPD and realized that she had never been working for Disney at all—had been, instead, working for the same shysters who had lately begun pulling the same fake Disney character scheme at famous spots like Grauman's and Times Square.

Musician

That time when, back in Tucson, she joined a friend's band as a second lead singer, becoming obsessed with downloading albums on Soulseek and acquainting herself with the entire catalogs of famous artists, like Dylan, whom she had previously neglected; ended when the band broke up, unremarkably, and she admitted to herself that she just plain fucking hated Dylan's voice.

On and on Kelly went, acquiring qualities, obsessing over each one for a couple months, until her interest combusted. Finally, twenty-nine years old, working a register—or, depending on the night, bagging groceries—at Safeway, saving up zero cash toward her eventual goal of returning to the University of Arizona (the whole fucking reason she landed in Tucson to begin with), she figured it was all over for her. She thought,

Here's my life. And then she got laid off. Who the fuck else would hire her? No qualities, no qualities...

Ah, *there's* the Armory Hotel, here on—what street is this? She search-es for a sign but can't find one in the dark. Forget it. Doesn't matter. When will she ever again in her life need to know the name of this street? She stands on the corner between the hotel and Crooked Mile, the coffee shop with the black metal tables outside. Those tables always wobbled, and whoever sat at one would have to put a personal belong-ing—an empty cigarette pack, or a rolled-up scarf, or some coins—un-der one of the legs. Kelly and Penelope used to come here; it was one of the few places they could go without running into Deering classmates. As the sun would set over this stretch of cobblestone street, the windows in the surrounding brick buildings all lighting like fireplaces, Kelly and Penelope would joke that it was Paris: somewhere that felt comfortable yet alien, as though their lives had taken a different shape but were still recognizably theirs.

Of the Armory Hotel, however, Kelly has a much less pleasant mem-ory. She had never really noticed this hotel until one afternoon when her sixteen-year-old ghost found the scrap of paper in Mom's bedroom. She'd gone in to snatch some money from Mom's wallet while Mom dozed, inebriated, on her futon, and upon opening the billfold, Kelly found a scrap of paper, printed on which were the following words: *Miles, Armory, Room 305.* It didn't take much to figure out what this meant. How many men could Mom have known named Miles? Kelly's father must've been in town, must've been staying at the Armory Hotel in room 305. Did this make sense? Of course it made sense, of course, of course. Hands shaking, Kelly dug around in Mom's jewelry drawer until she found the locket engraved with *K.B.*, which she hooked around her neck. Then she drove downtown, parked on Exchange Street, and walked. She sat at one of those Crooked Mile tables for a few minutes, massaging the locket, feeling the engraved letters under her fingertips. If Dad saw it, he would recognize his daughter.

She crossed the street to the hotel, walked past the black sedans and taxicabs in the roundabout, and approached the doorman outside, who opened the door cordially and said, "Good afternoon, miss." And Kelly could've just nodded and slinked inside confidently, like she was supposed to be there, and then she could have gone upstairs to room 305 and knocked. But instead of acting like she belonged there, Kelly turned to the doorman. "I'm looking for room three-oh-five."

The doorman raised an eyebrow, a gesture Kelly didn't know people actually performed in real life. "Three-oh-five?"

Kelly nodded. "My dad's room."

The doorman shook his head. "I'm sorry, but we don't have a room three-oh-five." He was a young dude with a ponytail, this doorman. Kelly doesn't know why she noticed, at that very moment, his ponytail. But she did. She noticed it. For a few seconds, it was all she could see, like the doorman was one gigantic ponytail.

Then Kelly shook herself free of the trance. "No. That can't be right."

"I'm sorry, ma'am."

"Well, I'll just go upstairs and look around then."

The doorman shook his ponytail. "If you're not a guest or meeting a guest, I can't allow you to wander the hotel." No, no. Wearing a wool cardigan was a bad idea. Her whole body felt hot. "I *am* meeting a guest. I'm meeting my dad. He's staying in room three-oh-five."

"There's no room three-oh-five. I can check the guest registry. But I can't let you wander."

Kelly felt as wobbly as one of those tables next door at Crooked Mile. Surely the doorman saw this too. He peered at her, inching his face closer to hers, like he was trying to see up her nose, or trying to check his own reflection in her eyes. "Are you okay?"

Kelly's hand fell and landed on the railing behind her. It was a lovely autumn day. The breeze knocked leaves from the trees and dusted the ground with them. But Kelly didn't notice any of this. All she noticed was that the railing was cold. "His name is Miles Bennett," she croaked. "Please, yes. Please look him up."

"And who should I say is asking?"

The words stuck in her throat: "His daughter."

Kelly waited on one of the benches in front of the hotel while the doorman inquired within about Miles Bennett. Near the bench, a well-dressed man stood with luggage, chatting up a bellhop, asking questions about the area: good spots to eat, good places to grab a cocktail, good sights to see, whatever. A tourist. Kelly didn't care. She waited, sitting on her own hands so they wouldn't flap around. When she thinks about this afternoon now, she remembers trying to light a cigarette and being unable to, but she didn't even smoke back then—she was only sixteen—and there would've been no smoking allowed so close to the hotel.

Kelly waited. No room 305? Bullshit. Of course there was a room 305. That's what it said on the scrap of paper. Probably Miles Bennett had tipped the doorman. *Anyone comes asking about me, tell them there's no room 305.* Folded $100 into the palm. *Yes, sir. No room 305.* And even, okay, so, even pretend for a second that Mom wrote down the wrong room number and there wasn't a room 305 but Miles was actually at the hotel, just in a different room—okay, so now the ponytail was going to call up to Miles Bennett's room and say, "Your daughter's downstairs," and Miles Bennett was just going to come down? Of course not. Her only chance was to surprise him. She knew this. Her only chance was to dive straight into that hotel, hurry upstairs, knock on the door. That was her only chance, and she'd fucked it up. Why did she have to ask the doorman about the room number?

She should've thought this through before arriving, yes—but she'd never quite realized how desperately she wanted to meet her father until she sat there on her own hands, a failure.

So she stood and turned toward the steps, toward the awning, toward the door; to hell with the doorman, she would storm inside, up the stairs she'd go, nobody would stop her. But before she could launch—both of her feet still pressed firmly against the cool brick sidewalk—the front door opened, and a man in shorts and a T-shirt emerged, looking out of place with the fading fall afternoon temperature and also with the swankiness of this place. He darted down the steps like a bug scurrying across a bedroom floor as the lights came on.

What did Kelly remember about her father? Nothing more than faucet drips. He used to call her *Girly*. He used to run his fingers up and down her arm until the bliss was like a blanket thrown over her eyes. He used to—what else? The memories were scattered, formed when Kelly was so young—only, what, three years old?—that she couldn't be sure of any of them, and so they became a mosaic, tiny fragments of her past that, when assembled, added up to something she liked to call whole, needed to believe was whole. But there was one thing she knew for sure about her father: the eyes, ringed with black—the feature that made Max and Kelly look almost perpetually sleepless.

And there Dad was, scurrying down the steps. After all, this man had those eyes, didn't he? At least Kelly *thought* she glimpsed them before the man reached for his sunglasses.

So, taking a step toward him, she said, "Dad?"

He didn't answer. Just checked his pockets like he'd forgotten something upstairs. Forgotten something in room 305.

"Dad?"

He looked up and seemed startled to see her, glancing over his shoulder to check whether she had her eyes on somebody else and he stood in her way. Then he smiled at Kelly a little nervously. "No. I'm sorry."

Kelly came to a stop and jutted her head forward. From her right, she heard somebody at the door—the doorman with the ponytail, in fact, returning from his journey to the guest register. "Young lady," he called.

"Take your sunglasses off," Kelly said to Dad. She had to see his eyes, had to make sure. Did his eyes have those circles? Was he looking at the locket around her neck? Had he figured out who she was? "Take your sunglasses off." She reached out.

"Young lady," the ponytail called before starting down the steps.

Dad caught her hand. Had K.B. tightened, somehow, around her neck? She felt strangled.

They fought, hand in hand, near the sunglasses. Kelly felt the man's fingers on her wrist, and she tried to remember how those fingers felt so many years ago, when they'd walk the paths the veins made up her arms. *Girly, Girly, Girly.* But she felt only the struggle, wrist twisting, skin burning. *Take off the fucking sunglasses. Take them off.*

And then they broke—not the sunglasses, but the hands, Dad's hand and Kelly's hand, they broke apart, and Kelly, backward now, into the pile of luggage that stood between the bellhop and the well-dressed man as they chatted about good places to eat. Somebody—either the bellhop or the well-dressed man—asked if she was okay, but she didn't answer. Somebody offered a hand, but Kelly ignored it and scrambled to her feet.

The ponytail took a step toward her. "We have no guest named Miles Bennett. We have no room three-oh-five. You need to leave."

She stood there, staring at the man in the sunglasses, unable to tell whether he stared back at her, those shades obscuring his eyes. He shook his head at the sadness of it all—some pathetic lost girl, probably crazy, looking for her father.

"I'm sorry, Mr. Melnicove," the ponytail said.

Mr. Melnicove shook his head—"It's okay, I'm fine"—and then turned from the scene and walked toward a taxi that had, apparently, been waiting for him this whole time.

Maybe he hadn't seen K.B. So she reached for it to make sure it hadn't fallen behind her sweater during the scuffle. But as she put the locket on display, the cab—and with it the man who probably wasn't her father—drove off. All Kelly could do was watch them go.

And then she just stood there, all those eyes upon her, everyone outside the hotel, everyone in the idling cars—hell, it even felt like the whole of Portland had stopped in that moment so it could watch. Her father, or at least the idea of him, had pulled away from her, robbing her voice, leaving Kelly unable to tell any of the spectators what was wrong.

It embarrasses her to remember a time when she'd acted so unhinged. And on account of so little too. A scrap of paper with some random words written on it. Without context, it could've meant anything. She feels a chill that has nothing to do with the breeze gathering handfuls of snow from the hotel roof and releasing them overhead.

But boy, it's pretty, this old brick building, the granite steps leading up to golden doors, the streetlamps glowing like something in a painting of a winter scene, the snow that lines the edge of the roundabout not yet brown with rock salt. The night holds still around her. Nobody wants to interrupt with noise the feeling of standing before the building. Even the voices of the drunks on Fore and Exchange Streets—just a couple blocks over—are no longer audible; they've bowed their heads in respectful silence.

And then Kelly squints and takes a good look at the awning and its gold cursive lettering: REGENCY HOTEL. Regency? She juts her head backward, away from the awning. *Regency?* And then she remembers: this hotel isn't called the Armory. That's the name of the hotel's *bar*, whose entrance is right around the corner. So now Kelly doesn't know what to think. Was *Armory* written on Mom's scrap of paper years ago, or *Regency*? Did Kelly know back then that this place was called Regency, not the Armory? Did Kelly go to the wrong building looking for her father?

Oh, what's the difference? She's the only one who cares.

Sometimes Kelly feels like she's locked in a dark room, able to hear thousands of voices beyond the walls, but unable to break through and touch any of those people's hands, unable to whisper into any of their ears. That must be loneliness, Kelly thinks: not being alone necessarily, but being surrounded by thousands of voices, knowing that thousands of people are there, yet unable to reach any of them.

M ax is fine, snoring, his cheeks puffy and raw, rising as he breathes like pulp in a glass of orange juice. For a moment, she stands over him, watching. If his skull was fractured, his brain in a state of concussion, how would she tell? Probably this isn't the case, and he will wake up tomorrow fine, if a little sore—although it does alarm her, the way he fell asleep with his TV off but his bedside lamp still on, the exact opposite of what she knows him to do. "Max," she whispers. Part of her wants him to flutter a bit, to snort, to roll over—something to let her know that he's okay, that there's still a glow there behind his eyelids—but he gives her nothing more than the steady whir of a man zonked. She'll hope for the best. Besides, for whatever happens tomorrow with Penelope, he'll need the rest.

She moves her hand to the lamp on the nightstand to kill the light, but stops when she notices the drawer open an inch. Through this crack, she can see something inside, glossily reflecting the illumination. So, as her brother snores, she opens the drawer, its rusty hinges yowling. Photographs in here—a smear of them, spread out haphazardly, looking recently disturbed. On the top, Kelly sees her mother and Max looking up at her. An old Polaroid, the two of them flanking a television, smiling. Max is probably ten here, and Kelly remembers this day, this gift, when Mom bought Max his first television, one with a VCR built in, which seemed so decadent at the time. She looks up from the photograph to Max's television. Same one. Kelly recalls some Christmas—didn't he get this television for Christmas?—but upon closer inspection of the photograph, she sees no lights, no tree, no other presents, no snow visible through the windows behind them. So maybe Kelly *doesn't* remember this particular day, but she remembers the gift. (A birthday maybe? No, because there'd still be snow visible, considering the twins' February date.) And Kelly knows something else: she must've snapped this photo. Who else would've?

She reaches into the drawer, gathers the photographs, and thumbs through the pile. In one, she observes Mom on the futon, wrapped in blankets, a glass—containing what Kelly will not guess—in her hand. In another, she observes Mom and Max in what looks like a proto-selfie, the two of them smiling in front of a movie poster, something retro with a blocky illustration of a man playing piano, the words TIREZ SUR legible before the edge of the frame severs the rest. In another, she observes Thai food on the table—just boxes, half-empty. Why? A photo of a decimated dinner, yet no photos of Kelly anywhere. Her only presence is behind the camera, and even that's the case in maybe only half of the images. She wipes her thumbprints off the top photo, then goes to return the stack to the drawer. But then she notices something else: a key. She picks it up, a small, pointy, old-looking thing, weighing in her palm no more than a penny. Odd, but knowing Max, there's some movie he loves where a guy, for some romantic reason, keeps a key in his nightstand drawer. Still though, it looks familiar, but she puts it and the photos back in their place and shuts off the light.

But hang on a minute, because outside, in the hallway, she stares at the door to her old room, locked. And she understands—or *thinks* she understands. At the very least, she regrets putting that key back.

Of course it works on the door to Kelly's old room—and of course there's no Tobias, no absent roommate, all bullshit—but she already knew that, didn't she? Instead, heading inside the room, flicking the light switch on the wall—to the right of the door, just as she remembers—she finds the place gutted, nothing that she used to own present. Sure, she'd taken a lot of it with her, but she had left behind certain larger things she didn't want to pay a moving van to transport—things like her armoire and her bed. The only thing left now: her desk, covered in chipped green paint, which went mostly unused back when she lived here. "Leave my stuff," she told Max eleven years ago; after all, she'd need to use it whenever she came back to stay. But then she never came back to stay, so after a while, he must've called the moving company himself, or however the hell one removes furniture from an apartment (another of her mysteries about adulthood).

In place of all that, one wall, covered, which she scans. Articles about *Land Without Water*, about Darren Stanford. One, a sheet torn out of a magazine, has that image of Penelope floating in the water and, written over her, *For your consideration in all categories.* Elsewhere, posters for Max's film, *The Glazen Shelves*, hand drawn, probably by Max himself considering the lack of artistic competency: in each of the illustrations, the text looks blocky and childish, and the people are nearly stick figures, sitting on what looks like a dock, water drawn in bright blue beneath them. Then stills: Evelyn sitting somewhere, the ocean behind her, hair blowing in the wind—images from the movie itself, Kelly knows, or at least what Max managed to complete of it. Probably fifty or so images, mapped out on the wall with lines drawn from each one to the next, a visual representation of the movie, shot by shot, moving from Evelyn, to the water, to Max, to the sun overhead. Next to these, more illustrations, frames drawn tightly around them, all done in pencil—more planned shots from *The Glazen Shelves*? One set of drawings Kelly gets close to: a building, labeled MUSEUM, and two stick figures outside, one in a dress, one burly and mannish. Then, in the frame next to this one, a man with Max's curly hair, looking ahead. Then, in the next frame, the woman in midsprint down the street. The last time Max saw Evelyn, Kelly remembers, outside the museum, now sketched here as another scene to one day film. There are newspaper clippings about Evelyn's disappearance, including a blank spot that probably contained the one Max now carries around with him, folded into that book, a pushpin stuck into the wall to hold its absence. Then maps of Portland, lines drawn through them, tracing Evelyn's path. And finally? That flyer, Evelyn's face. HAVE YOU SEEN THIS GIRL? The pin jammed through her forehead, her disappearance now one more element of *The Glazen Shelves*.

The lump in Kelly's stomach grows, and her fingertips go numb. She knows the feeling. She felt the same way earlier today when she talked to Chad at Casco Bay Books—when his exclamation point tattoos told her that Max had been kicked out of the place after unwanted staring. (She cannot bring herself to think the word *stalking*.)

Then Kelly hears something behind her—the sound of footsteps, or a door opening? She looks over her shoulder, expecting to see him, her brother, bellowing at her, *I told you not to come in here,* approaching with his hands out, his palms growing larger as they get closer, ready to fold themselves around her face and neck, her brother's skin warm, the rage and madness in every atom—but no one's there. Nothing. Still, her heart feels faster and closer to her rib cage now, its position jostled by the scare. She turns back to Evelyn's hundred faces, all seeming to stare just beyond Kelly, over her shoulder, as though someone hovers there after all, poised to attack.

She looks to her old desk. Piles of papers, many loose, some bound. More scripts perhaps? Closer, she sees a tattered old composition notebook with pages colored by exposure to sunlight. She picks it up, the cover feeling brittle and dusty with time, and she opens the book. Handwriting, ink that had bled into the pages and, on other pages, pencil marks smeared against the lines—the effect of a left-handed person scribbling and dragging skin over the fresh print. She reads the beginning of one entry: *I'm a little worried about Max.* This one dated April 4, 2001. She flips through the notebook, most of it empty, the last entry dated April 21, 2001. Between these two time stamps, the notebook catalogs nearly every day. But then nothing. It stops. Not much written here—an aborted diary, it seems—but the author is clear, the entire room a shrine to her: Evelyn.

Sometimes with Max, it's a little tough to determine the line between harmless obsession and something more like a well in its depth and darkness. Watching movies all day long? Probably harmless. Penning draft after draft of a screenplay for a film that will never get made? Maybe harmless, *mostly.* Protecting his space to the extent of lying about a roommate? Well, hasn't Kelly done the same, although admittedly under different circumstances? ("Can I come over tonight?" the guy might've asked, and Kelly would've said, "Sorry, [insert name of nonexistent roommate] is home.") Everyone has obsessions, Kelly knows—how many hours has she spent in the last five years digging backward through Google News articles regarding Penelope, from reviews of her movies, to the places deep in the morasses of the Internet, where all the zero-facts-checked gossip articles and blog entries reside? (Did Penelope *really* get caught in a nightclub bathroom with some white powder under her nose? Probably not, considering that the one time she and Kelly ever tried doing blow in high school, the movie-star-in-training spent nearly thirty minutes sneezing.) Of course, Kelly never printed out those articles and taped them to her

THE SADNESS • 109

walls, which would not have been a matter of idly passing the time, but would've been instead... well, what?

Because this room—*this* is not the sort of thing where the line between harmlessness and darkness blurs. This room, everything in it— Max has gone down the well, and here Kelly has found herself at the bottom with him.

A creak, over her shoulder, and Kelly cracks her neck looking. Nobody there, but the door wobbles. "Max?" she says. In his room, right across the hall, she hears movement too—feet against the floor and then rustling sheets. "Max?" she says again. She throws the diary on the desk, feeling furious at the condition of this place, at the lies, at her brother sneaking around. And in Max's bedroom—where she finds him with the lights out, under the covers, the blankets pulled way up over his head— she slams the key down on the nightstand and says, "Fucking *Tobias*?"

Her brother stays buried, and Kelly stands over him, looking at his form, an abstraction of him missing his face and his voice—nothing too different, it will only occur to her later, after her temperature has subsided, from the way she has been talking to him since Mom died: her relationship with him has always been yelling at an abstraction.

But now, she hisses, "Diaries? Photographs? What is somebody supposed to think, finding that stuff squirrelled away?"

No movement from the lump.

Kelly's face only feels warmer, and her body wants to spin, though there's nowhere to spin. "Why do you have this stuff? Why do you have Evelyn's diary?"

Still, nothing. And Kelly, not knowing what else to do, finds herself biting her lip, finds herself jutting her head in different directions with little spasms of her neck. Never in her life has she been able to make him talk, but she *needs* to make him talk. "How the fuck do you have her diary? Did you do something to that girl? You *need* to tell me. This is serious now, okay?" She swallows. "If you're a fucking lunatic—" As soon as she says this word—*lunatic*—she shuts up, scared she might be right.

His body hiccups, a jolt of the blankets, and he sniffs something back, she *hears* him sniff something back. "If I did something," he whispers, "why would I be trying so hard to find her?"

BRING
ME THE
HEAD OF
PENELOPE
HAYWARD

Here she comes, Penelope's assistant Chelle Ghusson, emerging from the door leading backstage, weaving through the crowd of people waiting for admission to the new auditorium. Kelly, staking out a spot near the entrance, didn't expect to see Ghusson—figured she'd be waiting backstage with Penelope—but the assistant holds a piece of paper and hands it to the girl whose job is to take tickets at the door, adding some tight motions of her mouth. Then she says a few things to the people with lanyards and badges labeled STAFF around their necks— things that she says while also gesticulating purposefully, an index finger in one direction, a tilt of a head in another. Instructions. Then she says something else, and one of the staff guys points toward the doors to the older part of the high school. Ghusson nods and heads through those doors, and as they close behind her, Kelly watches her duck into the bathroom on the right.

Kelly researched Ghusson online this morning at Kinkos while waiting for her business cards—which she hopes will make her appear more professional—to print. Ghusson's age startled (and, yes, angered) Kelly: she turned twenty-seven last month. How do others manage so effortlessly to cut through life's weeds? Of course, Kelly knows the answer just looking at Ghusson: money, lots of it. Even her skin looks like something bought on Rodeo Drive.

In the bathroom, Ghusson washes her hands. She seems dressed for business, buttoned up and severe. Kelly had decided to vamp it up and put on pomegranate lipstick, crisp jeans, and a dress shirt with the top buttons undone—the nicest clothes she brought, although her sneakers tell a different story—but now, seeing Ghusson, she feels inappropriately groomed.

"Hey"—Kelly draws this word out, voice slackening—"didn't think I'd see you again."

Ghusson scrubs her hands, barely looking up. "We met before?"

"We, yes, we—"

"Excuse me." After turning off the faucet, Ghusson approaches the dryer, moving Kelly around like a chess piece; she juts out her elbow to blast hot air.

"We met at Nosh. Yesterday. I used to know Penelope. We were friends."

The dryer goes quiet. "So?"

"I'm hoping to get just a second of her time, just to say hi. It'd mean a lot to me."

"We're done doing publicity."

"No." Kelly shakes her head. "You misunderstand. This isn't about publicity."

"Don't kid yourself, young lady."

Young lady? Young fucking lady?

"I didn't come out here to get accosted," Ghusson says. "You Mainers build a, quote, state-of-the-art auditorium, and then only put one bathroom backstage? Amateurs." Ghusson shoulders the bathroom door to push it open.

"W-w-w-wait," Kelly says, machine-gun-like, reaching out.

Ghusson flinches and backs up a few steps, perhaps expecting to see a weapon in Kelly's clutches.

"Let me just give you my info, okay?" Kelly finds the business cards in her pocket, which bear her name, cell phone number, Max's address, but no actual business or occupation.

Ghusson shoves the card into her blazer's breast pocket. Without smiling, she mutters, "Thanks," and pushes the door all the way open. Those business cards were a waste of a perfectly good twenty-dollar bill. Kelly had intended to spread them around to as many people working this event as she could, hoping that one of the cards would make its way to Penelope (Max's idea—and, yes, an odd one, considering who the fuck pays attention to business cards anymore?). This plan's success now seems dubious. As Ghusson leaves, Kelly glances down to the assistant's shoes, hoping to spot a stowaway piece of toilet paper. No luck, the woman from Hollywood immune to pedestrian embarrassments. The door swings shut, resurrecting the wall between them.

Kelly hears the drip of the faucet, so she strangles the lever until it quiets. Ahead of her hover tinted windows, which blur all shapes on the other side. She rests her head against one of these windows. As the sun dies in the sky, the plastic feels cold.

Her phone vibrates. She opens her eyes; the fluorescent lighting makes her vision spotty for a second. Her knuckles chafe against her jeans as she fishes out the phone.

It's Max, calling from behind the school, where she parked her Honda. She told her brother to wait in the car. Even left the engine running for him, like she was a mom stepping into the grocery store to grab one quick thing.

Kelly wants him secluded. In a crowd, he'd draw attention, with his battered face that looked worse this morning after sleep ripened the bruises. Kelly will find some way to get Max alone for a few minutes with Penelope, but it will involve hiding him from everyone else as though he were a madman chained in the attic. All morning, Max said, "I'm fine," as if last night he opened a window in his mind and let Mom and Evelyn and whatever else has haunted him for the past eleven years fly away. (Did she press him about the diary she found, or the photographs? Not exactly. How could she?) So what can Kelly do besides what she did earlier today: hug her brother to make sure he had nothing heavy and metal concealed under his jacket, strapped across his chest, ready to breathe fire onto a crowd of innocents—what else can she do? He's fine, he says, and she has no way of knowing what thoughts hide in his head.

On the phone, he asks, "Is everything going all right? Are the business cards working?"

If she tells him the truth—that things look unpromising—he'll throw a tantrum, rip apart the inside of her car as though a lion at a carcass, wrecking her means of transportation, which she needs healthy and in one piece. "Everything's great," she lies, entering the hallway, the bathroom door swaying shut behind her. The tile compresses under her feet; instead of spending money constructing a new auditorium, they should spruce up the rest of this dump.

"Okay," Max says, "but I have another idea."

Not if it wastes more of her money. "I don't need help," Kelly says.

Ahead, she hears the muffled voices of people awaiting the start of the event. She opens the door to the lobby, but freezes midway through, peering into the crowd.

Fuck.

Kelly takes a breath and creeps backward, letting the door inch shut.

"There's a big black sedan behind the school," Max says, "parked at the curb, security around it. I believe it's Penelope's car. I'm going to—"

"Don't do anything. Let me handle it." Kelly snaps her phone shut, stuffs it into her pocket, and presses her snout against the checker-patterned window. All morning she has ignored his calls. But there, in the lobby, lurks someone she *can't* ignore.

Garrett Labrecque has come hunting for her. Peeking through the glass, she spies him standing near the auditorium entrance, chatting with the young female ticket-taker, who looks up and smiles but shakes her head. He mutters angrily then walks off, kicking at the ground peevishly as the crowd of fifty or so people closes its jaws around him.

Kelly opens the door and tiptoes out.

The auditorium has yet to open to the public, so the early birds wait in the lobby, walking carefully on the unscuffed floors, breathing air that reeks of fresh paint. Many of them are students given free admission to this event and now spending Saturday afternoon back at school to see a celebrity. Many others are older, middle-aged or retired—school employees perhaps, or, more likely, local alumni. For these people, the event isn't about celebrating the arts. Like those newsletters from the University of Arizona that Kelly keeps trying to unsubscribe to, this event exists to raise money for Deering High. Kelly finds it disorienting, this sleek new addition to the run-down place through which she roamed during her teenage years. She hides herself near some overweight middle-aged couples who socialize near the entrance. Once it opens, she will force herself inside before everyone else.

Any minute now. Kelly scans the lobby. Any minute.

Then she spies Garrett as he reappears down the hallway, wiping his hands on his pants. She bends her knees and maneuvers closer to the entrance, crouched.

Finally, the auditorium doors open; in the rush of air, the foul new-building smell hits so hard that Kelly feels like she has tumbled into a vat of sickeningly sweet air fresheners. She bounces upward, bee-lining toward the entrance, cutting in line in front of some older people who mutter, "How rude." The ticket-taker takes her ticket, and Kelly jets inside the auditorium.

The seat doesn't squeak when she sits. Goddamn money. Keeps everything quiet.

At 4:07 P.M., the stage lights brighten as everything else tilts into darkness. Mr. Allen—the principal since time immemorial—appears before everyone in attendance, the applause polite but uninspired, and into the microphone he says, "Thank you, and welcome to opening night at the Penelope Hayward Auditorium." At the sound of this name, the applause rises in tenor.

Allen keeps his remarks brief and introduces the next speaker, Mr. Wheeler, English teacher and head of the drama club. Mr. Wheeler didn't work here in Penelope and Kelly's day, but this doesn't stop him from speaking for an interminable length of time, shifting his weak jaw in praise of the guest of honor and particularly that dreary, unendurable *Land Without Water.*

The next speaker Kelly remembers from years ago: Ms. Crookshank, the tenth grade biology teacher who doubled—and maybe still doubles—as the faculty adviser for the video yearbook. She looks ghastly, her skin a hollow white, her hair a nest of gray twigs; the voice that comes from her barely there body sounds digitally deepened, like she's on one of those true-crime shows and wants her identity hidden. But at least she actually knew Penelope, who was the student editor of the video yearbook senior year. Crookshank announces that her video yearbook students have produced a tribute to Penelope Hayward. Then darkness douses the stage as a screen lowers. Images flicker to life. Even Kelly's heart flickers a bit here.

Cheesy voice-over opens the video, the joke being that it sounds like that movie trailer guy: "This is the Penelope Hayward that America knows." A series of clips follows, showing scenes from Penelope's various movies—the sort of footage that plays during one of her promotional appearances on a late-night talk show or *The View.* Finally, the video freezes on an image of Penelope in her forthcoming movie, *Gretel*—a departure from her usual romantic comedy fare, in which she plays Gretel to some blond actor's Hansel, both of them killing witches with crossbows—and the voice-over returns, proclaiming in low timbre, "But Deering High knows a different Penelope." A new image shows Penelope in a school hallway, mugging for the camera, dishing on the awesomeness of school and how much she loves her friends and how sweet the teachers are: eighteen-year-old Penelope, filmed during her video yearbook days. "No better place," she coos, a star in training. "No better place on earth..."

Kelly never saw the finished yearbook—she skipped school the day of its premiere, as she was skipping most days at the end of senior year—but she does remember one comic sketch Penelope wanted to film: a parody of those dance competition movies, like *Bring It On* and *Save the Last Dance*, starring Penelope and Kelly as competing dancers. Recalling this, her stomach fills with rocks. This happened after Mom died, and Penelope and Kelly hadn't been spending much time together. Penelope kept calling Kelly and leaving messages—*let me know if you want to talk, I'm here for you, Kel*, etc., etc.—but Kelly didn't want to talk to a friend so moralistic, so judgmental, who treated her like somebody who needed help; she wanted to hang out with strangers in the backseats of their cars, in the basements of their decaying Parkside apartments—strangers who let Kelly do what she wanted, not conceptualizing her as a grieving daughter. With Mom dead, why would Kelly have wanted to move through her final days of high school under scrutiny? However, just to shut Penelope up, Kelly said, "Sure, I'll be in your yearbook thing," and the following Saturday, Crookshank unlocked the high school for the video yearbook staff. Kelly arrived at the gym to find Penelope and some fellow yearbookers setting up a camera on a tripod. Penelope rushed to Kelly and hugged her. "You smell high-proof," Penelope said, crinkling her nose. Kelly shook her head. Said, "Where's my costume?" Penelope handed over a gym bag, and Kelly went into the girls' locker room to change into the tank top and parachute pants. Then she steadied herself against a locker for a moment. She hadn't slept the night before. She knelt by the toilet in case she needed to throw up. False alarm. Kelly returned to the gym and saw the crewmembers tapping their feet and crossing their arms, like a parody of impatient people. They were ready to shoot—just waiting on Kelly, the hot mess. So Kelly and Penelope began to perform their dance moves, none of which was fancy or impossible for amateurs to master. Penelope nailed the routine, but Kelly wobbled and hurt her ankle and requested a break. "Are you all right?" asked Penelope. Kelly felt funniness in her stomach again and wondered, in a flash, whether she was pregnant. The girl manning the camera—some prissy East End bitch who had joined the video yearbook staff only to have another extracurricular activity bulking up her Yale application—made a snotty remark about how she didn't want to waste all Saturday doing this. Penelope pulled the girl aside, and Kelly watched as they whispered in the corner. *She's having a rough time,* Kelly knew Penelope was saying, *so kid gloves, please.* Kelly knew her friend was whispering this, and she hated it, she fucking hated it. Everyone thought she was having a rough time. Everyone offered pity, but she wanted pity from no one. She wanted them to know she was already stronger than everybody else, certainly stronger than Mom ever was. So Kelly quit rubbing her ankle and stood up. She was fine. She attempted a dance move by jumping into the air; then she fell on her ass and swore. Her stomach was stuffed with bubbles, popping. "We'll do it another day," Penelope decided, "Okay, Kel?" In her car afterward, Kelly lit a cigarette with fumbling hands and banged her fists against the steering wheel, growling. Then she opened the door and vomited onto a muddied patch of leftover winter, smothering in puke all the snow fleas.

Throughout the following week, Kelly practiced the routine in her bedroom, but her whole body felt cumbersome during this workout; she couldn't stand to watch herself in the mirror, fumbling. Dreams of Mom dead in a bathtub—a bloated corpse rising from the water, like in that horror movie Max loved about the haunted hotel—stole Kelly's sleep each night, and she began to feel as though her eyes were dangling in front of her on springs. Nevertheless, she practiced. She would show them. She wasn't feeble. They had no reason to whisper about her. No reason to go easy on her. The death of her mom would not define her. She would prove this to them. Would prove this to Penelope.

The night before they had agreed to film again, Kelly intended to stay home and rest, but she drove by Conor Martin's house on her way back from Hannaford supermarket, and she saw all the cars packed into his cul-de-sac driveway—saw fluorescent lights making his barn glow. A party. She could stop for a minute, she figured. So she parked on the street and went inside and awoke suddenly at noon the next day on the barn's floor, a few other headache-besieged folk lying around her. Upon checking her phone, an avalanche of missed calls from Penelope greeted her; she had missed the dancing. First, *fuck*; then, *oh well*. She stumbled into Conor Martin's bathroom, paying no attention to the shirtless kid with spiked hair throwing up down the shower drain. On the drive home, the car swerved; she still felt wrecked, entire body pulsing, a heartbeat in every part of her. Soon, she was standing on her porch when, behind her, she heard a slam. Kelly dropped the house keys. Penelope had been parked outside, waiting.

Well, they screamed at each other, and it was pretty melodramatic, as things always were with Penelope. Penelope screamed that Kelly needed to pull herself together, that her behavior was unhealthy; Kelly screamed that Penelope didn't know what the fuck she was talking about, etc. By the end of the shouting match, Penelope's face looked oily from tears. But now, eleven years later, Kelly can remember virtually nothing that either party said. Not specifics, anyway.

Probably they could've salvaged their relationship, but school was almost over, and Kelly didn't want anyone telling her how to behave—didn't want anyone judging her. Besides, they knew each other too well by that point, which Kelly hated. So she ran from Penelope, who continued to call and leave messages, zero of which Kelly bothered to return.

After the graduation ceremony, as all the children—because that's what they were: *children*—stood around in their gowns, smoking cigars and mugging for family and teachers, Penelope's parents forced their daughter and Kelly together for a picture. "Smile," Penelope's parents said, so the two best friends glued their heads together. Pictures were snapped. Kelly's face hurt. Then the future movie star looked at Kelly, red-eyed, and reached for her as though reaching for someone in the dark, pulling her close; they held each other. Into Kelly's ear, Penelope whispered, "I love you." Kelly only cleared her throat.

That was good-bye. By the time Penelope threw a going-away party for herself in August, Kelly had already left for Tucson, driving her dead mom's beat-up Honda across the country. And Kelly hadn't thrown any kind of good-bye party for herself, because who would've come? The last person Kelly saw in Portland was, strangely, Penelope's mom. Saw her in Hannaford, where Kelly had stopped to buy cigarettes and bottled water on her way out of town. She wondered whether she should say good-bye, maybe ask Penelope's mom to pass along a message to her daughter. Instead, Kelly hid behind a display of Nathan's all-beef franks; after all, Independence Day was right around the corner.

The video tribute ends; everyone applauds. Crookshank retakes the stage and says, "Please welcome Penelope Hayward."

The applause doubles as Penelope emerges, putting herself on display, skin frosting-white. She embraces her old adviser and then strides toward the microphone, looking so much different from that girl in the video. As the racket dies down, Penelope opens her mouth to sigh into the microphone, a spotlight shivering against her face.

Kelly had wondered what this moment would feel like, seeing Penelope in person. But the movie star looks so far away; even though she's right in the room, she looks like a face on a screen.

After nearly half an hour of Penelope's scripted remarks—platitudes regarding her love for Maine, how she hopes this auditorium will allow some teenager to discover his/her passion for the arts, etc.—Kelly has heard enough. Any emotion from seeing her old friend is over, dead and buried. If she leaves now, she can find a spot to try to grab Penelope's attention as she exits. So she stands, climbs over some legs, and ejects herself into the aisle.

In the lobby, Kelly loiters by an unmanned merchandise table, near which stand several posters on easels: MEMORIES OF PENELOPE one of them says, and it reminds Kelly of a funeral display. The photographs pinned to the poster boards show Penelope's evolution over the years, from a six-year-old in overalls to an airbrushed celebrity hogging the cover of *Vogue*. The bottom of this display says DEERING'S DAUGHTER. Really overselling this whole *it-takes-a-village* thing...

"Those pictures were donated by Penelope herself," the high school ticket-taker offers as she walks by.

Kelly turns to her. "Do you go to school here?"

"Yes."

"Do you like it?"

The girl makes a face, then laughs.

"Yeah." Kelly turns back to the board. "That's how I felt too." Her eyes land on one image in the upper right-hand corner: a group shot of two dozen teenagers standing on risers. Looks like a chorus photo from sophomore year. She scans the rows and sees, yes, herself, standing next to Penelope. "That's me, right there."

"Oh yeah? Neat." The girl smiles, her braces engulfing her entire jaw, all in the name of politeness. How unbearable this feels, the old graduate back at the school, pointing out some ghostly version of herself. How should the ticket-taker respond? Should she be impressed? Kelly warrants rote politeness, nothing more.

"Hey!" someone yells, and Kelly jumps.

At the other end of the hall, Garrett has reappeared. Kelly's breath thickens—syrup in her lungs. The ticket-taker plays with her iPhone, not noticing.

"Call security," Garrett hollers. "That woman's a thief."

The ticket-taker looks up, this accusation earning her attention.

Away Kelly flies, through the door to the old part of the high school, as Garrett pounds the hall behind her, each step seeming to rattle the building's foundation. She runs, instinct kicking in, knowing exactly how to reach the back lot where she parked, and then, near a display of amateurish watercolor paintings, she bends over, a knife in her side. Her lungs must be blackened from years of smoking, caked in thick tar. Inhalations are shallow; will she pass out?

No. She shakes her head, sweating. No.

Outside, the sun is long gone, but the parking lot's lampposts dot the ground with grungy yellow circles of light. The fourteen-degree temperature slams its palm against Kelly's face, almost knocking her back into the school. She zips her sweatshirt and looks up at her Honda, which sits there, cold. No exhaust emerges from its tailpipe. Nevertheless, she barrels forward and, upon reaching the car, bangs on the windows, a useless gesture. Where the fuck is Max? She told him to wait here. The steam of her breath hangs so heavily it almost blinds her.

Too dark to see. Can't feel her toes. She doubles over again, her fingers squeezing her abdomen like she's trying to tear loose a kidney.

Turning back to the school, she sees Garrett charging her. She puts up a hand. "Stop."

He doubles over too, hands on knees, panting. "*You* stop. I'm not the runner. I never run."

"Okay. I'm stopped. All right? Just—please don't call security, okay? I'm sorry." Kelly presses her hands together, palms flattened. "I didn't mean to take your ticket."

"You mean, you went into my kitchen and just accidentally stole it off my fridge?" He shakes his head and stands; then he curves his back, stretching after his workout.

Kelly squints, trying to think of a retort, but exhaustion has moved in, pressure has made a home behind her eyes. Wind comes through, rustling tree branches above, shaking free snow that lands on the back of Kelly's neck. She shudders, and Garrett, maybe reflexively, shudders too. She bats at the powder melting on her skin, twisting her head and looking to her left: there sits the track, a quarter mile around, reminding her of one of those ponds on which mechanized skaters skate in Christmas village decorations. It gives her a teenage feeling, standing out here at night, like she drove over to loiter with Penelope and listen to Built to Spill and get stoned in the dodecahedron, seventeen years old and mildly satisfied with life.

She gives Garrett her attention again, feeling vaguely repentant. "Let me make it up to you. I can take you to dinner some night. Give you good dirt on Penelope. Yeah?"

He blinks at her. "You realize how hard I worked for that ticket? I'm going to report you to event security. Will you please come with me?"

"Are you fucking serious?" She stands there, wide-eyed. "Why? You had absolutely zero chance of getting a meeting with her."

"Because you stole from me," he says flatly. "And stealing is a crime."

Before Kelly can tell him to go fuck himself, an echo hits the air, something metallic banging against something else metallic, almost like a car accident down the road—but no, not that, not a car accident. From this back parking lot, the front one is partially visible.

A news van has its door open while somebody hauls out equipment. Garrett squints and shields his eyes from nothing.

"What's that?" she asks.

"A news van."

"Yeah, but why are they unloading camera equipment?"

Garrett lowers his hand. "'Cause something's going on outside." After a few steps in that direction, his walk mutates into a clumsy sort of jog, his feet hitting the ground oddly as though running along the side of a hill. "Must be for Penelope."

But Kelly's first thought is a dreadful one: *What has Max done now?*

Lights make a semicircle around the high school's entrance as the local news team sets up monstrous camera equipment. The lobby is visible through the bay windows, and people file out of the auditorium, Penelope's appearance ended.

On Stevens Avenue, traffic slows as passing cars inch over the speed bumps, the drivers gazing at the gathering, maybe mistaking it for a candlelight vigil in honor of a mass shooting they've yet to hear about. Kelly senses the sound of bass faintly in the air: Do teenagers still hold those punk shows in that church basement down the street, on the corner of Pleasant?

Then rustling behind her. Kelly spins to find a line of folk flying like an arrow toward the front of the auditorium. Something is happening *right now*—this much Kelly gleans when she spots Ghusson leading the charge, dragging behind her a young man whose face bulges purple with bruises. At first Kelly doesn't recognize her brother here, untangled from his usually lonesome context.

"Max?" With her brother barreling onward, she might as well yell this at a passing train.

"I tried to tell you on the phone," Max calls over his shoulder. "The sedan was parked behind the school. I knocked on the window."

Ghusson notices Kelly. "Are you the sister?"

"Yeah." Apparently she has finally made an impact on the woman.

"You can come too, if you want. But make up your mind. We're doing this now."

"Doing what?" Kelly hustles to catch up with her brother, falling into lockstep next to him. "What are we doing?"

He keeps his head down. "We're doing a thing."

"What kind of thing?"

"Not him again," Ghusson says, looking over Kelly's shoulder.

Kelly strains her neck and sees Garrett trailing behind her. "What kind of thing?" he asks.

"You stay the hell away," Ghusson growls. "I mean it. I'm a cat. I'll give you a swat."

They come to a stop on the marble expanse in front of the auditorium; the people snug inside the lobby have a good view through the windows. "You over here," Ghusson says, positioning Max like a mannequin. Then she grabs Kelly's hand and drags her to the sidelines, near the news crew and their cameras and boom mics.

Digital cameras start flashing. The auditorium doors open and Penelope approaches, flanked by security. Elegant winter gear bundles her: a cute scarf and French-seeming jacket, each item probably more expensive than everything Kelly owns put together. She can imagine somebody complaining tomorrow: *Why wasn't she wearing L.L. Bean, like a real Mainer?* But Penelope looks good, close to Kelly now, smaller than her still. The movie star stands next to Max and waves to the crowd as the cameras keep snapping. Kelly watches her brother flinch from the flashes, his left eye twitching as he tries to maintain a smile, the flesh of his face battered. Why is he on display, chained up and shoved onstage? It terrifies Kelly, watching his twitching eye. Something is deeply wrong with her brother; he should not be around crowds, should not be scrutinized by normal people. When was the last time he had to pull it together? He isn't ready; for this reason, Kelly told him to wait in the car before. Lamely, Max lifts his hand and waves too, glancing at the movie star for cues on how to act. With all these cameras flashing, he looks on the verge of bursting free from the chains, climbing off the stage, rampaging through the city. But for now, he maintains his composure, hand trembling as he waves.

Kelly has no fucking idea what's happening.

"Thank you, everyone," Penelope says to the gathered. "I'm not used to these arctic temperatures anymore, so I'll be brief."

This feeble joke elicits some chuckles, but Kelly can hear one laugh above all the rest: Garrett's. She glares at the crowd, trying—and failing—to find him.

"I have family in Minot," Penelope continues, "a rural place, and one somewhat strange family tradition we have is the burning of old footwear at holidays or graduations or housewarmings or whatever other events we deem important."

More laughter, everyone finding this oh so quaint and rustic. How refreshing, a celebrity who hasn't forgotten where she came from! The only problem? Penelope's family resides in Camden, in a million-dollar house on the water; she has one uncle in Minot, but he spent a decade in jail for stealing methadone from a clinic and used to scare her shitless. And what's this nonsense about burning footwear? A Hollywood publicist's idea of a small-town upbringing?

"I decided to continue that tradition tonight in hopes of bringing good luck to this auditorium." She pauses—an applause sign might as well flash over her head—then puts her hand to her chest. "And outside, before the event, I was thinking about all the people who brought me good luck: old teachers, family—and, of course, friends. Which is why it was fitting that, by happenstance, I ran into one of those old friends, Max Enright."

Penelope reaches for him, putting her arm around his shoulders; he squishes his face, battling every urge to shrink away. Kelly can't stand to witness this for very much longer.

"Last night, Max came upon a group of scoundrels defacing a public monument to *Land Without Water*. He defended the film and me, incurring injuries in the process."

The next few camera flashes seem aimed at Max, bravery incarnate. What a joke—although Kelly has to admit she's almost impressed by the lie he must've told her.

"I am eternally thankful for the support my hometown has shown me throughout my career," Penelope says. "For this reason, I asked Max to join me in my tradition." She looks toward him and speaks more quietly—but still for the benefit of the crowd—"I know it was last minute, but are you ready?" Before he answers, someone steps forward and hands Max a staff, which he holds awkwardly, two-handed. Penelope lifts her foot, hopping to keep her balance, and yanks off one of her boots. She drops the boot onto the ground and someone else hands her a bottle of lighter fluid, with which she drenches her former footwear. Wincing, she says, "Look at what a girl of the wilderness I am!" Laughter. The same someone who handed Max the staff now hands Penelope a grill lighter, which she ignites, the flame just a bead at the end of the plastic snout, looking as small as a star in the sky. She inches it toward the shoe.

The flame catches; evening bursts orange.

The invisible applause sign flashes again as Penelope takes the staff from Max and inserts it into the shoe. She lifts it and holds the stick out for Max. His hand grasps the stick below hers, and the two of them hold the flame aloft. The crowd hoots, hollers, whistles. What a show! The reporters snap their photographs, preserving this event for historical record.

When Penelope looks toward the news team, Kelly glances around to identify the recipient of the movie star's attention; for a second, it seems so improbable that the focal point could be Kelly herself. Penelope makes sure Max has a grip on the torch and leaves his side. She heads toward Kelly. Who freezes. Luckily, the muscles in Penelope's face do the moving for both of them. Grinning, she reminds Kelly of a teenager released from school for the summer. "Kel?"

Beyond Penelope, Kelly finally spots Garrett as he walks away from the event toward a police cruiser—some officer working overtime on this Saturday—parked curbside. Kelly waits for the siren, waits for the cruiser to turn around, to mount the curb, to come for her.

She returns her eyes to Penelope, so close now they can smell each other's breath.

Meanwhile, Max keeps holding the torch; his eyes scan the crowd, which has more or less turned inward, the gathered beginning to chat with neighbors, family, friends. It seems a dangerous idea, giving Max fire to hold around people who celebrate someone and something he abhors, akin to leaving the family pit bull in charge of the kitten while the owners vacation.

Although Kelly originally envisioned a limousine conveying the group of them to one of the fancier restaurants downtown—Fore Street, or maybe even Hugo's—reality, as usual, proves much duller: they all merely march around the corner to the old cafeteria, unchanged in the last eleven years. One table is set extravagantly, with wineglasses and cloth napkins and sparkling silverware. Someone has paid for one of those fancy restaurants to come *here*.

Seated around this table on plastic chairs, the diners—Kelly, Max, Penelope, Ghusson, Allen, Crookshank, Wheeler, and five older donors who have probably never seen any of Penelope Hayward's movies—make polite conversation over salad, bread, and wine.

And then stupid Garrett asks, "So did someone forget to make a reservation?"

So, yeah, Garrett's here too, all because Kelly intercepted him before he reached that officer. She proposed a deal: If she got him a seat at the dinner table, would he drop his nonsense about reporting her? After shaking on it, Kelly walked Garrett like a dog to Penelope and said, "This is my"—the word made her feel faint—"*boyfriend*, Garrett. He went to school with us, remember?" Garrett smiled and positioned himself heroically, prepared for Penelope to embrace him or something. But the movie star maneuvered her ear closer like a hard-of-hearing grandmother and said, "Sorry, what was your name?" Garrett looked on the verge of vomiting.

Now, Kelly feels obligated to run interference for Garrett's passive-aggressive joke about the reservation. So she says, "It's a cool idea, having dinner in the old cafeteria."

"Isn't it?" Penelope looks delighted. "Isn't it more fun than some stuffy restaurant?" She turns to her right, where Max sits playing with his bread, squeezing off hunks and rolling them with his thumb and index finger into balls. "Isn't it marvelous to be back?" Penelope asks him.

Max strengthens his focus on the bread.

Mr. Wheeler leans forward and puts his hand under his chin as though posing for the cover of his autobiography, while the old woman next to him forks some salad into her mouth. "So you graduated with Penelope?" Wheeler asks Kelly.

Penelope answers, "She's my oldest friend," and refills her wineglass.

Kelly wishes she still had salad, like that old lady down the table—wishes she hadn't finished hers in a frenzy the last time she felt embarrassed, five minutes ago. So she puts her hands under the table and feels along the edge. Crusted boogers? Wads of gum? What kind of nastiness affixes itself to the undersides of tables in high school cafeterias?

"These friendships last an eternity, don't they?" Penelope throws her arm around Kelly again and squeezes her even more tightly than before. Kelly's chair rocks; for a moment, she thinks she's about to fall. To steady herself, she puts her hand on the table and hits the edge of an empty plate, flipping it upward and making a racket.

"Careful, you two," Ghusson murmurs, eyes downcast; she holds her iPhone under the table and moves her thumb.

Kelly holds her breath. As when caught in quicksand, stillness is the best strategy.

"Of my old friends," Penelope says, "Kelly and Max are the only ones who came today."

A waiter swoops in from behind and reaches over Kelly's shoulder to snatch the empty bottle of wine from the table. "Shall I open another?"

"Yes. Oh God, yes." Penelope relinquishes Kelly, who rubs her aching shoulder.

In a minute, the waiter returns with fresh wine. He grasps its neck with well-manicured hands, uncorks the bottle, and refills glasses, starting with Kelly's. She never asked for more, but probably he thinks she's important, given her proximity to the movie star. As the wine waters her glass, she stares at the tattoo on the waiter's knuckle. She knows it can't be, but it resembles a teensy-weensy scrotum. Other people around the table gesture for more wine. The waiter knocks the hair away from his eyes as he pours.

"So." Garrett extends himself across the table.

"Huh?" Penelope's focus leaps upward, away from the wine.

Ghusson perks up. Whenever Garrett begins to speak, the assistant raises her eyes from her lap as if suddenly blinded by her phone's LCD screen. Garrett continues: "Are you planning to attend Day Without Water tomorrow? And if so, what do you expect the nature of your interaction with Ford Hunter will be? Will you be attending his book signing?"

"We're not doing an interview right now," Ghusson says, squeezing her napkin.

Penelope glares at her inquisitor. "What'd you say?"

"Penelope." Lockjaw seems to suddenly afflict the assistant. "No questions."

"Let him repeat it," Penelope says.

"You don't know how much—"

"Let him repeat his question. I can handle myself."

Ghusson rolls her eyes, unclenches the napkin, and returns to the phone in front of her, madly manipulating its screen. She waves her other hand in the air. "Proceed."

All eyes go to Garrett, the character in this play on whom the spotlight has begun to shine. "Firstly, I asked whether you're planning to attend Day Without Water tomorrow."

Penelope's face turns lopsided. "Do you think I should attend, given everything that has been written about me lately?"

Garrett starts to speak. "You go every year, so—"

"Max." Penelope turns to her right. "Should I attend Day Without Water?"

Max lifts his eyes from the knife and fork in front of him, and he glances around the table, startled to see all these people here. "Should you attend Day Without Water?" His voice sounds like twigs snapped on a forest path. It pains Kelly to hear his voice crack. He puts his hand over the breadknife. How quickly can Kelly reach him if he weaponizes this utensil?

"What is Day Without Water?" one of the older women says at the end of the table. Out of touch, yes, just as Kelly suspected. Maybe she lives somewhere in the suburbs.

The eyes still on Max compel him to answer. "Day Without Water is an event that happens on the Maine State Pier every December."

Penelope widens her eyes. "On Darren Stanford's birthday, saints be praised."

Max nods. "It's a sort of festival. A winter festival. It used to be a Bloomsday sort of thing. Now, it's more about buying local. Craft vendors and restaurants set up booths on the Maine State Pier. They screen movies. Bands play. It's trying to approximate, say, the Old Port Festival, but smaller and during the winter instead."

"It might be too cold for me now. *Brrr*." Penelope rubs her own body, miming coldness for the benefit of—of whom, the hearing impaired?

"Yeah," Max says. "But the organizers bring in heat lamps and tents with thermal insulation."

"Basically," Penelope adds, "Darren Stanford is the James Joyce of Portland. Pity I never read *Ulysses*. Did you?"

"No," Max mutters, "but I saw the film version from 1967, which Joseph Strick directed. Also, there's John Huston's *The Dead*, his final work, which is a more famous Joyce adaptation but, uh, still not very good. There's something pretty untranslatable about Joyce into film. Huston has to remain faithful to the lack of dramatic tension that Joyce has in his story, but doesn't get to utilize interiority in the way that Joyce does—not, at least, until the clunky final narration, which is pretty embarrassingly bad. I never much liked Huston anyway, though. The French didn't like him either. The French critics, I mean, of *Cahiers du Cinéma*. They liked him even less than they liked the British directors, about whom Truffaut once famously wrote that the phrase *British cinema* was an oxymoron. So, um, yeah."

Nobody moves, not even to sniff or to swallow. Leave it to Max to drain all the energy from the room. As though knowing this, he lowers his eyes again, like a machine that has served its function and, therefore, powers down.

To kill the silence, Kelly blurts out, "My brother's really smart," then has nothing else to add.

Penelope puts her arm around Max and jostles him for a second, during which Max keeps his eyes lowered. Is she teasing him? Kelly has no clue. Maybe Penelope has no clue either.

"Ms. Crookshank," Penelope says, turning her attention toward the other end of the table, "do you remember how Max used to borrow film equipment from the yearbook staff?"

Crookshank nods, face hazy with memory. "Of course."

"He used to borrow cameras, microphones, all that stuff. He was Deering's resident movie guy. He'd seen everything."

Garrett flinches. All this attention for Max, but none showered on Garrett. Poor, poor boy—look at him pout. Kelly forces as much wine down her throat as she can handle.

"So," Penelope says, letting go of Max and looking at Garrett, her impromptu interviewer, "I suppose my schedule tomorrow—whether or not I attend the festivities—will depend on what Chelle says I can fit in. And what was the second part of your question?"

"Penelope," Ghusson hisses, one last effort to stop what's coming.

Garrett dabs his mouth with his napkin, even though he hasn't eaten or drunk anything recently. "I was just wondering, since Ford Hunter is going to be at the festival tomorrow, if you were planning to, I dunno—"

"Confront him?" Penelope raises her eyebrows.

"No, no. Just more in the neighborhood of, um, what's your take on his account of the making of *Land Without Water*?"

A laugh squeaks from between Penelope's sealed lips. Prying them apart, she says, "Well, first of all, that question is syntactically confusing. Here at Deering, I learned very sharp skills of elocution and articulation—skills evidently lost on you."

Maybe hoping to issue a lame self-defense, Garrett raises his hand.

The movie star steamrolls him, continuing: "Nevertheless, let me provide some context to those at the table who haven't read Ford Hunter's book." Her audience—even the older people—rapt, she clears her throat as though preparing to deliver remarks at a high school debate tournament. "Among other things, Ford Hunter wrote, '*Land Without Water*'s ultimate greatness is a miracle considering the difficulty of working with Penelope. Her performance succeeds because Darren Stanford and I knew how to manipulate her into what was needed: the embodiment of beauty and transcendence, both of which she, as a human being, so clearly lacked. Now, she's just another Hollywood bimbo who traffics in sexuality.'"

"Is that really a direct quote?" Mr. Wheeler asks from the other end of the table.

"But of course. I'm an actress. I learn my lines."

Turning to Garrett now, Penelope's eyes look wild. "These are the sorts of comments you're asking me to respond to, the assumption therein being that some truth must exist to these comments, otherwise why would you ask me for a response?" Penelope becomes expansive in her gestures, winding her hands up, swinging them around. She knocks over what remains—not much, just a centimeter—of her wine and doesn't seem to notice; instead, she points at Garrett. "When you ask that question, you give the benefit of the doubt to Ford Hunter. Sexism, pure and simple. I'm aghast. I mean, have you ever asked Ford Hunter to defend his book?"

Garrett shakes his head; his eyes dart around the table, maybe searching for succor. "I haven't asked him anything. I've never met him."

Probably an unfair amount of pent-up frustration has avalanched onto Garrett, but Kelly feels embarrassed that she brought this guy along—that people think she and he are *dating*. She wants to speak up before the disdainful glares turn away from Garrett and to Kelly instead. Never did she imagine how badly he'd muck up his opportunity.

"So," Penelope says, ignoring Garrett's meek response, "would I confront Ford Hunter? The answer is, I don't know. How close would he be standing to the water and how many years in prison would I get if I drowned the little piece of excrement?"

"When we choose to dignify that book with a response, we'll release a statement. If you repeat anything she just said"—Ghusson wags her finger in Garrett's face—"I'll be drowning *you*."

"So tough! Ooh!" Penelope shivers comically, then rolls her eyes. "It's just a movie. Max, you're a cinema savant. What do you think of *Land Without Water*?"

Max stares at Penelope with lips pulled back, teeth slightly bared. Then he looks down.

Heat rushes Kelly's neck and face. "Max," she says, hoping this syllable—merely his name, grunted—will communicate everything she needs to: that he can't pull his usual shit here, not only for his own sake, but for Kelly's sake as well. Where's that twin telepathy everyone always mythologizes? Max's fingers tap Morse code against the table. Everyone watches him, awaiting his answer. He squints as his fingertips dance. Kelly sees either fear or anger etched into her brother's face.

Which would she prefer?

After a moment, he lifts his eyes again. "I dislike *Land Without Water*. Darren Stanford seemed obsessed with the construction of something hip and cool, but not something honest. I see none of The Sadness in his film."

"Well, I thought it was very sad." Someone at the table's other end says this, but Kelly has no idea who: the older folk have all blurred together as wine and dread massage her temples.

Max puckers his lips but refrains from reaching for water or wine. Despite his discomfort, he says, "I didn't mean sadness. I meant *The* Sadness."

The elderly squint, puzzled, as though Max is an odd piece of hexagonal fruit placed on the table—a piece of fruit nobody knows how to eat.

"I apologize. I'm not explaining myself well. I know I seem queer to you all, but I don't have much practice talking to people. Sitting here is a little overwhelming—kind of like one of those films where everything blows up all the time."

Everyone chuckles. Everyone *chuckles*? The tension breaks. Kelly realizes that, at some point, she lifted herself an inch off her chair, ready to lunge. She lowers herself like an adulteress returning to bed at three in the morning, trying not to awaken her spouse.

"The Sadness," Max goes on, "is a notion my mom had of what great cinema contains. It refers to something that's offscreen, something in the soul of the director. Sometimes watching a film, it feels like the director was stranded on an island and starving and lonely and that cinema was his only way of escape. That's The Sadness. And so the presence of The Sadness redeems some films that aren't very well made, but its absence cripples some films that are. For example, David Lean's films are impeccably made, but contain none of The Sadness and are therefore inferior to John Cassavetes's films, which aren't terribly professional but are drenched in The Sadness."

"Huh. You know who he reminds me of?" asks one of the older people.

"Who?" asks another older person.

"He reminds me of that old actor who used to be in those black-and-white movies. I see him all the time on Turner Classic Movies. He spoke very precisely. Kind of a comic fellow. In, uh"—making a windmill of his hand while trying to recall—"in, uh, what's it called... *Ball of Fire*, that one with Barbara Stanwyck. And then another one with Bing Crosby, I believe."

"Richard Haydn," Max says.

"Richard Haydn?"

"Yes. He also voiced the Caterpillar in *Alice in Wonderland* and made a cameo in *Young Frankenstein*."

The older people look at Max like they've all just met an adorable new grandchild.

But Max shrugs—another gesture that reminds these people of Richard what's-his-name? "I've always liked films," he says, "ever since I was little."

How well Max has spoken! Kelly wants to hug him. She almost sighs, but instead stuffs her face with a gob of bread, chewing merrily.

Penelope laughs, which sounds like a chair squeaking against the ground. "Well, that was a very bright take on *Land Without Water*." She puts her arm around him once again.

"But I thought you were wonderful in it."

"Well, thank you." She releases Max and mock bows. Then she picks up the glass—the one she knocked over before, whose wine extends like a finger toward the center of the table. "Now, where's that young man with more libation?"

"You can have mine," Max says, pushing his untouched glass toward Penelope.

She screeches, "My hero," darting forward to plant a big wet kiss on Max's cheek, while he closes his eyes, probably praying for the invasion to pass. Penelope rubs Max's head, while Garrett crosses his arms, fuming.

The older folks smile. This isn't their party, they know. But still, they seem amused, thinking, *Oh, to be young again,* or whatever exactly old people think about youth. And Kelly, yes, Kelly indeed feels strangely young. She laughs, and none of the rest of it—her disappeared father, her dead mom, the failure of her life—exists. She laughs and realizes with some astonishment that she's actually enjoying herself.

"This is my new boyfriend right here," Penelope says, still tussling Max. "Chelle, can you tell the press that we're inseparable?" With this,

Penelope releases her wineglass and reaches out her other arm to cradle Kelly, pressing the brother to one shoulder and the sister to the other, collecting a full set of Enright figurines. "I never want to be far from these two again. I want to be part of this family." Penelope puckers her lips and slams them against Max's; then she re-puckers and smears wetness on Kelly's mouth. Penelope discharges them both, finally, and Kelly snaps into her original position. She licks her lips. The wine tastes different from Penelope's mouth. More sugary, maybe.

"I love these two." Penelope shakes her head wistfully. "At least Max doesn't suck up to me."

"Penelope." Wrinkles grow around Ghusson's eyes; perhaps she can will herself to age decades whenever necessary. "Stop it." She becomes a stern mother—something with which Kelly has little experience.

"Stop what?" Penelope cocks her head.

"Act like an adult."

"But I'm not an adult!" Her voice reaches crescendo. "I'm a movie star!"

"Dinner will be out in just a few minutes." The attractive waiter has materialized behind Penelope. Kelly never saw him approach, but now she looks up and notices a minuscule tattoo of a skull on his neck, just below his left earlobe. Tattoos seem to dot this waiter's body like specks of grime. Someone else carries a pitcher of water around the table, filling everyone's glasses.

Penelope rolls her head across her shoulders to look up at the waiter; she pouts at him and taps the edge of her wineglass. The awkwardness is a heavy fog.

"So," Garrett says to Ghusson, "as for the statement you mentioned before—the statement about Ford Hunter's book—when will I receive a copy?"

Kelly can't believe it—everyone had just managed to forget him! If the table were narrower, she'd kick his shin.

Ghusson sets her water glass down. "Why would you ask that?"

"Don't you want me to release your statement?"

"Why would we want you to release our statement?"

"You—you know I'm a journalist, right?"

"Oh no, I wasn't aware. Do you write for *Variety* or *Entertainment Weekly*?"

"I write for the *Portland Phoenix*." He swallows. "Well, sometimes."

"Oh. Okay. Well, I work in Los Angeles. Obviously it's no Portland, but I'll manage. Thanks for the offer, though."

"But aren't I getting an interview or an exclusive or something?"

"Who said that?"

Garrett looks at Kelly, who says nothing. "Well, no one I guess, but I—"

"That's right. No one said that. Not even as a joke. Which it would have been."

Garrett seems to move all of himself away from the table, as though pushing back his chair and standing up and walking out without actually doing any of those things. He sits there glassy-eyed for a moment before reaching for his wine and slugging back half of it in one go. When he puts the glass down, he shakes his head. "Well, I feel stupid now."

Ghusson looks around the table. *"Now?"*

This has become a merciless display. Kelly has trouble watching, and a chill hits her. "It's a legitimate newspaper," she says, feeling obligated to say something.

"Portland Phoenix? I've never heard of it."

"That's because it hasn't risen from the ashes yet," Max says.

The convulsion, which speeds around the table, surprises Kelly so much that, initially, she wonders whether someone made a joke that she missed. It starts when Penelope, in the middle of a sip, begins to make gagging noises, trying not to choke. Ghusson laughs sharply, high-pitched, a squeak of a laugh—the first time her face has looked like a human being's. Mr. Wheeler coughs, sputters. Around it goes, the laughter. Max smirks and surveys the table, assessing whether his joke landed. And it did, it definitely did. Kelly tries not to smile. After all, her brother's joke was mean, and she should apologize on his behalf. But the quip turns upward the corners of her mouth. She can't help it.

Max grins, feeding off this positive energy. He has had a good day—maybe for the first time in years—and it pleases Kelly to watch her brother shrug off the sullenness and make the table laugh, like he used to make his sister and mother laugh. Kelly taps her foot on the ground and wants to think of a joke too, which reminds her of middle school, when she and Penelope would crack each other up late at night on her basement floor, stifling their giggles because they knew they should be asleep, not wanting parents, lords of upstairs, to hear. Kelly closes her eyes, trying to concentrate. Being funny is hard. She had forgotten.

"A lot of newspapers are going out of business," Max says, "but Garrett's is actually growing. They're about to make the leap from using paper clips to using staples."

Eureka! The lightbulb over Kelly's head bursts into brightness, so to speak. "Also," she says, "they're launching an audio/visual component. Garrett's gonna interview a cardboard cutout of Penelope live." Everyone stares at her. "In front of his *grammy*," she adds.

This one doesn't land as well as Max's—too wordy, too much set-up—but that's okay; Penelope still chuckles. Kelly's joke was, by far, the meanest and most personal. But isn't that what makes good humor sometimes? Isn't good humor an Exacto with which one cuts away the false exoskeleton and frees the truth?

From across the table, Garrett stares at Kelly. He makes her feel guilty. So she looks away—and *presto*, the guilty feeling vanishes, like she felt chilly and simply added another layer. Easy as that.

"For his next celebrity guest," Max says, "Garrett will interview the homeless guy on outer Washington who looks like Nick Nolte."

His quickness annoys Kelly (did he come up with these beforehand?), but she smiles nevertheless.

"Okay, okay." Garrett nods and chuckles, sounding like he has swallowed a cork.

Oh man, Kelly can tell how worked up he is, which makes everything funnier. He wants to sound like he can take a joke, sure. But suddenly, Garrett is the fat kid here, and high schoolers—which Max and Kelly and Penelope might as well be, sitting in this cafeteria as if living out the year right before Mom died—love to gang up on the fat kid.

"Ha, ha," Garrett says, "we get it. The paper's small. Good one, guys."

"Your paper's soooooo small," Kelly says.

"How small is it?" Max says, mugging.

"Your paper's soooooo small that the paperboy and the milkman are the same person. He just tapes the paper to the side of the bottle."

Penelope snorts; she loves this.

Kelly remembers Mom: *Ooh, I'm Joe Cupo and I wish I were made of snow!* Max must too, because on the other side of Penelope he starts fluttering his palms—jazz-handing.

Garrett shakes his head. "A milkman? Who even has a milkman anymore?"

"Ooh, my name's Garrett," Kelly says, "and I think *I'm* what's black and white and read all over!"

This cripples Max; he bends forward, red-faced. Kelly feels so proud—victorious!

"That doesn't make any sense." Garrett frowns; he's stopped pretending to enjoy this and looks around the table for support. Meanwhile, Max, Kelly, and Penelope bust up, losing it like bored students at an assembly.

"Wrongs will be righted," Kelly sings, *"if we're united."*

"He left his newsboy cap at home," Max says.

Penelope makes a choking sound like she might throw up; Kelly knew the singing would work on her. They performed "Seize the Day" at one of the choral concerts during junior year, and Kelly and Penelope invented a funny dance, which they did until Mrs. Cantor threatened to keep them after school. They simplified the dance, making it easier to perform without Cantor noticing, until all that remained was a rolling of hands, which the two friends performed clandestinely during chorus practices while trying not to crack up. Penelope's present hysteria delights Kelly, sure, but she really hopes the movie star remembers to roll her hands.

"Okay, enough," Garrett says. "Stop it."

"Neighbor to neighbor," Kelly sings, *"father to son."*

"Stop."

"One for all, and all for—"

"Shut the fuck up!"

The table leans back. "Whoa," Principal Allen says, holding out his hand, "watch your language, mister."

Maybe sensing that his time has almost expired, Garrett turns to Penelope. "I can't believe you don't remember me."

Ghusson grabs his shoulder and says, "You need to leave," her face like iron, but Garrett snaps away, swatting the assistant's hand. Ghusson

THE SADNESS • 141

looks over her shoulder toward the security guards who stand across the cafeteria, near the door. She motions with her hand: *Come, now.*

"You must remember me," Garrett says. "The summer after graduation. You must."

Penelope shakes and bows her head.

Security lines up behind Garrett. It's unclear whom these men answer to—Hollywood or the school—but Ghusson says, "Can you remove him, please?"

"You must remember me. Our dates." Garrett's face twists and pales; every second he waits, blood leaks from his body. Kelly still doesn't get it. How do a few dates (even make-believe ones) mean anything in the scheme of a life—even a life as seemingly empty as Garrett's? Surely he's full of shit, yet he looks so earnest; he *believes* he's telling the truth, even though he isn't.

"Sir?" As the security guards fold all their arms, Kelly worries about what will happen next. She doesn't want to see a show of force—doesn't want to see them grab Garrett and hoist him from the chair and drag him out. No, she'd feel too responsible for that.

But something changes. Penelope raises her eyes, and when she lands them on Garrett, a fire lights in them. Her lower lip trembles. Kelly watches the movie star very closely, expecting to see a tear fall.

Holy shit. Of course, Kelly knew everything about Penelope, but that access elapsed the summer Garrett mentioned—the summer after graduation. Maybe something actually *did* happen between them, improbable though it seems to Kelly. And if so, Penelope's expression spells bad news for him.

"Remember you?" Penelope's voice cracks and her throat seems to bulge, as though memories are trying to bust through her skin. "Should I take a second to fill everyone in about what *really* happened?"

Garrett looks lost. "I'm sorry, but I don't—"

"Why don't you tell them how much you hurt me?" Penelope hisses. No longer does she seem wounded and scared. Still, she trembles, but because of the anger electrifying her body. "Why don't you tell them how impossible you made it for me to ever be the same again?"

Garrett stares at her with his mouth open, his eyes wide. "I don't know what I did."

"You know," Penelope hisses, shaking. "You *know* what you did."

His face is that of a man remembering every awful thing he has ever done. The broken shards of his life—at least those that Kelly has glimpsed in the last forty-eight hours—come together in this moment, revealing nothing but questions. Why does he live with his grandmother? What happened the summer after graduation? How did he hurt Penelope?

But before Garrett can say anything—make any sort of confession to the waiting priests—Kelly looks down at Penelope's hand, her fingers draped over the edge of the wineglass that Max gave her, the tips of those fingers wading gently into the liquid. The movie star's whole body shakes, but not her hand; she wants to avoid spillage.

Kelly understands the punch line to this cruel joke.

Sure enough, only another second passes before Penelope widens her eyes and cocks her head, smiling. All the electricity leaves her body like a citywide blackout. She winks at Garrett before looking around at the rest of the table. "Not bad, huh? Maybe Ford's wrong about me. Maybe I *can* act."

The table launches into uproar, with Wheeler even clapping childishly. What fun! Penelope's display has delighted and charmed everyone— everyone, of course, except Garrett, who sits stiffly, the wide-eyed victim of a prank show, while the security guards remain vultures at his back. After a moment, he shakes his head and wipes his eyes. His hand flies to his mouth to push his reaction back in, but it's too late. It's coming out.

Kelly can't bear to watch him anymore. So she lowers her eyes. Hears his chair scrape against the ground as he stands. As he leaves. She should follow him into the hallway, apologize for everything. She knows she should.

Instead, Kelly looks at her brother, who scrunches his face, maybe trying to think up another joke.

"I don't remember much of this." Penelope glances inside the classrooms, which house test tubes and Bunsen burners and smocks hanging on hooks. "It feels like walking around the set of a movie I made years ago, trying to run my lines."

After dinner, at the actress's special request, Penelope and Kelly wander the school's empty hallways. But now, immersed in all this space—this playground for her to chase memories—Penelope seems to recall little of it.

Kelly fills her lungs with the empty hallway. This is the old part—the familiar part—of the high school, and they walk through the darkness that stretches from wall to wall, knocking it away as though passing through cobwebs. With the lights out, Kelly has trouble seeing her past hung on the walls, scattered on the floors. Penelope drags her knuckles against a bulletin board, rumpling the flyers pinned there.

"You really don't remember?" Kelly asks.

"I remember the *idea* of it," Penelope says, creeping up to a door and cupping her hands around her eyes to look through the tiny window, "but I'm drawing a blank on specifics."

Kelly feels momentarily lost, so it startles her when Penelope spins and presses her index finger to her lips, shushing. They stand still for a few seconds.

"Thought I heard footsteps," Penelope says.

"A ghost maybe?"

"I'd prefer a ghost to Chelle. She's probably already leaked this to the press. 'Penelope takes nostalgic walk through high school with friend.' *See, she's just like everyone else!*"

Kelly smiles politely, while noting that Penelope said only *friend*—not *best*. "Can it still be nostalgic if you don't remember it?"

"Nostalgic in theory, at least, if not in practice."

Instead of continuing their walk, they both plant themselves in this narrow hallway, leaning against the walls opposite each other.

"But," Penelope says, "I've been forgetting things all week. So what do I know? I stopped by Silly's to sign a headshot for the wall, and I heard this voice, kind of scratchy, calling my name. She was... let's see... she said she taught here, and she had this slicked hair, so black it looked spray-painted over—"

"You saw Mrs. Hodgkins?"

"Holy shit, you remember her? I didn't at all!"

"Oh yeah, sure. I bet." Kelly makes a droopy face and rolls her eyes, then follows this with a chuckle. *Of course* Penelope would have remembered Mrs. Hodgkins.

"Really!" Penelope joins in the laughter. "Should I remember? Did I take a class with her or something?"

Kelly's good humor wilts as she realizes they find different things funny about this. See, Kelly remembers the obsession Penelope had with Mrs. Hodgkins throughout high school. First of all, there was that absurd skullcap of black hair. But then Penelope caught Mrs. Hodgkins miscounting three cookies on a plate during parent-teacher conference week and concluded she must be delusional. (There were three cookies on the plate, yet Hodgkins kept saying to herself, "Two cookies. Only two cookies remain," in the clutches of a serene sort of lunacy.) From that point forward, Penelope researched Mrs. Hodgkins, learning: her marital status—divorced; her car—a Geo Prizm; her home address— North Street. When Mrs. Hodgkins gave Kelly and Penelope an inexplicable C-plus on their *White Noise* presentation—which they'd worked on with rare focus—they used all that personal information to drive to the teacher's house and stick plastic forks in every inch of her lawn. She left her job not long afterward, likely for unrelated reasons.

Kelly decides not to mention any of this, however. What would be the point? Penelope seems so similar to how she used to be, but not quite—a version of her that exists in the uncanny valley, that looks and acts like Kelly's old friend, but just... *isn't*.

For Kelly, catching the right scent or hearing the right song opens the door to her past and carries her through. The smell of a room stuffed with sweat and the fresh air-blast of a newly opened window; or the sound of boats, their wood rocking in the water, like signals from across the world; or "String Bean Jean" by Belle and Sebastian, a band she barely thinks about anymore, coming softly from a pair of headphones that hug someone else's ears—these things take Kelly's hand and guide her into the past, depositing her in one of millions of particular memories. Hell, she even remembers her father from fingertips on her arm, from the word *Girly*. But it's not so simple for Penelope. The entire city of Portland has pulled up to her, waiting, at her memory's disposal like a chauffeur asking, *Where to?* But she has been laid into cement, immovable, stranded in the sidewalk—in the present. How sad that must be. Maybe for this reason it seems so easy, the two of them falling once more into the rhythms of closeness. Maybe it's easy for Penelope because she can't recall how the friendship died.

Slouched, the movie star looks like she might sink into the ground. After a moment, she laughs and waves her hand in the air. "Well, I didn't remember her." The final word on the matter.

Kelly grunts, feeling suddenly shy.

"So you don't still live here, right?"

Kelly shakes her head and picks some skin off her lip with her teeth. "I've been moving a bit. Tucson. Vegas. Around the Southwest, pretty much."

"And everything's been going well?"

Kelly stares. Of course she could answer this; oh, Kelly could sit Penelope down and relate the sour history of her last eleven years. But a weird thing happens to Kelly, watching her old best friend droop against the wall and bend her back, stretching uncomfortably. Kelly—who usually wants to dip into her reserves of memory; who usually wants to live there, even if the memory is unpleasant; who usually wants to talk about herself to anyone who asks; who usually wants to dwell on her own misery to the exclusion of all other people and things—well, now, Kelly wants to tell Penelope nothing.

So Kelly simply says, "Yeah. Everything's been going great."

"Penelope? Penelope?"

This voice echoes down the hallway, and the sound seems to sober the movie star for a second; she snaps her head to the left. "That's Chelle," Penelope whispers. "Please don't make me go back there. Please."

Kelly looks to some doors to their left—doors that lead into the stairwell, where there's a spot to crawl under the staircase and sit. Kelly remembers this secret place, sneaking off there with Penelope to sip a whiskey-filled water bottle in the sophomore days when they started experimenting with booze.

"Come on," Kelly says, and takes Penelope's hand.

"Where are we—"

Kelly puts her index finger against Penelope's lips and feels moisture. "Shh." They hold for a second, touching, in some kind of cloud.

Then off they go.

Moments later, crammed under the staircase, they cannot hear Ghusson's probing voice anymore. No one will find them here. No one ever found them here. Kelly feels Penelope's small body pressed into her; they fit together beautifully, whispers intertwining like hands.

"You know," Kelly says, "I see your movies, and I wonder whether you remember me."

"Of course I remember you, Kel."

"You seem like you haven't changed."

"I think I have. Probably. But coming home makes me into who I want to be." She takes a breath. "I don't want to do this anymore. I don't want to be that person I have to be out there. I want to quit, come home. I feel like whatever Penelope Hayward is, I'm only her shadow."

This vulnerability surprises Kelly—how openly Penelope shares her feelings. And Kelly tries to think of something to say, some way to reciprocate, something that will demonstrate her own vulnerability.

But before she thinks of anything, Penelope sighs. "But it's fine, right? Never feel sorry for a man who owns a plane."

Kelly blinks. "I don't get it. Who owns a plane?"

"It's from a movie I saw once. Listen, hey, let's go for a walk around Monument Square. Want to?"

"Would Chelle let you?"

Penelope makes a farting noise with her lips. "I'm flying out tonight around midnight. A red-eye."

"You're not staying for Day Without Water?"

Penelope shakes her head. "Chelle withdrew me. 'Personal reasons,' she called it. Given the attention on Ford's nasty comments, she doesn't want me anywhere near there. So Chelle won't want me out on the town for long. But to hell with her, right? You and I can go for a drive downtown. It'll be quick. I just want to look at the Christmas tree."

Kelly squeezes her eyes shut, her face feeling numb. What Penelope proposes, it does sound nice. It always delighted Kelly, how excited Christmas lights made Penelope. They were the same every year, the lights, but that didn't matter. And Kelly wants to go for that walk around Monument Square. She wants to spend as much time with her friend as she can, even if it's just one more hour. She wants to linger here in this vision of what her life used to be like. It feels so warm to linger here, just a little longer.

But she can't. As nice as this feels, it isn't the point of today. So she opens her eyes. "You know, I would, but I'm really tired. I bet Max would love to go with you, though."

"Oh yeah?"

"Yeah, he loves the lights. I'll loan him my car. You guys can drive up there, then he can drop you off at the hotel, whatever time Chelle wants. He'll get a kick out of it, I'm sure."

"Okay. Yeah. Great." Penelope sounds so happy. "That's tremendous. Thank you."

"Yeah. And maybe some other time you and I can have a dance-off."

"Oh, sure!" Penelope laughs.

Kelly feels something harden in her throat. "You do remember, right? When we tried to make that video of us dancing?"

"For what?"

"For the video yearbook," Kelly says. "It was going to be a joke dance-off. Like, a joke version of the big competition at the end of one of those cheerleader movies or something."

"Oh yeah." Penelope nuzzles up, putting her head on Kelly's shoulder. They used to do this sometimes at night, when they sat on the couch in Penelope's basement watching movies. They used to sit like this. Fall asleep like this. Kelly remembers so vividly. Only in those days, it was usually Kelly who put her head on Penelope's shoulder.

In all the years that she has stared at Penelope's face on a screen, Kelly has never quite remembered their past together—never quite remembered how much she always loved Penelope, always wanted Penelope to love her too. But Kelly remembers it all, right now, with Penelope's breath against her body, feeling the small girl shake and sigh like a child. Kelly recalls so much of what they used to be like. For a second, she fools herself into thinking Penelope does too.

Why didn't Kelly return Penelope's calls? Why didn't Kelly ever try to contact Penelope in the years that followed their friendship's dissolution? Maybe it's because, after landing in Arizona, Kelly felt that Penelope, along with Max and Mom, was part of her old life—felt that she was supposed to face the future alone, or some bullshit like that. But how cruel of her to not say good-bye. Maybe Kelly never called because she didn't want to admit the truth: that she herself was to blame for how the friendship died.

So if Penelope can't remember the worst parts of Kelly, then Kelly doesn't want to remind her. Frankly, she's still too ashamed.

"Yeah, that was fun," Penelope says, "our dance-off. That was really funny."

"Yeah," Kelly says, "makes me smile just remembering it."

That was pretty. Very pleasant. Thanks for driving.

All right.

So how's everything going with you? Do you still do stuff with movies?

No.

No? But you were always so good at it.

No, I wasn't.

That's not true. Don't say that. What discouraged you?

[No response]

Well, whatever it was, just remember that nobody ever got anywhere being discouraged. Besides, I have connections. If you ever want to come out to L.A. I could get you a job as a production assistant or something. Nothing fancy, but who knows what could come of it. It's a start in the indust—

Why did Darren Stanford thank Evelyn Andersson at the end of the film?

Who?

Evelyn Andersson. I'm asking about Evelyn Andersson.

I don't remember.

t isn't until Kelly reaches the corner of Salem Street—after a calming half-hour walk from Deering—that she realizes she doesn't have a key to the house. The spare is with her car keys, which she loaned to Max. Sure, the back door might be unlocked, but instead of traipsing around like a criminal, Kelly decides to have a drink. So she stops at Ruski's and sits at the bar. Ghusson set a curfew of nine for her movie star, and it's half past eight now. There's really only time for Penelope to look at the tree in Monument Square and then for Max to drive her to the hotel. It shouldn't take long. But then Kelly thinks of her old room and what Max has turned it into, and she begins to worry. What the hell is Max doing with Penelope? What kind of conversations could they possibly be having?

After consulting her beer, she ignores her concerns and focuses on developing a plan. As soon as Max returns her car, she will learn the location of her father, per their agreement, and she will visit him tonight. Then she will drive toward Tucson until she finds another spot along

---

She went to high school with us. Her real name is Evelyn Romanoff but her stage name is Andersson.

I don't remember. Maybe she knew Ford? Might've been one of his slutty groupies from his Rocktopus days. They were always hanging around.

She wasn't one of his—

You know, I really can't believe that guy Garrett asking me about Ford. What an embarrassment. Coming home, I thought I'd be treated like a human being, not made to feel stupid.

I don't care about that. I care about Evelyn Andersson. Do you remember—

I'm so stupid, Max. I feel so stupid all the time.

[No response]

I'm just smart enough to realize how stupid I am. Every time I open my mouth I think I'm wrong about whatever I'm saying.

[No response]

The great Saint Ford who still resides in Portland. Something or someone always comes along to make me feel stupid. He's a Janus. You know what Janus means?

the highway that has a better vibe. She will take I-40 across the country, passing through Nashville, Memphis, Oklahoma City. There must be somewhere along the interstate for her—for the new version of Kelly that will exist after she finally meets Dad.

She kills over an hour drinking two beers and chatting aimlessly with the bartender, Louise, and then she leaves a little before ten, her feet feeling like water balloons. Maybe she drank those beers too fast, especially considering the wine from earlier. It doesn't take much to wreck a puny girl like her.

For this reason, Kelly thinks she might be hallucinating when, approaching the house, she notices a taxi idling right outside. The driver, a mammoth man with full sleeves of tattoos, reads a magazine in the glow of the overhead light. Apart from the purring of the engine, the night is quiet, like someone turned it off. Then some asshole pounds a fist against the front door of the house.

"Can I help you?" Kelly jogs ahead, full of boozy bravery. But she comes to a stop when she identifies the visitor.

Ghusson.

Although Kelly shivers like crazy, Ghusson stays composed, unaffected by the winter; feeling chilly must rank low on her to-do list. Uncoiling, she storms down the driveway. "Where's Penelope?"

Yes.

It means two-faced.

Well, Janus had two faces: one to the past, one to the future. But he was more about new beginnings.

See? There I go. Can't get anything right.

I'm very familiar with Janus.

We used to go to Ford's house all the time. We'd take breaks from shooting and smoke joints out his window. We'd order takeout from Tandoor and eat it on the floor in the living room. It was our production headquarters. They treated me like a princess on that movie, Darren and Ford. Those boys fought over me. Piled gifts upon me. Ha. It was kind of embarrassing actually. They used to bring me breakfast and flowers. Sure, that probably spoiled me a bit. I was young.

Why did Darren Stanford disappear?

I don't know. He was a strange guy. Deeply neurotic. I could never wrap my head around the fact that he was both the most talented and most insecure person I'd ever met. But he vanished. The "reclusive genius responsible" is what the title of Ford's book calls him, right?

Have you talked to Darren Stanford in the last several years?

Numbness infests Kelly's body; she has trouble understanding this question. "The hotel?"

Ghusson widens her eyes, the grid of seriousness that usually strains against her face disappearing; then she smacks her palm to her forehead. "Well, gosh, gee, thanks a bunch." She says this with a slight southern lilt, making fun of Kelly for something she doesn't actually sound like. "Penelope never came back to the hotel, and she needs to be on a plane in two hours. This isn't pretend. What happened to my movie star?"

Kelly shakes her head. "She—I don't know. She went off with my brother. He said he'd drop her off at the hotel."

"Well, he didn't."

Kelly blinks. "I can, uh..." Her shaking hand struggles into her jeans and emerges a second later with a cell phone. "Let me call him." In a minute, Max's voice mail comes on: full—probably from years of voices unlistened to. "I can try again," she says.

Ghusson rolls her eyes.

"Or we can go inside and wait."

"*You* can go inside and wait," Ghusson says.

"Look, she's famous. She can't just disappear."

"Unless someone hides her in a supersecret place."

"You think I'm hiding her?"

No. We lost contact after he vanished from the film world. Rumor has it that he does some ghostwriting.

But you don't know where he is?

No. He went off the grid, as they say. One rumor was that he moved to middle-of-nowhere Vermont. Why are you so interested in him?

I'm interested in Evelyn Andersson.

Well, I'm sorry, but I can't help you with that.

But you must remember—

I really don't. Okay? Can you drop it?

Don't talk to me like that.

Excuse me?

You're a celebrity. What else do you have to talk about?

Why would you say that? I was trying to talk to you before, to tell you something honest.

But you spend your life making people think what they want to think about you. Maybe you're just doing that with me too. Maybe your quote-unquote honesty is another performance.

That's cruel of you to say that. That hurts my feelings.

"Are you?" Ghusson cocks her head and watches Kelly, trying to see through her.

"Look," Kelly says, "they probably just lost track of time."

Ghusson raises an eyebrow. "Lost track of time?"

"Yeah. Or maybe Penelope wants to stay in Maine. That's what she told me earlier."

Ghusson exhales a storm cloud and looks up at the sky, clear and sparkling; then she looks at her wrist, even though she wears no watch. "Look, I'll make this quick. I'm a simple person, okay? I work, eat a bagel for dinner, watch *Letterman* before I go to bed, et cetera. But the fussiest I ever get? Morning. I need my coffee, and I need my amaretto creamer. If I don't have it: watch out. Now, Penelope in the morning— you know what her amaretto creamer is? Her amaretto creamer is a gentleman named Derek who comes into her bedroom with a full breakfast—bacon, French toast, a beautiful omelet, pancakes with blue-berries the size of pearls. *Bravo!*" Ghusson makes a kissing noise and a gesture near her mouth as though tasting something delicious. "We're talking the sort of breakfast you and I only eat on the specialest of spe-cial occasions, and Penelope gets it every. Single. Morning. And you know much of it she eats? She eats precisely two lemon wedges. *Two.* She doesn't touch the rest of the food. She just likes the smell of it. First morning we were here, she wouldn't get out of bed because there was

---

People fawn over you, give you whatever you want. And you whine about feeling stupid?

You really think I don't feel anything missing from my life? You don't know... that's the hotel, Max.

[No response]

Max, you passed the hotel. I'm at the Eastland. Remember?

I don't want to make films anymore. Mom always told me I should make films. Mom always believed in me. But I wasted too much time, see? After she died I wasted so much time. So I failed at that. But now there's something else I need to do. Something I won't fail at. So I need you to come with me to just one more place. Just a mile away. I need you to come with me.

Max, I—

One more place and then that's the end of it. I promise. One more place and it's over. I'll take you back.

But it's already nine. We'll be late.

Where we're going, we won't be long.

no Derek. So now we pay for the hotel to bring up an entire continental breakfast each morning so that Penelope can enjoy her lemon wedges. Then we throw everything else away. Meanwhile, I went around the corner to buy my amaretto creamer at a 7-Eleven. Get the gist? Penelope's not staying in Maine. She just wants attention. To get it from you, she acts one way. Usually though, she acts another way."

Kelly feels the cold breeze like tongues lapping up and down her arms.

Ghusson bites her lip and nods. "But you know what? I believe you. If you were hiding Penelope, you wouldn't have made yourself so easy to find." She holds up the lame business card that Kelly handed her earlier. How fucking embarrassing.

"You know," Ghusson continues, returning the card to her pocket, "when you first said you knew Penelope, I thought you were nuts. But then she spoke highly of you. Told me you were best friends. A genuine person, she said. She has a good sense for that sort of thing, even though she lives on another planet. So do Penelope a favor and help me find your brother."

"He's not dangerous," Kelly says weakly.

"Well. Let's be on the safe side. I'll call you if I find her. You do the same."

Ghusson turns and walks down the steps. The slam of the taxi door seems shockingly loud out here, where nobody makes any noise, not even to breathe.

Is it really like Ghusson says—that Penelope will regress into her life of glitz and lemon wedges as soon as she returns home? It seemed so heartfelt before, how Penelope said she wanted to leave all that—how she articulated her desire for an exit. If what Ghusson says is true, then it's tough not to feel a little sorry for Penelope, beating on the door back to reality—a door that will not budge. Maybe the way Kelly feels toward Penelope right now resembles the way Penelope felt toward Kelly on the front lawn all those years ago: sad about her friend's future, afraid of what will happen to her, and, above all else, frustrated by her own inability to help.

But maybe it's like Penelope said: *Never feel sorry for a man who owns a plane.*

Alone in the cold, silence wrapping its hands around her ears, Kelly listens for the sound of any approaching cars. When will Max return?

Where has he gone with Penelope? Curtains obscure the windows, but the house glows, turning the cloth a pulsing sort of yellow, the color of a candle in an illustrated children's book.

Kelly traipses around back, crushing frozen shrubs and fighting through low-hanging branches, making a racket. As a teenager, there was this one way she always used to go, sneaking in at night, not wanting to unlock and open either of the squeaking doors that might wake Mom, that might force her to confront Kelly for her lateness (on those rare occasions Mom herself wasn't too wasted to wake up—or when she'd care about lateness at all). There was a rock behind the house, under which Kelly hid a spoon. Using her cell phone light, she illuminates the ground. Much weedier, more overgrown back here than before. But then there it is, the rock, a thin slab. And when she flicks it over? Little pill bugs go running but, Jesus, there it is, the spoon, the long cooking spoon, still here after eleven years. She picks it up—so cold, the metal, it cuts a freezing line down her palm—and she finds the right window in the back, the one with the indentation toward the bottom, just enough space to wiggle the long spoon in and use it as a lever on the unlocked window. And up it goes, silently—so much more silent than either door ever was. Kelly hoists herself to the window, squeezes through it. More beer weight on her now than when she was a teenager, but still, she fits, just *barely*, she fits.

Nothing looks out of the ordinary in the kitchen, which is to say that everything still looks out of the ordinary, but not in any way different from before. She calls her brother's name, but hears nothing apart from the echo of her own voice pinballing wall to wall.

Earlier today, Kelly thought Max was normal again as he sat at that table making jokes, turning all those people Penelope especially—into admirers. He seemed fine again, transformed from the person who started the crazy fight under the Casco Bay Bridge and then tried to make a crater in his own face—transformed from the kind of person who kept diaries and photographs hoarded in the upstairs room. It seemed, momentarily, like a triumph, some proof that he could be okay again, could get control of his life again—and if he could do it, couldn't Kelly do it too? She thought for a second that maybe they weren't stuck in place, that maybe there was a way back to find themselves again, to find the people they were before Mom died, to find the people they *could've* been had life gone differently. Was she wrong?

She steps through the kitchen and into the living room. Mom's futon sits unfolded against the wall—the futon on which Kelly rested last night; she'd struggled to fall asleep, trying to ignore those voices upstairs that belonged to whatever Max watched before bed, the sort of white noise chatter of a movie or television show left on after the viewer has fallen asleep.

Thinking of this, she goes to the staircase, stares at the tarp of darkness thrown over the upstairs landing. "Max?" she calls, tossing her voice as though casting a fishing line off the edge of a boat. She draws in a breath and listens. Then she begins her ascent, one foot after another, just like she learned as a kid.

In Max's room, she checks the bed for a body. On the bureau next to his turned-off TV sits a video camera with red, yellow, and white wires plugged into the television's inputs. She hits the power button, revealing a black screen, the words AV INPUT green and blocky in the upper right-hand corner. She picks up the video camera, afraid to see what Max has been watching each night. Eleven years ago, he crept into Kelly's room to film her as she slept; what has he taped since?

She presses play.

What happened to Mom was this: she died. No mystery to it. She asked Kelly to deposit the cash, but Kelly never deposited the cash, not wanting Mom to waste it on wherever she had gone and whomever she had gone there with.

Six days after that last call—six days after Kelly "accidentally" dropped Max's phone in the toilet so that Mom couldn't contact him— the police called the Salem Street house, and they explained: Mom had gone to stay with a man at his roach-infested apartment on Cumberland Avenue, a mile away from home. They drank for weeks, until he came back from 7-Eleven with some orange juice one morning and found her in the bathtub. She must have passed out, drowned in dingy water. The police determined Mom's death accidental—but Kelly knew there was nothing accidental about it.

At one point, Mom had been in New Hampshire—she had withdrawn her last batch of cash from an ATM in Bedford, after all—but then she had come north again, to Portland. In her last days, she was close to home, probably waiting for Friday so she could sneak to the house, intercept the mailman, and abscond with the next installment of cash. Portland looked beautiful that April. The sun came out and melted most of the snow quickly. The boats rocked on the water and bells sounded from cathedrals, echoing between the brick buildings. The pollen turned the air dream-sequence yellow. The breeze gathered salt from the ocean and flew it inland. The whole city looked and smelled like a memory. And Mom was so close. If Kelly had called the police, they probably could have found Mom easily. But she never called the police. Never even told her brother—not, at least, until too late. At the time, Kelly told herself, *It's not serious, this sort of thing has happened before, Mom will come home.* Sure, she was worried—but then, she'd spent most of her adolescence worried. She thought she was

---

Casco Bay Bridge. This was the last place she was seen.

The last place who was seen?

And look. Up there. See that painting of you? Up there underneath the bridge. See it?

It's dark. I can't see anything.

Evelyn was down here because you shot the film down here. The end of Land Without Water. *The film made her do something to herself because she had something to do with the film. She had—*

[No response]

Why are you looking at me like that?

I'm sorry, but I don't understand what you're saying.

Evelyn had something to do with the film. What did she have to do with the film? Did she work on it? Did she help Darren Stanford with it?

I don't know—

She's thanked at the end of the film! Look. This is her. See? This is her right here on this flyer. I just want to... I want to see her. I want to find her. Someone needs to find her. And she went missing because of your film. Because of—

[No response]

Stop looking at me like that!

Can you drive me back please?

Not until you help me. Not until you tell me the truth.

doing the right thing by not panicking, by keeping it from Max, by getting him dressed, by making him go to school each day; she thought she was protecting him from Mom's wreckage. But now, Kelly wonders whether there was something else in her mind. If she had told Max, he would have gone looking for her, just as he now looks for Evelyn, and he probably would have found her too: Mom was only a mile away, after all. So maybe Kelly told nobody about those phone calls from Mom because, really, she was hoping the police would call instead.

When the day of the funeral came, Kelly wanted to avoid it, wanted to wait it out at Ruski's until someone stopped in later to tell her Mom was in the ground. Of course she went, but she compromised, sitting in the back with Penelope. Kelly desired invisibility. Didn't want anybody to ask about her—how she was doing, what she was feeling. Meanwhile, Max sat up front with Evelyn. Kelly watched them huddled there, grieving. That afternoon, Evelyn cried for Mom, and she held Max's hand, and it felt to Kelly as though she were watching an actress playing her, playing the role of sister—the role of daughter. It was the

---

I'm sorry, but I need to go.
Wait. Who are you calling?
If you won't take me back then I'll call Chelle. She can send a cab.
Put the phone down.
Calm down.
Put it down.
Stop it. Back off. Get away from—
Put it down.
What the fuck was that?
[No response]
[No response]
It's busted. Don't bother. It's soaked through. You'll be down here until I want you to leave, until I let you leave. Do you understand?
What if I scream?
You think anybody will hear you with the traffic overhead?
[No response]
[No response]
What do you want from me?
Do you know this person?
I don't—
Look at the picture. Do you know this person? Do you remember this person?

oddest thing really, almost as though Evelyn, out of some great unintentional kindness, gave Kelly the memory she would later want to have of the funeral—the memory that Kelly was in no position, back in those chaotic days, to give herself. Strange, how little Kelly has remembered this girl in eleven years; whenever Kelly thinks of Evelyn, she's thinking of an alternate version of the funeral, in which *Kelly* got to be the good daughter whose eyes turned to oceans, who looked after her brother—didn't *pretend* to look after her brother, didn't hide behind the *idea* of looking after her brother, but truly, in a moment when it mattered, *looked after* her brother.

What does Max think about when he sees Evelyn's face? Not the same thing, Kelly supposes. But he still has the tapes from *The Glazen Shelves*—puts them on when he needs to sleep, the sound of this footage a lullaby. Kelly sits on the edge of Max's bed to watch.

She has never seen any of *The Glazen Shelves* before—never even knew the plot, really—but despite its unfinished status, the professional quality of the visuals surprises her. Evelyn sits on a dock, hair glowing in the sunlight, ocean in the background—the waves a lovely sort of

---

She's missing. I'm trying to find her. I'm trying to save her. Did she know Darren Stanford?

Your mom was missing too.

Don't change the subject.

You need to find this girl or you need to find your mom?

[No response]

Your mom's dead, Max. I'm sorry but your mom's dead.

My mom loved Evelyn. My mom wanted us together.

But your mom doesn't need you to do anything. You can't do anything for her.

[No response]

If you take me back to the hotel I can help you. If you take me back to the hotel right now I'll help you find someone who can help you through this. Because you need to talk to someone. You can't chase this person. Finding this person won't bring your mom back.

Stop condescending to me.

What?

You've been condescending to me all day. You think I'm cute.

I don't think you're cute. I think you're hurt.

You don't know anything about being hurt. Worst thing ever happened to you is some guy wrote a book where he made you feel stupid. You don't know anything about being hurt.

white noise—while the actress, alone, applies makeup to her face and says, "I just don't want to look cold. It's supposed to be summertime." She dabs her face. "You look fine," Kelly hears Max say from offscreen. How many people were on this dock, involved in the making of this scene? Kelly has no idea, but from her perspective, it seems like there were only two people: Evelyn and Max—only those two, shutting out the rest of the world. "Okay," Evelyn says, putting her compact away. Max says, "Pick it up from the beginning of the speech." Evelyn shivers, then lowers her head for a moment to draw in a deep breath. There is a moment of silence on the tape, except for the sound of the waves in the background. Then Max whispers, "Action." Evelyn raises her head and looks slightly to her right, pretending to address somebody who sits next to her. "The cruelest thing I ever did to somebody?" Evelyn smiles. "Oh God, I don't know... there was this boy a few years ago—this boy I met in New York—and..." Evelyn continues to speak, speaks for about one minute, delivering a monologue about some experience she had trying to make some guy jealous a couple years before. Was this from Evelyn's own experience, or did Max write

---

It's cold out here. Let's go back to the hotel. You can come in. We'll talk about this.
I need to find her.
We're not finding her out here. You need to take me back before Chelle sends people looking for me.
What's Evelyn's connection to Land Without Water? How did she know Darren Stanford?
I'm sorry, Max, but you aren't making any sense. You're talking in circles.
I'm not.
I'm freezing. Please take me back. Please.
I don't care about your opinion of me. You're a movie star. Nothing more. This is all you have to offer, helping me find Evelyn. This is the only thing you'll ever be good for in your life. And you are *stupid. You* are.
Okay. Forget it. I was trying to help.
Where are you going?
I'm not playing around.
You're not going anywhere.
I'm... no, wait. Wait, wait, wait. Max, what are you doing? Get out of there. You'll freeze.
What does it matter? If I can't find her, whatever happens to me, it doesn't matter.
Max, I'm scared.

this speech? Either way, it's pretty unremarkable—cliché and unconvincing. Oh well. Her brother was only eighteen. Kelly can't expect genius—probably, she has to admit, wouldn't be able to recognize it anyway if she saw it. But she knows that Evelyn has a lovely presence, and she delivers each line of dialogue with precision. It makes total sense to Kelly as she watches this footage: What young man wouldn't have fallen in love?

Despite the obvious skill of Evelyn's performance, Max cuts her off before she finishes:

Max: "What you're saying about him, there's too much pride in it. I think you need to focus on regret. Zero in on regret."[14]

Evelyn: "But regret doesn't make any sense. I mean, Natalie would feel amused by this story, if anything. She's not prone to guilt. This is her just kind of... amused. Human nature, whatnot. When Welles comes in and laughs and the guy goes, 'What's funny?' and Welles just shakes his head and says, 'Old age.' Remember that?"

Max: "But in terms of narrative, this needs to be a turning point."

Evelyn: "Well, what I could try is to work my way into the guilt, if that's really what you want. 'Cause she wouldn't start at guilt, I don't think. But she might get there by the end."

Max: "Maybe she starts amused and then something shifts?"

Evelyn: "Yeah. When she says, 'I was a little girl. I realize that now.' When she says that, she knows it's true. That might be the moment. Because, see, I don't want her to feel regret that she made the New York guy jealous. That's out of character. But she might feel regret that she was so young."

Max: "Regret about never being smart enough?"

Evelyn: *"Exactamente."*

Max: "Okay. Whenever you're ready."

So Evelyn takes a minute, lowering her head, drawing another deep breath. When she tries her speech again, Kelly can't hear much of a difference from before. After a minute, a low rumbling emerges and grows louder and louder, until the sound of a plane overhead drowns out Evelyn's dialogue. She rolls her eyes and throws her head back, casting scorn upward.

Kelly notices something previously hidden—something that hangs around Evelyn's neck, a sphere of sunlight against her pale skin. Pressing her face close to the television, static tickles Kelly's nose. On screen: a locket, gold, glimmering. K.B.

Mom's.

I'm scared too. I'm scared of what's happening to me. So tell me something.
Tell you what?
Tell me something to save my life.

IMAGINE
YOURSELF
A CAMERA

April 4, 2001

I'm a little worried about Max.

Dr. Dipshit says I need to worry about myself instead of other people, but fuck him. Max's hands have started shaking so much that he can't hold the camera steady.

Because of his shaking hands, Max has enlisted Jake as his director of photography, which seems like a haughty title for somebody who keeps staring at my cleavage (seriously?). This dress Max has me wearing throughout these dock scenes is ridiculous. Why so low-cut?

Plus why the hell am I even wearing a dress in the first place? We're still shooting at the end of Town Landing. The pier seems to extend a mile over the ocean. I have to fight the wind. My dress blows all over the place. A woman as dignified as myself (ha!) should not be sitting in the cold wind like that (what can I say, sometimes it's fun to play the diva).

When Max calls "Action," I have to will myself not to shiver. When he calls "Cut" (so funny that he calls "Action" and "Cut," even when it's just the two of us), I put on a sweatshirt. We've been shooting these dock scenes for the last month. (YOU try sitting on a dock in early March in Maine wearing a sundress.)

Max said the whole film would just take a few weekends to shoot. That was back in December. I thought we were just going to shoot in some bedrooms and basements and living rooms. Everything interior. But the script kept getting longer. And then Max decided the exterior scenes should take place during summer (even though we were filming in winter). And then Max wrote all this dock stuff. When we first started shooting here last month, we had to be careful not to accidentally film any stray patches of snow, this supposedly being summer and all.

When I tell all this to Dr. Dipshit, he says I can back out any time I want. He says that I'm sticking with the film because I feel bad for Max. But that's not it at all. I'm sticking with the film because, in spite of everything, it's a valuable experience. And even though I've been doing theater this year, I've started to feel more kinship with film acting than with stage acting. I like the opportunity for small gestures. I think The Glazen Shelves will be good. At least good enough to use when I apply to Tisch next year.

I have one last thing to say about Jake: it's weird having a third person around. Before, the film felt like a secret, just Max and me. I haven't bothered to tell anyone about it. They'd think it was weird that Max Enright would ask me back in October to be in a film. But you don't even know him, they'd say. True. But the film sounded interesting and we bonded quickly over directors we both loved. It surprised me, really, that we hadn't become friends earlier. We started going to the movies. Mulholland Drive was a kind of awkward first one to see together, but it was fun. Nice to have company, really. Sure, he might be crushing on me. I don't know. What does it matter really? He's never weirded me out.

But our new "DP" weirds me out big-time.

The only good thing about Jake being on board is that now we can do some of the shots that contain Max and me at the same time. For the last months, we've just passed the camera back and forth, filming each other (Max rarely wants steady tripod shots), but with Jake, we can start doing some steadicam-style stuff following us down the dock. (And no, Max definitely doesn't want to use the wheelchair-dolly trick. He thinks JLG was a hack. Some people. Tsk tsk. I mentioned to Max what Dan Domench told me, how the Coens apparently attached a camera to a board and carried it between two people for the tracking shots in Blood Simple, but Max seemed indifferent. If we did either of those tricks, Max would have to "hire" someone new.)

On Monday I called Max to make sure we were still scheduled to shoot in the afternoon, but he didn't answer and didn't seem to be at school either. Then at 2 P.M., he e-mailed me like he'd never heard my message. Said the shoot was canceled. Still on for Tuesday, though. Also, he said that I needed to give him a ride. Most of the time he borrows his mom's Honda. Usually when she goes somewhere—like Brian Boru, or that place with the thumping music next to Portland Pie Company—she walks, which means the car is often up for grabs.

(It makes me remember when I first starting hanging around Max, and his mom invited me out to go drinking and dancing with her and some other thirty-something women. When I reminded her that I was only seventeen, she seemed unconcerned. Then she invited me to Boston for the weekend with her and her friend Melanie. I politely declined both offers.)

Anyway, so Max asks for a ride, which means the Honda must've been occupied. (Mom on one of her trips again? And to think I didn't get an invitation!) I pick Max up and we head toward Town Landing. I ask, "Where's your mom?"

He tells me she's away, at some job interview in Massachusetts, but he's rubbing his eyes and his hand's twitching even more than usual. When I ask how long she'll be away, he just says "awhile" like it's a specific unit of time.

He doesn't say where in Massachusetts either. Boston? Western Mass? But he doesn't know. He's hasn't been the one talking to her; instead, all of this info comes from Kelly. Ten days (ten days!) she's been gone. I tell him he should call his mom. He has a right to talk to his mom. But he doesn't have a phone right now; Kelly's broken it—"an accident."

I gave up on the interrogation when we crossed Martin's Point Bridge into Falmouth. It felt like we were driving into the sky. Max kept his forehead pressed against the window.

So then the other day I notice Kelly sitting in the corner with Penelope during lunch. Then I pass her in the hallway and I say hello and she asks me if I know where Max is. No hi, no nothing. Just "You know where Max is?" I thought for a second she was going to push me up against a locker, shitty-high-school-movie style, and spit in my face or something. I should have asked her what was going on. I didn't.

Kelly scares me. She barely looks at me. I'm just her brother's friend, maybe. But it's not like a dismissive-big-sister thing (even though they are twins and pretty much the same age). It's just like total indifference. Have you ever noticed that? Indifference is the scariest thing in the world.

But Kelly understands Max. At least seems to. And the truth is, I don't really understand Max, even after all this time working on this film. I don't understand him at all. So what do I know?

I hope everything's okay with Max's mom. He worships her. I don't understand it, but that doesn't make it any less true. I can't imagine what would happen to him if something happened to her, like something's bound to happen to her someday. Like something's bound to happen to every last one of us.

But Dr. Dipshit told me yesterday that I shouldn't think such thoughts anymore. You know, the pessimistic ones about the world ending, and the lives of the people in it ending, and all of that. He upped my dosage. But I'm still tired. I need to feel okay.

I'm trying to feel okay.

April 21, 2001

I've been to three funerals in my life.

Okay, maybe my grandmother's funeral doesn't count, because I was only four.

But definitely Uncle Jimmy's counts, 'cause that was just a couple years ago. My dad asked me to read a passage from the Bible (weird, how us nieces and nephews of the childless Jimmy had to participate like it was some kind of family relay race). Reading the passage made me uncomfortable because I don't know anything about the Bible. But I read it anyway.

And now, here, I add a third: Max's mom. (That's why I didn't write in this notebook last week, MOM AND DR. DIPSHIT, in case you're reading this right now.)

Everything happened so quickly with Max's mom and none of it makes much sense. She was never at a job interview. She was missing. Kelly knew and lied about it. And then they found Max's mom dead. The details are disturbing to me. I don't want to go into it.

I don't have much to write about any of this, I guess. I'm shocked. Especially shocked that Kelly knew their mom was missing and didn't tell anybody. Didn't tell Max. Apparently Max really did think that his mom was interviewing for a job somewhere, although if you ask me, the way he's been acting the last few weeks, all twitchy and removed, leads me to believe he at least suspected something was wrong

I've always thought that their relationship was close. Max and Kelly, I mean. But she didn't tell him about any of this. And even if he suspected something, he didn't ask.

But how could she hide this from her brother? Their mom goes missing and she doesn't tell him? I can't get over it. What kind of person does that? Maybe it's wrong, what people say at school. Maybe Max isn't the sibling with issues.

Max is broken up about it, of course, but he won't talk to me. He just asked if we could take a week off from shooting. Only a week? I was surprised, but I didn't say that. Instead I said of course we could take a week off. Did he need anything from me?

He said, "Will you come to the funeral with me?"

Well, I was already planning to go to the funeral. But the phrase "with me"? Strange. I didn't know what to think of that. Like it was a date or something. Like he'd asked me to prom.

I'm not sure what I was expecting exactly when I agreed to go. Part of me thought that maybe I'd get to sit by myself toward the back. But instead, Max dragged me up front with the family/friends. Of course Max belonged there. But how could I sit there? I was a fraud.

There were people from school there too. Deering let anyone who wanted to go to the funeral miss second period. A lot of people went because they hadn't done their homework and wanted to skip school. So all THOSE people saw me too. Am I paranoid? Am I narcissistic? I don't know, but I felt people scrutinizing me out of the corners of their eyes.

As for Kelly, at first I had no idea where she was. Did she miss her own mother's funeral? Well, I spotted her eventually. She decided to sit in the back, next to Penelope. I kept my eyes pointed toward the front, but I kept picturing the two of them back there, giggling and passing notes. Probably just my imagination.

The funeral itself was nice, but brief. I found myself thinking about Max's mom. What did I know about her? Of course she was around when I'd go over to the house (we shot some of The Glazen Shelves *in the living room, on the futon where I sort of suspect she used to sleep since I never actually saw her bedroom). She was nice enough, I suppose, and I know that Max loved her. He would always tell me how wonderful his mom was, how encouraging, how creative... but I wasn't sure I ever saw that side of her.*

Once, when I looked at her Easy Rider *and* Zabriskie Point *posters and told her I didn't like either film, she asked me my favorite. I said, of course,* Cries and Whispers. *I guess this is my go-to choice these days. (Is it really my FAVORITE film? I don't know. Maybe I just like saying it is. It certainly haunts me, certainly sleeps beside me at night.) To which she shook her head as though thinking,* Ugh, kids these days. *She never seemed like the kind of person who wanted to talk about something if she didn't like it. Didn't want to hear anything negative about something she liked either.*

Anyway, during the funeral, I looked down and saw Max's hand. It had crept very close to mine. And with a startle I realized that he wanted me to take his hand. He wanted me to hold hands with him. My palm started to sweat. I didn't know what to do.

Take his hand? No, of course I couldn't take his hand. I didn't want to. I felt uncomfortable with it. I felt uncomfortable with the whole situation. I felt trapped. After all, what had Max been doing to me for months? He kept putting me in situations I couldn't get out of because I felt like I needed to be "nice" to him. Was I being too nice? Pity is a bad emotion to get trapped in. But how could I get away from any of this?

When we first started shooting The Glazen Shelves, Max said it would take us just a few weekends. But he kept writing more scenes, kept asking for more of my time. In the original script, there were more characters, more actors. But soon it became clear that the film was just going to be the two of us—just going to be me, really. (Not even Jake works on it anymore. He only lasted a week.) Then Max started asking me to improvise, started making me get more and more personal with what I did for the film. And eventually, four months had passed, and there was no sign of the film getting finished. Whenever I'd go over to the house, the way Max and his mom looked at me, both with their eyes glowing... what was that? What kind of world were they trying to invite me into?

I should've walked away from the film. Walked away from Max. Escaped.

But what could I do? He seemed so lonely. And I didn't want to be cruel.

But maybe it was nice to be wanted. And, of course, I thought I could get something out of it. I'm selfish for thinking these thoughts. (And yes, Dr. Dipshit, selfish thoughts ARE bad, despite whatever crap you say.) Of course I thought that I could use The Glazen Shelves sometime in the future, whenever I decide to apply for college. (Tisch? Yeah, right. Try USM. So much for my brilliant career in film.) But it got more and more obvious every day: Max was never going to finish The Glazen Shelves. He was going to drag it out, write more and more scenes. He was going to keep us together as long as he possibly could.

When I saw his hand there, I realized how stuck I was in his world. It was a terrible time to realize this, at his mother's funeral. But I felt blackmailed. And I felt angry about it. And then I felt bad for feeling angry.

And then I—God—and then I held his hand.

Dear Penelope,

Nobody sends letters anymore, I know, I know, but it's all I can do, on ac-
count of I lack the Internet. Can you believe it? I remember when I was young,
scavenging at Videoport for VHS tapes of old films. I'd watch things in dreadful
quality because it was the only option. Now, on the Internet, with all these
streaming services and the like, one can access any film one wants. But to tell
you the truth, I can't remember the last film I watched.

It might've been Approach the Bench. *Seems you're doing well for yourself,*
making money, giving interviews, and posing for magazine spreads. You were
funny in ATB. *Always charming, of course. You have the ability to move be-*
tween weightlessness and thereness. Do you understand what I mean by "there-
ness"? I'm not sure the director of ATB *does. Honestly, dear, what are you*
doing in movies like that? Do you need a better agent, or has fame just become
a porch light around which you flit, mothlike? If you keep giving performances
so weightless, you'll float off.

Please take that in the good humor it's meant. You must understand what
an enormous fan of yours I am. Always have been, and still am, which is why
I have written you this letter in the first place. I want to warn you. (Cue omi-
nous, discordant violins.)

Ford Hunter has written a tell-all book (God, what a moronic phrase) about
LWW *that is not particularly kind toward you. It's a short book (130 or so*
pages), about which you haven't heard yet because Ford has declined to publish
it with any major New York publishers (or, rather, they declined for him, but
that's another story). Instead, he will self-publish his meisterwerk *and distrib-*
ute it around Portland, where he thinks it will generate interest.

What interest it will generate, I have no clue. Does anyone still care about
our little film? Probably not. Perhaps you will never hear anything about this
would-be controversial book. Perhaps this letter is for naught. Perhaps Ford's
book will be justly received with a grain of salt.

(If you ask me, an entire pound of salt is necessary for the working title alone:
The Reclusive Genius Responsible. *Get it? That's yours truly. Duh.)*

Regardless of the outcome of Ford's foray into the world of publishing, I
wanted to warn you. I believe it proper to do so. Ford doesn't think so. I am
breaking from my ranks, so to speak. You didn't hear any of this from me.

Anyhow, I hope your handlers pass this letter along. I hope they do not think me some insignificant fan. I thought about tweeting @you (or whatever), but a regular old handwritten letter will have to suffice.

Furthermore, I hope that, as you read this letter, you imagined me standing before you, addressing you directly. Imagined yourself a camera. Imagined me staring right at you, reading these words. That's what I would've liked.

*Bergman does that in one of his films—*Winter Light, *maybe, when the minister reads a letter from his wife, and Bergman visualizes it by having the wife (played by I forget which Ingrid) address the camera. (Am I wrong about this? I haven't seen it in years.) Or, did we ever watch* Two English Girls *together? I believe Truffaut reaches for the same effect in his film, breaking the fourth wall to replicate the reading of a letter. Makes a lonely act feel less lonely.*

Maybe one day our paths will cross again. Doubtful, but who knows? Next time you're in Portland, stand at the midpoint of Park Street. I will give you no information more detailed than that about my whereabouts, but doesn't mystery make it more fun? Anyway, if from the midpoint of Park Street you start yourself a-yellin', maybe I'll hear you, dear. Maybe I'll come running, dear.

Your reclusive genius,
D.S.

DAY WITHOUT WATER

M ax sits naked at 9 A.M. in the thick of Day Without Water, the heater spewing warmth, the car seat sticking to his bare skin. So what he's still naked? He isn't crazy. He treated Penelope as needed. It wasn't easy on him, being in the water. That's why he stripped off his icy clothes and blasted the heater to thaw out his body, skin turning from blue to red to pale again.

The last hours dealt an epiphany, a shade pulled up to drive spikes of sunlight into the room: Darren Stanford still lives somewhere in Portland, somewhere on Park Street (the cat nuzzled Max's legs in the doorway, Harry Lime smiled), though unfortunately Penelope didn't know exactly where. *He sent me a letter last year, that's all he said. But Ford probably knows.* And where was Ford? Max wanted to know. Where did Ford live? *I don't know anymore,* Penelope said, *but he'll be at Day Without Water.* And Max, having staked out Day Without Water in the past, knows where the talent parks: on the top level of a garage near the pier. How to find him? Max remembered something from his times reading through Ford Hunter's book, a sentence designed to contrast the author's humility with Penelope's pampered lifestyle: *Me? I took nothing fancy from my time working on the film. Even now, I still drive the same old car, my wood-paneled station wagon I've driven for years.*

Now, Max waits with his hazards on near the garage at the waterfront, where the celebration began hours ago. The camera shows him in jump cuts. (Max can play Belmondo, yes?) He waits for the station wagon—the one he will follow inside the garage. He watches the vehicles crawling the streets, fighting through pedestrians. Please let the camera treat Max kindly as he waits: show only his face and the top of his bare chest, not his splotchy skin, not the acne staining his shoulder blades and lower back, not the celluloid—cellulite?—caking his upper thighs.

Max has been parked here all morning. Pedestrians passed, but nobody wanted to look at his body—nobody ever wants to look at his body—often the camera tracks right and away, to fix upon an empty hallway instead. Evelyn never wanted to look, did she? Evelyn was the camera. Evelyn tracked right.

Cinema had always captivated her, as much as it had ever captivated Max and Mom. Watching films always seemed for Evelyn a fervent act of worship. Max designed *The Glazen Shelves* in the grand tradition of the filmmakers to whom he devoted himself (ones whom Mom had extolled), and Evelyn understood immediately. Once, there was Mom and Max and Evelyn; after Mom, there was still Max and Evelyn. They were so close throughout senior year of high school, so close when Mom died, when Evelyn attended the funeral. Kelly refused to sit up front, which enraged Max (he felt that furious Altman feeling: cinematography growing muddy, sound blurring and overlapping, the edges of the world hard to define). But Evelyn intertwined her fingers with Max's— even squeezed his hand as they sat together on the pew at the very front of the church—and it felt like a moment of love between them, a moment when they decided not to see their children, decided to dance at the hotel instead. Yet nothing else ever came of it, this moment. Sometimes the story of love is the story of something unrequited. The last thing Evelyn ever gave him was her diary, the one she kept from April 4, 2001, to April 21, 2001, at her therapist's instructions. "Hold on to this, please," she'd said. "I think my mom is reading it. I can't have it in the house. Can you keep it for a while? I'll get it back later. Please don't read it. I trust you not to read it." But she never came back—neither for the diary nor for him. Unrequited, see? Now, Max checks the expiration dates on pineapple cans.

And no, he never read it, because she asked him not to read it. Whatever she asked him to do, he did. He keeps it still because he always thought one day she'd come back for it. But he has never read it.

Post–high school, Evelyn started busying herself with classes at USM and acting in local plays. And Max kept trying for a year, trying to get on with *The Glazen Shelves*, until one day Evelyn told him (and this was one year after Mom had died), "I think we shouldn't spend so much time together anymore," told him this as she finished her clove cigarette outside Casco Bay Books, where she had started working. Max issued a sudden response: he broke into shards a standing placard outside Casco

Bay Books, stomped it to pieces, the face of the wood bloodying under his feet, *way down below the ocean, I didn't want to get blood on your floor*. A passerby grabbed Max's shoulders, pulled him away from the placard, told him to settle down (though Max heard him say, *Take a swing at me the way Sam Spade would*), and once Max stopped flailing, Evelyn told this passerby that she was all right, thanks. Calmer, Max sat with her in her car, breath thick in the air, and she said, "If you can't handle me having my own life then I think we need to sever our relationship," like that (for the record, she was crying; it seemed a difficult subject for her to broach, but did that matter?). Max said, "What about our film?" Evelyn said, "We both know we're never going to finish it. It's been over a year. Let it go." Max said, "Are you saying this because I got mad today? Because I won't get mad again. I'm sorry, I'm sorry." Evelyn sopped tears with her sleeve and said, "I've wanted to say this for a long time now. And as for today, you shouldn't act like that. Have you ever thought to talk to somebody?" No, no, talk to somebody? What had he been doing for years? He had talked to Mom, had talked to Evelyn; he had always talked to somebody, so the problem wasn't him. The problem was, the people he talked to kept abandoning him. "Can I still come to Casco Bay Books?" he asked her. If she'd said no, he would have stopped, he *knows* he would've. But she said, "Yes, you can come." Even if she was there? he asked. "It's fine," she said. So he went whenever he could; it was the only place he liked anymore. He missed Evelyn, though; it was hard for him to watch her there.

And then? What happened? After a few months, she quit her job, moved from her apartment, left school. Max had no way to find her anymore except to keep visiting Casco Bay Books, hoping that she would return, dreaming of those afternoons on the dock making *The Glazen Shelves*, when they were both eighteen. Life was so much better before. But after Mom died and Evelyn turned away from him, there was nothing left. His dreams of film disintegrated. Nothing left but a shell of what his life should have been. Ossification. Now, he eats ramen, steals books from the used displays outside Longfellow, sneaks into films—anything to live cheaply. He has worked a handful of jobs, but nothing serious or long term. He has never gone to college, has instead spent a lifetime (at his mother's encouragement) pursuing one goal, because

Mom thought her son was brilliant enough to reach it. But Max Enright is not brilliant. Not special. Top of the world? Nonsense. (Thank Christ Mom died before she saw him this way.) The only thing he has left is to find out what happened to Evelyn. And after he fails at this, as he fails at everything he does? He doubts much energy will remain in him then. (Hey, Frankie Five Angels, what was it the Roman peasants used to do in the bathtub?) These days not even cinema comforts. Max is no great filmmaker. No great anything. No great son.

But enough of this wallowing. Cut back now to Day Without Water.

Through the fog of festivalgoers, a Cecil B. DeMille crowd on this *Ordet*-colored day (the festival always reminds him, to some degree, of some forgotten Hollywood film directed by Dreyer), Max sees it, sees the wood-paneled station wagon, the license plate reading AGAPAO, a word he doesn't know. Max shifts his car into drive, but he cannot go anywhere. People cross in front of him, waves of people wash up from the sea and flop across the street. Wind and celebration spit winter people in every direction. Max is not crazy. When people get close to the car, they glance inside and see Max naked, his eyes bloodshot and features manic from twenty-four hours of wakefulness, from defrosting all night, almost as though after being with Penelope Hayward in the water, he came out of an eleven-year cryogenic freeze, ready to find Evelyn, not just wait there at Casco Bay Books for her, to really fucking find her this time. He has nowhere left to hide. But what does he care if these people see him sans clothes? It makes no difference, affects him in no way whatsoever. Where is Ford Hunter? He was right here. The crowd parts. Oh, there he is.

Right blinker on. Into the Casco Bay Parking Garage, near the Maine State Pier, near the boats tied up, bobbing their heads to the rhythm of the ocean. Max follows Hunter into the garage's gaping mouth. They curl around the corners, ascending. Hunter drives higher and higher until the darkness breaks. Max follows Hunter's car across the roof of this parking garage, the surface looking clean but probably pocked with landmines of black ice; he follows Hunter across this expanse, the two of them specks in a CinemaScope wide shot. Hunter snags an empty spot. Max notices a kitty-corner vacancy, so he slides in, imagining the motion in a triple cut, closer and closer, Saroyan's finger to the buzzer, one, two, three. Doesn't matter that this spot has a sign: RESERVED PARKING. He won't be here long.

Once situated, Max lets the engine run and readjusts his rearview mirror so he can watch Hunter's car, whose tailpipe pumps pollution into the air. Better it'll happen up here, whatever is fated to happen, away from the festivities below. Now that Max has Hunter alone, will he harm him? If necessary, yes, Max will convince himself that Hunter deserves harm—that he is the sort of man who would plow his car into a child and not turn back, whose own teenage son (if he had one) would wish him dead—Max will convince himself that Ford Hunter, this man, must die.

When Max climbs out of his car, he will be able to look over the edge of the parking garage, will be able to see the people lingering on the heated dock below, shuffling around, eating food, buying knickknacks, listening to live acoustic music from the stage. Does Ford Hunter attend Day Without Water every year? Max has no idea. Maybe Hunter walks among the winter people annually, waiting for someone to recognize him, feeling like a celebrity again. Maybe Hunter needs to come here and receive praise for the performance he gave five years ago, his only goddamned accomplishment, his *Glazen Shelves*. And who knows: given the revelation that Darren Stanford lives in Portland, perhaps the director too stalks Day Without Water to hear encomia for him and his film. He must be vain enough, mustn't he? Max would be were roles reversed.

As soon as Hunter steps out of the car, Max will make a run at him, will learn the precise whereabouts of Darren Stanford. Max feels the breath from the heater smothering his body, and, sweating, he keeps an eye on the rearview mirror, waiting for Hunter to head his way, waiting to repeat what he did to Penelope Hayward. Waiting to find Evelyn. It's what Mom would want him to do. Mom would want her son to find this girl. It's the final way he can please his mother after all the ways his life has collapsed. He has come this far. It's the last thing he can do to please Mom, to make her proud.

The station wagon's door opens, and Hunter's long legs creep into the cold air. Strands of his hair wave, beckoning Max forward. Max turns off the car and the heat dies, and instantly goose bumps erupt all over his skin. Hunter stretches as though trying to crack his back. He hisses teakettle steam into the air. Between his fingers he holds a cigarette. He stares out over the ocean and takes a couple more drags before flicking the cigarette off the edge of the roof, sending it toward the waterfront, as if trying to burn the festival tents. Max prepares himself for the cold that will assault his body in a second. He inflates his lungs with breath. He counts down from five. He opens the door and steps, nude, into the December morning, his bare feet hitting the pavement, his bare soles burning against the frozen ground, but in just a moment he cannot feel anything anymore. He knows the air laps at his skin, but he cannot *feel it*.

Hunter fishes through his pockets, checking for something, then returns to his car.

Max looks over the garage's edge, but not at Day Without Water; instead, he looks into another parking lot below, looks down at some teenagers who loiter around a car, one of whom happens to look upward (the parking garage stands four stories high) and, upon seeing Max, points with his cigarette. The others turn and laugh, hoot, holler. Max looks at the clouds. He feels so close to them, like the weather hangs low, heavy in its stomach. Below, a couple more people—a mother with a stroller, a man with a hot dog—have stopped to stare upward at the naked man on the roof. The teenagers cheer, probably mistaking Max for a publicity stunt.

Hunter leans half his body into the wood-paneled station wagon, rooting for something. Max turns his ass to the spectators below and storms forward, approaching Hunter, who pulls out of the car and slams the door in time to see the naked man stampeding his way. At first Hunter laughs, a sort of disbelieving chuckle, but then Max lifts off and, for a moment, flies. When he lands, he knocks Hunter against the railing, the top half of the actor's body dangerously close to the edge. Max wraps his hands around Hunter's neck.

A shout rises from below.

Max looks beyond Hunter, out over the Maine State Pier, where everybody watches someone floating in the water, near where the boats are tied. Max holds Hunter steady, his hands around the fucker's neck. Someone shouts, "Oh God, it's Penelope Hayward," and the camera cranes up, up, up, away from

On foot, Kelly has been going in circles for hours now, yes, just looping around Portland's West End, hoping to spot Max coming home—but this loop around feels different, really it does, because she sees nobody when she turns onto State Street, just a vacant city block. Even at four in the morning, there were some drunks slumped under awnings and a couple college kids dancing in the streets, dueling each other with trash can lids. Now, at half past nine, nobody. How densely do citizens pack Day Without Water? It must be freezing. Nothing stupider than the idea of a winter festival. Her gut tells her that Max went down there. Maybe brought the kidnapped Penelope Hayward with him too. Lord knows what he has planned—how his outrage might extend its talons into a public event. Kelly imagines her brother on a rooftop, stuffing gasoline-doused rags into bottles of high-proof alcohol—something, surely, some movie has taught him to do—and hurling his makeshift Molotov cocktails into the celebration.

So Kelly keeps circling, searching—until, on Congress Street, hunger hits her; continuing will be impossible unless she eats something. She spots that place Nosh, where Penelope had her event the other morning, which now looks open for breakfast. A burly man, shivering outside in short sleeves, stands up a sign advertising French toast and bacon-dusted home fries. Kelly wants nothing so elaborate, but maybe they have simpler items too. Plus, coffee sounds so extraordinary that she might kiss whoever delivers it. She will sit, drink a cup of coffee, eat something, form a plan. Yes. She likes the sound of this.

Polished black marble decorates Nosh's interior, making it look less like a restaurant and more like a store model of a chic urban dining room. Kelly pulls out a chair at the bar and sits, the only customer. A couple employees—one of them the burly guy from outside; the other far skinnier with an old-timey mustache twirled up at either end—

huddle in the corner, speaking in hushed tones. A TV plays commercials. Kelly lays her head on the table.

Footsteps approach, and in a moment, she senses someone hovering. Opening her eyes, she feels like a child staring at a grown-up.

The burly man wipes his hands on his apron. "Water? Coffee?"

"Both."

He grabs a pint glass, which he loads with ice and water. Watching him do this, Kelly wonders whether she should also order an Allagash. She shouldn't start drinking so early, she knows. But then again, she never went to sleep, spent all night—well, at least since two, when she finally gave up in the face of insomnia—looking for her brother. So isn't it technically *late*?

In a moment, her coffee arrives, along with some sugar pouches and creamers. "Looking to eat something?" the burly man asks.

"Uh," she wavers.

"Waiting on some kitchen staff. Might be a while before we're up and running."

"Do you have just chips or cereal or something?"

For a second, his eyes dart downward toward the menu. "We might have some oatmeal."

"Perfect." Kelly tears into one of the creamers, squeezing it empty over the coffee, before beginning to drink.

"We're back with our coverage of the Day Without Water tragedy."

Kelly raises her eyes and looks over the mug's rim at the television, her lips contorted into a kissy face to sip the scalding coffee. The burly man stands next to his mustachioed counterpart again, staring at the television; apparently he forgot about the oatmeal.

The local reporter—a beer-glass of a man, unibrowed—goes on; apparently, he's standing far from the heated portion of the Maine State Pier, for his gloved hand shakes the microphone and his mouth pours steam: "To recap, a body was found floating in the water near the Maine State Pier just forty-five minutes ago. There's no official word yet on the identity of the deceased—"

Kelly hears nothing else; she can confirm the identity, can't she, even if the news can't (or is reluctant to). She sets the coffee down, afraid she might spill it, and shakes her head as though talking to somebody about this tragedy and trying to communicate her shock and sadness.

The burly man returns his attention to her. "Cinnamon-apple okay?"

Kelly murmurs a response that she immediately forgets, then tips her eyes downward to focus on the speck of white—dandruff, maybe—rowing across the coffee's surface.

Even though Kelly has imagined this worst-case scenario all morning, it still astounds her: Penelope Hayward, dead, floating in the water. Since she arrived in Portland, Kelly has been trying to figure out precisely how dangerous her brother has become. Now she knows.

She can't quite move yet. The television fades from her attention. Ghusson has seen this news, no doubt, and has notified the police about the Enrights. This new reality waits for Kelly beyond Nosh's door. So let her banish this outside world and rest here, just for another moment. Let her enjoy this silence, with her coffee and her water and the promise of some oatmeal, warm and friendly with cinnamon—the sort of oatmeal a mother should make. Let her enjoy this moment before she drags herself through the cold to the police station to tell them what she knows, lest the officers waste too much time this morning hunting for her instead of hunting for Max.

But couldn't she jog a few blocks west to the Greyhound station and catch the next bus to wherever? She has about $100 left in savings, and maybe she could—

No. In a day, she'd be broke. And in worse trouble than now.

She can smell the first whiff of the cinnamon wafting from the kitchen, and as she breathes this deeply—this scent visiting her from some imagined past—it's hard not to think of how life would have gone if only she'd done the right thing and told Max and the police about the phone calls from Mom. They would have found her, of course, and she would have gotten treatment for her problems with substances, not to mention whatever other problems—psychological or whatnot—hidden inside the holes in her brain. Mom would have emerged from convalescence feeling all right and, tethered to reality, would have encouraged Max to apply to college after a gap year post–high school. Max would have been accepted somewhere—NYU, or UCLA, or maybe even somewhere like the University of Arizona—to study film. And, sure, chances are slim that Max would have become a famous director like those he and Mom idolized, but at least he would have left home. At least he would have made friends and business contacts at college. At least he would have stopped obsessing over Evelyn, some girl whom he believed—*believes*—was his soul mate. At least Max would have stopped kissing the lips of a ghost before bed each night. If Kelly had told somebody about Mom's phone calls—such minimal effort that would have taken—instead of rationalizing her own inaction, then she wouldn't have landed in this bar, watching the news that Max has committed murder. That Penelope Hayward is dead.

But it's a dream, that other life, and dreams are useless—that much she learned from her mother and Max. Kelly knows what she has to do, and it's exactly what she deserves. Everything is her fault.

The old lady on the other side of the bulletproof glass wears earrings bigger than her ears—earrings so gigantic they seem to emit a frequency that deafens Kelly. She barely registers this white-haired lady's question: "How may I help you?"

A fully uniformed officer enters the booth from the doorway on the other side of the glass; he begins sorting through files.

"I need to speak to somebody," Kelly says, hoping this is specific enough.

"Okay..." The earrings hang there, waiting for more.

"I have information about the body this morning." This is the most precise way Kelly can communicate her purpose; she feels uncomfortable using the word *murder*, akin to using the L-word too early in a relationship.

"What's your name?" the earrings ask.

"Kelly Enright."

"And what kind of information do you have?"

Her mouth feels like the recipient of a Novocain injection; she can barely move her jaw. But she tries—maybe, as a result, overenunciating her declaration: "I know who killed her."

"All right." The woman with the earrings picks up the phone. After a second, she says, "Hey, Karl, we got a girl here says she knows about the body this morning. Yeah. Okay." She hangs up the phone and, with her other hand, gestures outward toward the lobby. "Take a seat. Someone will be right down."

Kelly sits against the window on a bench, whose cushion feels like a high school gym mat. She looks around the Portland Police Department, a four-story-tall brick building near the water, a couple blocks away from Casco Bay Books. Kelly has never been here before—has never been in any police station actually, except for the one in Tucson, which she was too drunk to remember. She inhales the lobby, her nose filling with scents of leather and metal. Elsewhere hover the crackles of voices on radios, but she has trouble identifying where the sounds come from. On the brick wall across from her, two portraits—they look almost like school photos—hang with black print above them: CITIZEN OF THE MONTH and OFFICER OF THE MONTH. Kelly almost wants to inspect them while she waits, just to move around a bit, just to do *something*. Another radio crackles—"702"—and the officer and white-haired lady chuckle, probably unrelated to those meaningless-sounding numbers from a second before. "Seriously," the officer says, "the guy was naked, I guess. In this temperature? Can you imagine?" The woman with the earrings says, "It's amazing what some folk'll do for attention." They laugh again while Kelly's legs fidget, dancing in place on the ground, tap-tap-tapping. With every second that Kelly waits, her brother gets further away from humanity. Kelly feels frantic, like her skeleton is trying to crawl out her mouth, and it takes every effort to keep it inside.

After a few minutes, a portly man in a necktie enters the lobby. "This is her?" he asks the booth people, who nod. He approaches Kelly and extends his hand; as he leans forward, his jacket opens, revealing a radio and a gun in a shoulder holster. He introduces himself: "Detective Rybeck. Follow me, please."

The detective holds the door open. Kelly's footsteps echo in the police station—echo along with all the radio crackles, which sound like ghosts whispering behind the walls.

The officer says, "You taking her up to CID?"

"Nah, just down here."

"All right, Karl," the officer says. "If you get in trouble, send up a smoke signal."

Down the hall, Rybeck ushers Kelly into an interview room, flipping on a light that gives everything the tint of sun-baked paper. When he closes the door behind them, Kelly takes a seat, stretching her arms across the table instinctively, expecting handcuffs. Rybeck stays on his feet. Kelly feels so much lightning pulsing through her that she worries she'll knock over her chair and tumble to the ground.

Rybeck leans against the door with his arms crossed. "State your name, please."

Kelly clears her throat and complies.

"Date of birth?"

"Uh." It takes her a second.

"Address?"

"I, um, I don't really have a home right now."

"You don't have a home?"

"Can I give you my brother's address? For where I'm staying?"

"Okay."

She gives him the address.

"Phone number?"

"Phone number?" Kelly taps her feet on the ground. "Why do you need that?" Don't they know how important this is? Here they sit chatting, while elsewhere lives may be at stake.

He stares at her and sighs like he would prefer any other job in the world, so boring he finds this one. "You *do* have a phone, right?"

Fine, whatever, she tells him her phone number.

"Place of employment?"

Is he kidding? She opens her mouth, but doesn't know what to say.

After a second, he shrugs, giving up. "Just tell me what you know."

"All right." Kelly leans forward and folds her hands together, trying to hold them still. "My brother—I mean, our mom died years ago and—well, Penelope, see, I knew her in high school and, um, my brother's friend—my brother used to want to be a director, so he..."

Rybeck shakes his head and pushes himself away from the door. "Please, step by step, tell me what information you have about the body."

Kelly feels overheated. "I'm sorry. I haven't slept." She takes a deep breath. One thing at a time. Focus on what's important. Focus on the murder. Focus on finding Max. "My brother's name is Max Enright. Our mom died many years ago and he's had violent outbursts ever since. I think he hurt her."

Rybeck narrows his eyes. "Hurt your mom?"

"Hurt Penelope Hayward. I think he killed her and put her in the water. He would do that, see. He hates that movie, *Land Without Water*. He killed her, I think, and then put her in the water so she'd float there like at the end of the movie. You've seen it, right?"

Rybeck stares.

"Well, that's how it ends, with Penelope Hayward floating in the water. So I think he re-created that today as some kind of sick joke."

"You think your brother killed the actress Penelope Hayward and put her in the water?"

"Yeah." Kelly blinks.

Rybeck nods as though expecting this, and he chokes the doorknob. "Someone else will be with you in a sec."

"Wait." Kelly untangles her hands and lifts one of them, though she can't tell which one; she regards the quaking appendage, feeling unattached to it. "I don't know where he is. I don't know where my brother is, and I'm really scared he's going to hurt more people or hurt himself."

Her voice sounds like somebody else's voice. Kelly has nothing inside her body. She rocks forward then back, scraping the chair's legs on the ground.

"Try to calm down." Rybeck flattens his voice like a doctor announcing a diagnosis. He leaves, letting the door hang open behind him, the stuffy air evacuating.

Kelly extends her arms across the table again and puts her head down, mimicking her exhausted posture from before, when she was at Nosh and didn't yet know how the world had changed. She can't keep going like this much longer, can't keep trying to explain herself to people who refuse to listen. How hard can it be to get somebody's attention? She wants to scream and pound her fists on the table: whatever it takes to bring a whole parade of officers to her. She opens her mouth and smells her own breath. Awful. She can't recall when she last brushed her teeth.

What could have happened between Max and Penelope that led to her floating in the water? She must have mentioned something about *Land Without Water* to him that he didn't like. Yes, that must have been it; movies—and whatever anguishes they represent regarding Mom and Evelyn—have always had the potential to enrage him. Yes, it must have been like that, Max overcome with fury, Max pushing Penelope into the water, Max holding her head under the surface until her legs stopped kicking, until—

Kelly's phone vibrates in her pocket. At first, the sensation feels unfamiliar. She lifts herself up and, keeping her eyes pointed toward the open door in anticipation of Rybeck's return, kneads the phone out of her jeans. The number is unfamiliar; nevertheless, she answers.

"Well," Ghusson says, like they already have a conversation in progress, "we had a pretty hectic night, so I forgot to give you an update. Penelope and I just landed at LAX. And I'll tell you something: your brother's real goddamned lucky Penelope doesn't want to press charges, you—oh, here, she wants to say something."

After a few seconds, a new—which is to say *old*—voice needles Kelly's eardrum: "Hey, Kel." Penelope sounds shaky, hushed, overwhelmed by airport noises.

"Penelope," Kelly says—*states* it, the answer to an unasked question.

"Have you seen your brother?"

Kelly opens her mouth to speak, but only air emerges, like a mattress that has sprung a leak. Finally, she gathers the wherewithal to shake her head and then, remembering this gesture isn't enough, to say, "No."

"Something happened when we were together. You need to talk to him."

"I don't know where he is."

"I think he went to Park Street. I don't know the exact address, but maybe you can find him."

"What happened? Where were you?"

"Under the bridge. He went in the water, he threatened to drown himself. I went in after him. He wouldn't get out until I answered his questions."

"Are you okay?"

"He's not a bad guy," Penelope says. "He just needs help. He needs you."

Look after your brother—Mom's words stick like plugs in Kelly's ears for a moment, blocking out the other sounds. When it all comes back to her—the clatter of the police station beyond the door, the whirring of a vent overhead—she says, "Park Street you said?"

"Yes," Penelope says. "He's trying to find Darren—"

Penelope cuts off; Ghusson's voice returns. "Did some girl die at Day Without Water?"

Kelly flinches, still dazed. None of what she has heard makes much sense. "I don't know."

"I despise your town." The phone clicks off.

When Kelly looks up, the uniformed officer from before enters, holding a pad of paper. Compared with the roly-poly Rybeck, this cop's upper body appears almost comically sculpted; he looks like a strawberry strolling on stick-figure legs. The chair screeches against the floor as the cop pulls it out to sit. "So you wanna make a statement? Brother's missing?"

And then Kelly realizes whose body was actually found.

*H*ow long since I ever wrote a diary entry? A note about myself? How long since I ever wrote anything at all?

The first time I ever kept a diary, it was 1997, when I was fourteen, after my first time at Maine Med. Dr. Dipshit assured my parents that it was "a cry for help," the most condescending of euphemisms for depression-related activities. Was it a cry for help? Who knows. That term means nothing anyway. Somebody who's tied a cinder block to her leg and dived into the ocean might cry for help. But she'll still die.

The P-Town Players returned my audition tape today with a form letter of rejection. I have gone smaller and smaller with my submissions. Aimed lower and lower. I can't even count the rejections any longer. Now, here's one from a local company so minor it doesn't have a website. So what does that say about me? What am I doing wrong?

Recently, I was listening to an interview with an actor I don't really like, talking about when he was starting out. He said that the cliché about rejection strengthening you is true... but only up to a point. Eventually that rejection no longer strengthens, but starts to make a little nick on your body each time, until one day you realize all the blood has drained from you.

Those weren't his exact words, but that's my interpretation.

The first rejections made me feel happy almost. Made me feel tough. But now it's been years. Now I'm out of blood. So you tell me, dear reader: Thoroughly rejected as I am, what else can I do? I'm seeing things very clearly today. I understand that I've failed. I understand that I don't have any options left. I can imagine somebody saying to me, But you're so young! You have so much life ahead of you!

Yeah? Is it all going to feel like this?

The other day, I ran into Jake Lunt outside the Irving in Falmouth. I drove over there for the hell of it, stopped inside to buy a pack of clove cigarettes. I was feeling nostalgic, I guess, after listening to songs about Paul Le Mat in 1980 and two-headed boys, while the wind swirled snow against the windshield.

I took my first drag of the clove cigarette, which tasted disgusting and different, now wrapped in cigar paper (per ludicrous federal law), still crackling but not as sweet as before. I took my first drag just as I heard somebody say, "Whoa, Evelyn?"

I had a couple minutes, so why not chat with Jake Lunt while I finished my cigarette? I hadn't thought about The Glazen Shelves in a very long time, but Jake, former DP, reminded me. The Glazen Shelves was the only thing we ever had in common, after all. He used to creep me out like crazy, I remember, but why? He was a strange young man in high school, but now he was coifed and sort of handsome in a boring way.

So yes, dear reader, we chatted. Oh, did we chat. Turns out he's a professional photographer now. Can you imagine? In fact, early next year, he's doing a shoot for an Urban Outfitters catalog, which is a big break he said.

"You know what?" Jake added. "Doing that weird movie with Enright really sparked my interest in photography, I think."

"Cool," I said. What else could I say? At least somebody had gotten something out of it.

"So what are you up to?" he asked. "Do you still act?"

I nodded. "Mais oui! I'm in the touring company for the revival of Harold Pinter's Betrayal *right now. We have one more show tomorrow evening, then onward to Harvard Square!"*

For a second, it felt good to say, felt good to pretend. I felt profoundly grateful for my life, which gives me so much, blah blah blah.

I saw Land Without Water *today. It was time, finally. Time to imagine myself in Penelope's role. To imagine myself saying her lines. To imagine how my life would have been if only Dr. Dipshit hadn't signed my future away with an eight-month hospital stay. If I knew where Darren Stanford was, I would write him a letter and explain it all. Explain why I vanished. Explain that it wasn't my fault. But I doubt he would remember me. After all, he found somebody else to play my role. He found Penelope. He moved on. I was too embarrassed to find him and explain myself back in 2007 when I got out of Spring Harbor—too embarrassed to do much other than drop off a box of my things at Acoustic Coffee.*

Of course, what I actually know is this: I will finish this letter, or note, or whatever it is, and then I will burn it in the parking lot. I won't give it away to anyone—not like last time. I will destroy the whole goddamned thing myself. And already, the writing of this feels so pointless, so dramatic. I'm rubbing my hand against this page. My skin is flaking off. If I keep writing, I will erode bit by bit, until one day I won't be here anymore. But that seems too slow.

In any event, dear reader, I report with sadness that Agnes and Ingmar were dead wrong. Life, in fact, gives not much at all.

Time, dear reader, for the flames.

PROUD

PARENT

OF AN

HONOR

ROLL

STUDENT

For a moment, the screen goes black—a rich, liquid darkness—and stays that way, making the audience wonder whether the film might have ended, making the audience check its collective watch to see whether two hours have passed already.

Then, interrupting the darkness, a man steps into the frame in extreme close-up, his bare shoulders only partially visible, his glabrous scalp (not from hair loss, but shaved clean) filling the screen (always powerful in a theater, isn't it, when a face blows up so big you can see the pores?). This man, he looks directly into the camera and, showing his white teeth, says, "The name's Darren Stanford. Pleasure to meet you." His voice comes out almost as a hum. He stands so calmly, yet when he speaks, something seems to vibrate in him, like some kind of sleep machine meant to make a comforting sound—an ocean, perhaps? He looks offscreen, hums: "Could you fetch my guest a blanket from the closet at the top of the stairs?"

The voice offscreen, the one that responds: a familiar voice, but familiar not from real life, familiar from its use throughout *Land Without Water*, the voice of its central character, the voice of Ford Hunter, who mutters a series of angry whatnots, surliness blurring his speech into incomprehensibility—"you've gotta be fucking kidding me," "un-fuck-ing-believable," gibberish like that. He passes in front of the frame, which acts as a wipe cut to:

Yes, finally, here he is. Max. The hero. Looking heroic (right?), even though his body remains uncovered, cold air rubbing his bare skin. (Amazingly, no shivering; the discovery of the body in the water, the trial of tackling Ford and shoving him into Kelly's car, and now the surreal situation of standing here before Darren Stanford—well, all of this has sped up the boy's blood, and to hell with the cold, he feels like pure heat, the world around him as gauze-covered as the Vilmos Zsigmond cinematography in an old Altman film, the haziness thick enough to be boiling fog.) Anyway, in this shot, no nudity is visible, framed tastefully to include Max's face, his hairless chest, and nothing else.

Offscreen, more rustling, more of Ford Hunter's pissed incoherence, then the creaking of stairs. He holds out a blanket. Max takes it (never removing his eyes from Stanford, mind you) and wraps it around himself.

And now, a cut to a wider shot, now that all the R-rated parts are covered, with Max and Stanford staring at each other, the director shirtless too but wearing gym shorts, the whole of his body on display now, all of it clean and gelled and muscular; he has the appearance of a 1940s strongman. He gestures to another room. "Shall we?" Max nods, and the three of them—because yes, irrelevant Ford Hunter remains (hasn't he fulfilled his purpose, leading Max here?)—trundle into the living room, camera following to reveal the whole of the space.

And what a mess, this space. Christ. All the blinds are closed, and some sunlight sneaks through a few exposed areas, shooting beams that illuminate the airborne dust motes as though spotlights on thousands of indistinguishable film stars. Stanford seems quite the collector of film memorabilia, but he has given no order to any of it. Instead, it's a hodgepodge of posters on walls, some in frames and some not, and other posters carpeting the floor, and pipes and rings and a few moth-eaten suits (memorabilia from what film not even a viewer as astute as Max can determine), and, most conspicuously, surface after surface covered with film books (many of the same ones that Max owns) and stacks of *Film Comment*, *Sight & Sound*, *Cineaste*, and numerous other magazines that Max never had the money to subscribe to (though he would read them when they showed up at Casco Bay Books—before the tyrants kicked him out, anyhow). As Max walks, he trails his fingers on glossy covers, leaving tire marks in the snowlike dust.

Then Max stops, one framed poster in particular catching his eye from its spot on the wall: *Land Without Water*, complete with the image of Penelope Hayward floating in the water at the film's end. And right next to this *Land Without Water* poster? Why, one of the missing person flyers, Evelyn's black-and-white face, her tight smile, her eyes looking about as tired as Max feels. The same poster he'd tacked up in his sister's old room. HAVE YOU SEEN THIS GIRL?

"He jumped me in the garage," Ford Hunter tells Stanford (though Max doesn't bother to look his way, eyes on Evelyn instead, as alive in this image as she is now in reality). "I'm supposed to sign books there, for God's sake, they're probably still waiting for me, probably a line, clogging everything up, wanna know how this fucker knew about you living here, Penelope told him, can you fucking believe that, she knows him somehow, and how the fuck does she know you live here, anyway, did you tell her, you told her, didn't you, after all I've done to keep you hidden," on and on.

But Max pays no attention—not even to the part where he's a fucker. He grabs that awful image of Evelyn and clenches it into a ball, which he throws across the room. It feels like... something. Really, he doesn't know how it feels. But some heat leaves him; he thinks so, at least. And he squeezes shut his eyes as if in pain, waiting for something sharply wrong with his stomach to pass. He turns, hits the wall, and slides downward until he's on the ground. Melodramatic? Perhaps. But he imagines himself a grief-stricken Brando. And though Max can't remember any particular scene in which Brando slid down a wall, he's sure Brando must've known a little something about sliding down walls.

Stanford's body seems to stop humming as he notices what Max grabbed. He takes a step toward his seated guest and says, "Evelyn Andersson? This is about Evelyn Andersson?" But Max avoids looking up, keeping his eyes closed, keeping his face contorted. Stanford turns to Ford Hunter. "Give us a minute?"

Ford Hunter stares, chewing on something—gum maybe? Did he have gum before? Did it just appear there like the world's most banal magic trick? "Fine. Whatever. Your kitchen's a pigsty anyway." And with that, he leaves—an exit punctuated a moment later by the noise from a faucet and the clattering of some dishes. Ford Hunter, wifely, cleaning.

Alone now, Stanford crouches in front of Max, knees bent, uncomfortably bearing the bulky weight of his upper half. "Do you know her? Do you know Evelyn Andersson?"

All the heat has left Max, and his blood has stilled. Weakly, somehow, he manages: "They found her body this morning."

And what does Stanford do with this news? Shout? Cry? Or something incongruent but lifelike—laugh, maybe? No, none of that. He shakes his head and uses his legs to lift his muscular torso off the ground (it looks mechanical when he does it, like machinery at a construction site raising a bulbous ornament to sit atop the building). His next mission: the retrieval of the crumpled paper—the ball Max threw in the most athletic action in his life. Stanford flattens the paper against the wall, trying to get the creases out. "Somehow I knew that already," he says. "Not sure how I knew it, but I did." He stares at the face on the poster for another second, and then he puts it down (facedown? Max can't tell from where he sits) on a nearby desk. "Who are you exactly?" he says, back still turned to his guest. "Why are you here?"

Max answers his question with a question—though when Stanford fails to respond immediately, Max asks again: "Why did you thank Evelyn Andersson at the end of your film?"

"Because I didn't know her real name. Not until I saw the flyers, read the newspaper. Evelyn Romanoff."

"How did you know her?"

Stanford turns back to Max and crosses the room, dragging his feet. Off a chair he grabs a bathrobe that looks like bearskin. "Cold," he mutters, sliding his arms into the sleeves, tying the fur together at his waist. When he reaches Max, he stands over him a moment, his shadow a second blanket over the seated man's shoulders. "I didn't know her," Stanford says.

Max squints, opens his mouth to say something—and if he says anything, it gets lost in the sound of Stanford sliding his back down the wall, the rustling at high volume, until he has landed right next to Max, their knees nearly touching. "I didn't know her at all."

With that preamble, Stanford tells Max his story of Evelyn Andersson, which begins, of course, with a cut to black—

TITLE CARD:Portland, '06

INT. ACOUSTIC COFFEE — AFTERNOON

The light in Acoustic Coffee is dim, making the dive feel like a dungeon. No windows. Few people inside. A couple of young men set up on the stage, amps and a drum kit and stuff, for a show later in the evening.

XCU: Two cups of coffee on a platter, being carried by a waiter. CAMERA tracks with the coffee cups until they are placed on a tall circular table, around which two people sit:

Stanford (24), skinnier than we last saw him, with a full head of hair and color in his face.

Hunter (24), looking as before.

> STANFORD
> (to O.S.)
> You sure you don't want anything?

> VOICE (O.S.)
> No, no.

The waiter moves out of the way to reveal a third person, Evelyn (23). She shakes her head, smiles politely.

> EVELYN (cont'd)
> I'm fine, thank you.

She looks around the place.

> STANFORD
> Are you all right?

> EVELYN
> Yeah, no, I just thought...
> (shrugs)
> Just thought more people would be here.

> HUNTER
> Frankly, we did too.

Stanford shoots him a look.

> STANFORD
> He doesn't mean to be rude.

> EVELYN
> Am I the first?

> STANFORD
> We've seen some other actresses.
> (beat)
> This is a real film we're making, in case
> you're worried. With real money.

> EVELYN
> Oh. Good. Not Monopoly money then.

Their rapport is easy. This dialogue should be fast,
ping-pong, like Cary Grant and Rosalind Russell.

> STANFORD
> Do you want to proceed?

> EVELYN
> I'm here, aren't I?

> STANFORD
> Yes. But perhaps you believe there's something
> underhanded happening here. Perhaps you're uncom-
> fortable.

> EVELYN
> Is that what I am? Always good to learn.

                    STANFORD
        Are you uncomfortable, here, with us?

BEAT. They stare at each other in alternating CUs.
Neither of them seems to blink. Something passes between them here.

                     EVELYN
              That depends.
                 (beat)
           Are you underhanded?

Stanford smirks.

                 STANFORD (V.O.)
                 So she read.

INT. ACOUSTIC COFFEE — MOMENTS LATER

CAMERA pans around the table as Evelyn delivers a
prepared monologue, WITHOUT SOUND. Eventually, the
CAMERA settles on Stanford in CU as he watches, rapt.

                 STANFORD (V.O.)
    And suddenly, it was like the whole film, every-
    thing I had dreamed of, everything I wanted it to
   be, was in front of me. It seemed almost pointless
   to make it anymore. She was the film, embodied. When
    I watched Evelyn read, I saw for the first time how
        good Land Without Water could be.

SOUND comes up as Evelyn finishes her monologue.

                    STANFORD
                 (stunned)
                 Thank you.

                              (beat)
                    What's your name again?

                              EVELYN
                       Evelyn Andersson.

                             STANFORD
                     Well, Evelyn. Thank you.
              Another BEAT as they stare at each other.

                              HUNTER
                           (to Evelyn)
                     So we'll let you know.

With one glare, Stanford shuts Ford up, and then turns
back to Evelyn. It seems clear enough that he has already made up his mind.

                         STANFORD (V.O.)
                I offered her a role on the spot. But
                first, I knew I needed to work on the
                              script.

DISSOLVE TO:

INT. STANFORD'S HOUSE — NOW... but the film stops, because
nothing seems worthy of celluloid on this day in Stanford's house, such
a graveyard of a place. The director sits next to Max, the two of them
leaning against the wall, Stanford's face drained of color like a gunshot
victim losing blood to the floor.

"I'd already written a dozen drafts, including the one that my fi-
nanciers had agreed to," Stanford tells Max, because more story still
possesses him—he has yet to pass the ghost to his visitor, "but I had
it all wrong, the way I'd imagined the character of Angela. I imagined
her as corporeal, sensual, a counterpoint to Erica's ethereal, ghostly
character. But it needed to be the other way around. Now that I'd seen

Evelyn read, I knew: Angela was the one who needed to be a ghost." He draws in a breath between the spaces in his teeth. "Evelyn seemed born for the role of ghost. So I wrote. Hundreds of pages. Feverish. And then, a few months later, we were all ready to begin. So I called the number Evelyn gave me. *Disconnected*." This last word he says as though uttering a curse.

"I went to Acoustic Coffee. Asked if they knew who she was. They didn't. So how could I find her? All I had was a nom de plume. No goddamn good to me. But I looked, and I waited. Waited as long as I could. And then I couldn't wait any longer, see. I had professional actors ready to go—actors who needed to shoot in a tight window so they could get back to real jobs. I had the money that Sony Pictures had offered, all because Todd had vouched for me, come on as a producer. I couldn't wait any longer, because it was my moment, my chance to make the film I'd always wanted to make. Except it wasn't the film I wanted to make anymore.

"By then, I'd cast Penelope too. Penelope was remarkable as Erica. Really wonderful in the film. Down to earth. Honest. Like somebody who lives in your building who you always look forward to running into. But for the role of Angela? Penelope was... adequate. Could anybody else see that but me? I don't think so. But it's all I could see. Every time a critic praised her performance, every time she won an award, every time somebody raved about the choice of casting Penelope as both Erica and Angela... every goddamn time, I was faced with it. *Land Without Water*. God. The failure. How could I have ever made a second film? I never even finished my first."

Here, Stanford seems to lose himself, and Max wonders whether he has finished—not with the story, but with words in general. But after a sigh—the sort of sigh that seems to come from a place deeper than lungs—the director turns to Max and says, "So who the hell are you? What's your story?"

Max opens his mouth, but no easy words form. Whenever he used to remember the time he and Evelyn shared, it seemed so special. Now, this question posed with such bluntness, he stumbles—feels like he never knew her at all—feels, in fact, like he knew only her absence. It was eleven years ago that she turned away from Max and *The Glazen*

Shelves, and five years ago that she ran from Max, plunged herself into the darkness across from the Portland Museum of Art, and was gone.

"I've been trying to find her too," Max says. "I knew her in high school. That's all."

From the kitchen, the faucet noise expires, and seconds later the back door opens. Stanford bends his head, trying to peer into the kitchen. "Ford, you going out for a cigarette?"

"Yeah."

Stanford climbs to his feet, stretching his legs awkwardly—a man standing for the first time. "There's a Tupperware in the shed marked *E.*" He wanders toward the desk. "Could you bring it in?"

"Whatever."

"Oh, and leave the rest of the dishes. I'll do them later."

"No, you won't." The sliding door slams.

Stanford stares at the desk. He pokes at an automatic pencil sharpener. For a second, Max wonders whether the filmmaker plans to insert his pinkie and carve the flesh into a point.

"So," Max says, "Evelyn is the reason you look like an alien?"

"An alien?" Stanford smiles, his teeth as white as his head. "Is that what I look like?"

"You look like Kola Kwariani ready to start a fight in a bar."

"Ha." Stanford's version of a laugh is just to say this one word.

"How do you pass the time?"

Darren Stanford shrugs. "I lift weights. I read. I watch DVDs."

"A life spent watching films doesn't sound so bad."

"Films?" Stanford shakes his head. "No, no, sir. I haven't watched a film in ages. I watch television shows. All the good filmmaking is on television anyway. Between you and me, I'm doing a little writing for a new show. Ghostwriting. You might know the program." He tells Max the title. Gibberish.

"Good directors work for television," Stanford continues, almost like a spokesperson. "Fincher, Soderbergh, Demme, Scorsese, Todd Field. If you want to sit down for a few minutes, I can show you what I mean. We can watch an episode of something together. Unless you want to leave." Stanford stares at Max, his eyes wide. He seems to want Max to sit—to keep him company.

Little of this makes any sense to Max. What magic does television hold, such crass entertainment, broken up by idiotic commercials with obvious narrative arcs and zilch for aesthetic value—what magic does television possess that eludes the cinema? Max looks around again at the inside of this place, at the film posters on the walls and issues of *Cineaste* and *Sight & Sound* and *Film Comment* piled everywhere. He had felt such odd kinship walking into this place; now, these materials are moot, simply aftershocks from the earthquake of *Land Without Water*—the earthquake of the cinema—that ripped through Stanford's life.

A paucity of inspiration or a rotting financial floor suddenly collapsing under the weight of the filmmaker's dreams: in Max's mind, these are the only two reasons to not make more films. Had *The Glazen Shelves* succeeded as thunderously as *Land Without Water*, Max wouldn't have been able to stop.

"You must have at least had an *idea* for a second film," Max says.

Stanford rolls his eyes. "Oh, Christ, don't tell me you're a *Land Without Water* fanatic."

"I hate it."

Stanford nods and runs his fingers across the surface of the desk. "So, are you going to tell anyone about me?"

"I have no one to tell."

"Fair enough. Although I doubt anyone would care anymore."

The back door opens and Hunter grunts his way into the living room, odoriferous with cigarette smoke. Down in the middle of the room he sets a Tupperware container the size of a milk crate, the top of which a strip of masking tape marks. Written in permanent marker there? E.

"Someday I'm gonna start charging you for my services," Hunter says, out of breath (although Max doubts the lugging was too strenuous), before shuffling back into the kitchen.

Max nods to the Tupperware container. "What's all that?"

"A funny thing happened about... I'd say, probably five years ago. I got a call from a friend of mine who worked at Acoustic Coffee, who let me hold my auditions there. This was after *Land Without Water* had been out for a little while. He said there was something for me." Stanford kicks the box; its innards jingle. "There was a note inside. It was from

Evelyn. It said these items were for whenever I made another film. *So I can be in one of your films after all,* she wrote." He shakes his head. "But I'm not making another film. And seeing as you were her friend, maybe you can take what you want. Take all of it. I don't know."

Max tumbles forward, onto his knees. He sorts through the box, which contains photographs, ticket stubs, and some jewelry.

There, among assorted trinkets, Max sees his mother's old necklace, K.B. During the filming of *The Glazen Shelves*, Max and Evelyn raided Mom's jewelry box for whatever the character of Natalie might wear, and Evelyn fell in love with this necklace. "It's yours," Mom said. "Keep it." But Evelyn didn't keep it. Apparently she didn't want it.

"Want to stay?" Stanford falls onto the couch. "Want to watch something with me?"

Max tears additional items—scarves, a pack of Djarums—out of Evelyn's box, searching for something. But what? His search has ended. He has nothing to find anymore.

He stands and looks at Stanford. Seeing the lonely man on the couch, beckoning his new friend forward with the remote control outstretched, Max forgets that *Land Without Water* exists. Even *The Glazen Shelves* fades in his memory.

Or maybe he just stops caring.

F ucking *finally*, Kelly finds a bit of luck.

She spots an Arizona license plate tucked into a driveway on the other side of Park Street—her Honda, stowed next to the end portion of a brick row house. She starts toward it, her left foot skidding over a streak of black ice, almost tumbling her into oncoming traffic.

The driveway appears recently plowed, but the wind has knocked snow from the trees, sprinkling the ground. Footprints are stamped into this light dusting, leading from the car to the porch steps. Two sets of footprints, in fact: one set normal looking, but the other set alarmingly small with well-defined toe marks. Whoever left them wore only bare feet.

On the porch, Kelly presses her ear against the door, trying to hear something inside. Shades cover all the windows; no natural light brightens the interior of this house. She knocks on the door. Waits. When nobody answers, she makes a fist and punches the door, a noise that inside must be impossible to ignore. Still, she hears nothing. Maybe Kelly has the wrong house. Maybe her brother left the Honda parked here as a diversion as he spiraled toward his next location. Maybe Kelly has arrived too late, Max having vanished like old breath.

Shivering, she steps away from the door and notices the curtain on one of the front windows pulled an inch back, with an eye pressed against the revealed glass, watching her. Then the curtain falls back into place, the spy retreating.

"Hey." Kelly reaches over the porch railing to hit the window. "Hey, is my brother in there? Max?"

She should wait for an answer—but she's sick of waiting.

Next to the porch, she finds a brick and picks it up. The wire fence alongside the house proves easy to climb, and she drops onto browned snow. Does that eye monitor her progress? She holds the brick like a ten-pound weight as she walks alongside the house, looking for some window that isn't completely covered. Under her feet, snow cracks.

One of the windows has Venetian blinds with a few rungs bent backward, allowing her to peer inside. A long-haired cat jumps onto the windowsill. Kelly rockets backward. The animal rubs its face against the glass and meows.

Composure regained, Kelly reapproaches the window and sees inside. Someone sits on a couch, wrapped in a blanket, watching television. She can't see his face, but a tuft of familiar curly black hair is visible. She bangs on the window. "Max? Max?"

The figure in the chair turns, and she sees him clearly—her brother.

She waves. "Are you all right in there?" She bangs some more, but Max doesn't budge. Kelly wipes her breath away from the glass with her sleeve. Then she holds up the brick. "I'll bust the window, I swear!"

Before she decides whether she means this threat, someone whispers a few feet away: "Psst, hey." A lanky man has appeared outside. His eyebrows angle, cartoonish with frustration, his entire face scrunched into a fist. "Hey, shut up, okay?" He gestures for her to follow him. When she doesn't move, he adds, "Come on already."

With her brick ready, she follows him around the corner of the house and onto the back patio, hidden by a wooden fence and trees. The lanky man stands near the back door, holding it open, saying, "Come on, Michelangelo," until the long-haired cat storms out. The lanky man eyeballs Kelly. "Coming or going? You're worse than the cat."

Kelly says nothing and starts inside.

The lanky man clears his throat and motions to what she holds. "Seriously? Leave the brick outside. It's filthy."

Kelly glances at her weapon, then tosses it onto the patio before going in.

"Last thing we need is more filth in here." The lanky man closes the door and latches it; then he proceeds to the sink, where the faucet runs. He's in the middle of doing dishes, it looks like, one side of the sink filled with food-encrusted plates and bowls.

"Hey," Kelly says, "aren't you in that movie?"

He turns from his dishes and smiles at her like a middle-aged professor greeting an attractive young student in his office. "Yeah," he says. "Do you want to talk about it sometime? I love chatting up fans."

"Uh, maybe later."

His face sinks, and back to the dishes he goes.

Kelly looks down at the grime-covered floor; as she walks forward, her feet stick and snap. In the corner sits a litter box with spillage and pellets of dried shit lining the perimeter. Underneath the dim overhead light, Kelly cannot see the dust that surely flits around.

The lanky man gestures toward another room. "Your psycho brother's in there."

Yes, he is, wrapped up in a blanket, staring at the television; on the couch next to him sits a big bald man. A show or a movie—Kelly isn't sure which—plays on the screen, in which a different bald man digs around frantically in a crawl space under a house while a blond woman looks down at him. Kelly has seen this bald, goateed man before, his face on posters and T-shirts usually worn by college dudes who came through her line at the grocery store.

"Max?" Kelly says.

Her brother keeps his eyes on the screen. The bald man next to him has folded his legs knee over knee—a feminine posture—revealing fuzzy slippers hanging down from his bathrobe.

"What's going on?" Kelly takes tentative steps deeper into this cavern.

The bald man puts his index finger against his lips. "Shh." He points that same finger at the television and nudges Max. "Are you watching? This is astounding directing. The framing of the shot. That piercing sound in the background, building, building. The whole pacing of this episode, the journey to this moment right here. I mean, Christ, better than anything in cinema today." The man in the crawl space begins to weep—no, wait, begins to laugh, cackling horrifically, as somewhere else a phone rings.

Kelly looks around this living room. It's stuffy in here—one of the grossest places she has ever entered, the air reeking of body odor and spoiled food. Whoever lives here never leaves. The furniture looks cheap, and books and magazines cover nearly every surface. There's a stool to Kelly's left, on top of which is a stack of something called *Film Comment*. The one on top shows an image of an actress Kelly recognizes—Kirsten Dunst—wearing an old-fashioned gray wig: *One Long Party*, the text on the cover reads. Underneath this, the stack of magazines looks a foot deep. In the middle of the room, close to the couch and the television, sits a Tupperware container with junk spilling out of it, clothes and jewelry and papers. On all the walls, almost like wallpaper, movie posters hang. The colors in most of them have faded, and Kelly knows few of the titles: *The Naked Kiss*? *Winchester '73*? *La Notte*? *Heart of Glass*? Oh, *The Shining*—Kelly knows that one. And Kelly knows another one too, partially obscured by some other posters: *Land Without Water*, featuring the brilliant floating face of Penelope Hayward. It's disorienting to see her old friend revert back to an image on a piece of promotion.

This room reminds her of Max's bedroom during high school, but far worse; really, it looks like what Kelly always feared Max's bedroom would become. She kneels next to the couch, her mouth level with her brother's ear. He holds the blanket shut around his body, bare shoulders partially visible. "What happened to your clothes?"

Bald man hisses, *"Silencio."*

On screen, the blond woman backs away from the crawl space toward the ringing phone.

Kelly asks her brother, "What are you doing here?"

"Jesus Christ!" The bald man jumps as though shot, gesturing wildly. "Couldn't you wait? There's one minute left." His words sound like gobs of spit.

"Oh, forgive me," she says—the same tone of voice she would use on Max in high school whenever he'd freak out at her for interrupting one of his strange activities.

"So rude." The bald man heads to the staircase and stomps upstairs, his housecoat trailing him like a wedding dress. Even after he disappears, Kelly can still hear him pacing, muttering.

She turns back to her brother who, in spite of all the commotion, still hasn't looked away from the television. "Hello?"

"She's dead." Max mutters this as the credits start their crawl.

"I'm sorry." Kelly turns from him and looks up at the ceiling, her eyes settling on mildew; she takes another deep breath of this place. There's so much she needs to ask Max, but she has no idea where to start. The last twelve hours feel so obscure, so hidden. But right now, the most important question seems to be this one: "Do you have my car keys?"

Max nods so slightly that, at first, Kelly misses the motion. He points to a table in the corner. Kelly finds her keys among some magazines and wadded-up tissues. "Okay, come on. Let's get out of here, let's go home."

"I'm not going home."

"What do you mean you're not going home?"

"Darren said I could stay here, so I'm staying here."

"Why would you want to stay here?"

In the kitchen something shatters—a plate maybe—and Ford Hunter swears.

"Those are her things," Max says.

Kelly's eyes return to the box in the middle of the room and the mess strewn from it. "Whose things?"

"Evelyn's. They've been sitting here all these years. Sitting here—"

But she stops listening to her brother; among the mess, she recognizes something—recognizes K.B., the glitter of it—so she leaps forward, pulling the necklace from the box, untangling it from other pieces of jewelry, chain clasped between her index finger and thumb.

Max lunges for his sister to stop her, but Kelly stands again, pulling away just as he lands on his knees. She stands over him, holding out the necklace. "You gave this to Evelyn?"

Max stares at her. "Mom did."

"But—no. It was mine."

"You never wanted it." Max looks away, his gaze falling to the container, to the floor.

Kelly jingles the necklace in front of him. "How would you know I never wanted this?"

Max's eyes jump up and widen. "Because you let her die."

The force of these words dazes Kelly; she shakes her head. When she speaks again, her voice sounds like somebody else's voice—like mumbling heard through a door. "Where's Dad?"

"You can't give him that necklace. He can't have it. That's Evelyn's."

"I don't give a fuck about Evelyn. Where's Dad?"

Max stares widely. After a second, he snaps out of it. "I don't know."

"What do you mean you don't know?"

"I mean"—Max sounds out of breath—"I don't—"

"No." Kelly shakes her head. "That's not it. No." She takes a few steps toward him; he has to bend his neck backward to look up at her. "You said you knew where he was. You said if I helped you with Penelope you'd tell me."

"But you didn't help me."

"What?"

"I was the one who got her attention outside the school."

Enough of this. Kelly shoves Max, her hand a spider on his forehead, forcing him against the couch. The necklace, still in her grip, drips down his nose. "Where's Dad?"

Max opens his mouth and catches the metal.

"Where the fuck is he?"

"I don't know. I don't know." He sounds panicked.

Kelly wants to smother him right here. She feels his face getting hot under her fingers, like she's putting her hand over a stove burner.

"Don't hurt me," he says. "Don't hurt me." His lips suck on the necklace. She should shove it right down his throat.

But she doesn't do anything, except take her hand away and back off. He pulls the blanket around his body more tightly than before, a child trying to make the monsters go away, and shakes against the couch, avoiding eye contact with his sister—his *sister*, of whom he's terrified right now. For years, Kelly has believed Max the crazy one—the dangerous one. For years, Kelly has been afraid of her brother. But it never once occurred to her that maybe her brother has been afraid of her too.

Maybe Max looks at Kelly and thinks, *She would've let me die too.*

And you know what? Max is right. Kelly doesn't care about him. All she wants is her father's address, wants only to go to Dad's house, to greet him at the door with this necklace, to see how badly he still wants it, how much he's willing to pay for it.

Max shudders against the couch. Kelly stares at him, waiting for him to look up. But he closes his eyes, lips and limbs trembling. "Okay." She shakes her head and takes a deep breath. "I never want to hear from you again. Do you understand?"

She wants him to look up. If he looks up, maybe she'll change her mind, maybe she'll see something in his eyes that will remind her of what Mom told her to do: *Look after your brother.* But Max has reneged on his promise to his sister, so why shouldn't Kelly renege on her promise to Mom? What good is a promise in this fucking family anyway?

Kelly hurries toward the door, stuffing the necklace into her jacket pocket, holding her car keys like a weapon.

So what choice does she have? With $100 in savings and Mom's necklace in her pocket, she decides to revert to the original plan: visiting her list of Bennetts, knocking on their doors as though selling magazine subscriptions. She has come all this way across the country, across the years of her life, to arrive here in this city of memory. This cannot be another interest—another goal—that she abandons. No. She cannot have come all this way only to fail like before. She cannot live another day as a woman without qualities.

The car starts, and radio static gives way to local news: *"... continuing coverage of the Day Without Water tragedy..."* Kelly flicks the dial off and embarks for Baxter Boulevard.

As a teenager who wanted to stay healthy—back before beer distended her abdomen—Kelly jogged Baxter Boulevard, sometimes running the three-and-a-half-mile track twice in one hour; she doubts she could make it around even once now. After exercise, Kelly often sat in the car and stared out at the ocean—especially on stormy days, when she couldn't see across the bay and might as well have been in the middle of the sea, watching nothing but rolling waves.

She could revisit some of these sensations—hell, she could drive around the boulevard and catch a vision of the squat city skyline from Payson Park—but really, she just wants cigarettes. And to tear a page from a phone book, a necessity since she left her original printout of Bennett names at Max's apartment (no fucking way is she going back there). So she drives, ignoring the view, ignoring all the houses, which she doesn't know how to describe anymore except to say that she will never live in houses like those—and, in a minute, she pulls into the Hannaford parking lot, which crawls with Sunday afternoon shoppers pushing their carts into corrals or abandoning them in the middle of parking spots.

Inside, most registers are closed. Kelly stands in one of the lines with people who cross their arms and roll their eyes and bitch and moan under their breath about the wait. Her legs wobble. She fetches a bottle of water from the cooler and, after drinking half of it in one swig, feels better. The line takes five minutes, but it's worth it. Like a starving woman with food, she peels the plastic from her Camels and lets it flutter to the ground. She lights a cigarette before she makes it through the automatic doors.

A pay phone stands against the brick exterior of the grocery store, and Kelly grabs the dangling phone book. Many Bennetts greet her. Are these the same names she carried with her across the country from Tucson? They all look different, unfamiliar; her Bennetts have left and new Bennetts have arrived. She tears out the page. Embers fall from her cigarette, making pinprick holes in the thin paper—little dark eyes staring at her.

The first Bennetts are Amanda and Shelton; they live around the corner actually, on Falmouth Street, behind the university. Was Shelton on her list? Who the fuck is Shelton Bennett? If Shelton answers the knock and Kelly identifies him as a relative of her father, what will he say? Will he feign ignorance? Probably, probably—whole goddamned family will feign ignorance, will protect its own. And what if he isn't home? What if none of the Bennetts is home? She'll need to leave notes, but she has no paper. From a basket near the front of the Hannaford, Kelly grabs a free weekly, Garrett's fucking *Phoenix* of all things. When she reaches her car, she will scribble a note, something to leave on Shelton and Amanda's door, or in their mailbox, or somewhere. She isn't even sure a note is the best idea but feels too drained and too desperate to come up with a better one. So what should she write? *Where's my father?* Bullshit. He wouldn't respond. She should think of something else to say. Some lie. Maybe she's a city official who needs to get into the house to inspect something. But then why would she be writing a note on the back of newspaper? Kelly should just wait outside their house. Unless they've gone somewhere for Christmas. But there are other Bennetts, so Kelly can pay the others visits, then can try Shelton later. What good would a note do? Why would anyone respond to—

"You wanna wait here, Girly?"

"Want to, Daddy, *want to*. And yes."

"I'm just grabbing one thing. Lock the doors."

Kelly drops the cigarette from her hand. She looks down at it, then looks up at the minivan in which this man, this father, has left his daughter.

Girly? Kelly heard him clearly—at least, she thinks she heard him clearly, although the wind might as well be a pillow tied around her head. *Girly?*

The father heads toward the Hannaford entrance. Kelly squints, still grasping the free weekly, which flaps in her trembling hands, but can't catch a good look at this guy, let alone a good look at his eyes, which she needs to see—needs to see whether they have those dark circles like her own eyes, like Max's eyes. She takes a few steps forward. Calls to him. "Dad?" But he cannot hear, does not turn. Did that man call his daughter *Girly*?

An engine starts and headlights somewhere break the surface of the overcast afternoon. Kelly shakes her head, performing for someone else's benefit. No, not Dad, how could it be Dad? Many people probably use that word, *Girly*, a common term of endearment. Still, Kelly will await his return. She fumbles for another cigarette and, hand shaking, puts it between her lips. When she sucks in smoke, it feels like someone jamming her mouth with cotton. She heads back to her car, catching a glimpse at the bumper stickers on Dad's—rather, *this stranger's*—minivan.

One of them: ROMNEY / RYAN.

Another: THE FRESH TASTE, OAKHURST DAIRY.

Another: PROUD PARENT OF AN HONOR ROLL STUDENT.

Then Kelly sees *Girly*, the silhouette of her head bobbing in the passenger side, alone.

Kelly drops her eyes from this minivan and, head down, walks toward her Honda. She'll keep watch from a distance. But it must be Dad, right? The Oakhurst sticker, too big a coincidence, and Kelly doesn't believe in coincidence. No, Kelly believes in cause and effect. She chose not to act, not to save Mom, which has led her here. She walks past her car, then turns around, making a circle. No vehicles coming. She can make a circle. She can pace. Cause and effect, cause and effect. Because she chose not to act, an entire life has happened to her, to Max. But what can she do now? It must be Dad, it must, leaving his daughter in that minivan all alone; it has to be her father going into the store. Proud parent of an honor roll student? That girl looks too young to attend any school with an honor roll. He has another child? How many children? Did Max say anything about Dad having other children? Then again, can she trust Max at all? If she waits for Dad to return with his groceries, she can corner him, *you're my father.* But he will say no. Christ, in front of his daughter? Of course he will say no. Kelly stops walking. She drops her cigarette again. She fumbles for another, but drops that one too before lighting it. She puts her head down on her trunk and puts her hands in her hair, squeezing her forehead, making marks on her scalp with her fingernails. She drags her fingers through her hair as though trying to comb out a nasty knot. Her fingers are threaded with the hair she tore out, didn't mean to tear, but he will say no wherever she questions him, even if she waits for him to go back home, even if she questions him at his front door. She looks at the sky and exhales a cloud of steam, convincing herself for a second that she managed to light that cigarette after all.

What's the fucking point of this trip if he's just going to say no wherever she asks him, whenever she asks him? Miles Bennett will not leave Kelly as easily as he left Mom. She will show him the necklace. But first, she needs his attention.

She shuffles to the minivan, scanning the entrance, about fifty feet away probably, for any sign of him, keeping an eye out. But she can't see him. She doesn't know what she's going to do. She hasn't thought about it yet. But it makes perfect sense, what she's about to do. That's all she knows about it. Perfect sense, whatever it is.

Not many people around. A woman a few spots away, loading her trunk with groceries. Another guy pushing his cart back to a corral. Dad has yet to return. Kelly squeezes next to the minivan, up to the passenger-side door, and sees the little girl in the car. She looks seven or eight and keeps her eyes on her book. She's wearing cute little kid clothes, puffy, turning her into a ball. Her hair is dark, like Kelly's hair, but her eyes don't have those rings yet. Knowing who her father is, she'll earn those rings in a few years.

Kelly knocks on the window. The girl tears her eyes away from the page and sees Kelly. She looks startled. "Hey," Kelly says, knocking again, "don't be scared." But despite this assurance, the little girl looks scared. Kelly fogs the window with breath, then wipes it clean. "Is your name Girly? Is that what Dad calls you?"

Girly stares; then Girly, almost invisibly, nods.

This little girl: her sister. She has Kelly's blood in her body.

"Dad's inside, he told me to come get you. He fell down. Dad fell down. We're calling for help and help's on its way." Kelly glances around. The woman a few spots over has finished loading her groceries and, with her trunk closed, pauses for a moment next to her car. Kelly turns back to Girly. "Your dad said, 'Get Girly.' He told me, 'Get Girly.' You need to open the door."

"What's the secret word?" Girly asks.

Kelly wipes her breath off the window again. "What?"

"What's the secret word?"

"He didn't tell me a secret word, okay?"

Girly stares at her. She doesn't cry. Face turns to stone. Does not cry.

Kelly shakes her head and claws at the window. "Dad's hurt. You need to open the door."

"Is everything okay?"

Kelly snaps away from the window and turns to see the woman looking at her, the woman who just finished loading her trunk. She's older, a little heavy—no other features register. Kelly feels like she sees through this woman, just sees a shape, just an outline of a woman floating there, as though the woman ran away really fast in one of those old cartoons. "It's fine." Kelly puts up her hands. This should make things look fine. "I'm her sister. I just—"

"No she's not," Girly shrieks from inside the car.

"I just got locked out, it's okay."

"No she's not, no she's not."

Kelly starts to back away, hands still up, nodding, trying to look normal, trying to catch her breath. "It's okay." She backs away, the outline of the woman approaching. "It's okay," Kelly says, "I think I have my keys over here."

"No she's not, no she's not."

"What's going on?" Someone says this somewhere else. A man's voice. Kelly doesn't know where, except it's somewhere else.

The outline of the woman turns its head. "Is this your minivan?"

Dad?

"No she's not, no she's not, no she's not." It sounds like Girly is triumphantly singing the chorus of some pop song on the radio.

Kelly rushes off. The outline of the woman yells, "Wait." Kelly slouches as she goes. Her body feels like nothing but air right now. Maybe she'll float away. "Wait," Kelly hears, and she runs. Footsteps behind her. She darts between some cars, trying to keep her body low. Reaches her car, yanks her keys from her pocket, drops them. Footsteps, voices behind her. She crouches to pick her keys up, then stays crouched, holds her hand over her mouth. The outline of the woman hurries past, followed by someone else. Was it Dad? She can't get a look. Their footsteps grow fainter and Kelly stands, unlocks the door, and gets inside. She sinks in the seat just as another person passes, the shadow cascading over her body. Was this person looking for her too? She doesn't know. Trying to breathe—*breathe, breathe*—she turns on the car, surprised by the heat, by the noise of it, and she throws it into reverse and backs out, looking over her shoulder for anyone coming. To her right, an aisle away, she sees the outline of the woman looking at somebody else and shrugging—*I don't know where she went*—and Kelly drives past, across the parking lot, and makes a right onto Preble Street Extension. She didn't even check for oncoming traffic. Pure luck, really, getting back onto the road without an accident; pure luck that nobody was winding that corner when she pulled out. She drives, not going too fast, keeping her eyes in the rearview mirror. She waits for somebody to pull out after her. She feels certain somebody will pull out after her. But she sees nobody. Just as before—just as all morning, in fact—the streets are empty. Kelly feels like this whole thing has been a scene in one of those movies Max watches, when an entire sequence of action takes place in just one long shot, the camera darting, dexterous (she has been spending too much time with her brother). But now it's over. She checks her rearview mirror. Nobody coming for her. No sirens. Nothing has happened. It's over. She checks the rearview mirror again, keeps her eyes on the rearview mirror. Nobody coming. Over now. The camera can cut away.

Kelly drives up Preble Street. Her breath feels short. Everything is starting to come back to her. This whole way, she's been on autopilot, not paying attention to streets, to signs, to other cars, to pedestrians. But now she's fine. She checks the rearview one last time, she promises, one last time.

Her phone rings, the vibration a startling tickle against her thigh. No way anybody from the parking lot has her number, right? No, of course not, just paranoia talking. She struggles with her cell, eventually prying it from her jeans. The screen says RESTRICTED.

Restricted? Who calls from a restricted number?

Kelly hears the horn before she sees the driver coming. When she looks up, it takes only a nanosecond to determine what happened: she blew through a stop sign. Jerking the wheel, her Honda hits a patch of black ice or something, because the car barrels forward, knocks over the street sign, and rams the brick wall across the street from the Preble Street Resource Kitchen, where homeless people wrap around the corner, shivering, waiting to enter and eat lunch. The first thing Kelly notices is the broken windshield—shattered really. Then the smoke, thick and black, looking like pubic hair, billowing from the hood of Mom's eighteen-year-old car. Kelly starts to choke. She sees smoke and chokes on smoke before she smells smoke.

In the moment after a car accident, everything feels indescribably wrong.

The person from the other car comes to her window. "Are you okay?" He looks like even less of a person than the parking lot woman looked like. This person looks like a nonperson. "Are you okay?" But she doesn't know. When she answers she cannot hear her own voice: "Do I look okay? Do I look okay?" She feels all over her face, dreading that she won't feel a face at all. The person—a man, she sees now—tries to open her door, but it's stuck. "Push," he says. She pushes. The door opens like an arm being snapped, a bone being broken.

One last time she checks the rearview mirror. Almost forgets what she's checking for.

The rest of it happens quickly: 911 is called. The police, when they arrive, are indifferent. The paramedics check a few of Kelly's vitals in the back of the ambulance and then give her an ice pack for the air bag burn.

Her car is towed—"Probably totaled," one officer says, "old junker like that," but she'll have to wait for the insurance company's verdict. Kelly turns down the cops' offer for a lift somewhere. She has nowhere to go.

Besides, maybe she'll awaken at any minute—awaken in Arizona weeks ago, before a phone call told her that her father still lives in Portland.

She waits for it. Waits to be *before*. Waits to be elsewhere.

But after slogging a block up the street, she can't avoid where she is, where she *actually* is, because she recognizes a building: 131 Cumberland Avenue. She believes in cause and effect, yes, but this seems like too much.

Mom died there.

Kelly knows nothing of the man in whose apartment Mom's life ended—the man who found her in the bathtub where, inebriated, she had passed out and drowned. Never did Kelly get the chance to ask him anything; after all, the asshole lacked the decency to reach out to the family, or to attend the funeral.

Then again, what could he have said or done? Kelly isn't sure. But he should've said something, should've at least tried.

After Mom's funeral, Kelly decided she wanted to meet this man. So she went to his home, a stout house converted into four apartments. Stepping into the first-floor hallway, her foot crunched something on the ground—a cockroach maybe, although the absence of light made it tough to see. Ahead of her was a steep wooden staircase, so thin and rickety looking it could've been an architectural detail in a horror movie. The place scared her, but if Mom could enter, so could Kelly. She took a few steps, but before she made it far, an apartment door opened a crack. Kelly stopped. The face of a man appeared, craggy and veined, his skin almost translucent. Against his cleaved throat he held an electrolarynx. "Hey," he purred in mechanical monotone, "can you come here for a second?" Kelly stared at him. "Don't be scared," he said, "come here." A sound like running water started, and Kelly looked down. A puddle of rusty liquid came from under his door, hissing warmly. The man kept the electrolarynx against his throat and opened his mouth, but said nothing. Kelly backed off, bolted into the night. How could her mom have let herself die in such filth? Kelly didn't need to know. Lots of things Mom did weren't good ideas; spending time in that building was one additional example.

Today, 131 Cumberland looks mid-disintegration, the shingles flaked off and scattered in the yard. Has anybody tended to this house in the last eleven years, or has it simply been allowed to sit here, to crumble? Kelly climbs over some orange construction tape. Looking up, she sees that part of the roof has been torn away. Someone has pinned an official notice to the door: eviction, condemnation, etc. Soon, the city will tear this place down, will uproot this awful building, wrenching the ghosts away from the land. Kelly hopes this action will contain Mom's spirit— bury it even—and not simply free it to wander elsewhere, following its daughter wherever she goes, curling under her bed, wherever her next bed winds up being.

It looks like an ax has cracked the front door, and Kelly sees inside in slants. She doesn't even need to turn the doorknob, needs only to push, and the door swings open, creaking, the hinges rusted, wearing away. Once again, she steps into the front hallway. This time, Kelly finds another sort of roach: small burned remnants of joints litter the floor, along with cigarette butts and empty cans of PBR and other things probably for drug-related purposes that Kelly doesn't recognize. People break into 131 Cumberland, crawl around the floors, hide from the weather—all until the city of Portland swings a wrecking ball at this building, cracking its head down the middle. Kelly listens for a moment, but she can't hear anything except for herself, except for the rising and falling of her chest as she breathes deeply, her hoodie rustling. She steps forward, over the paraphernalia littering the ground, and she finds the right apartment: number 2 on the first floor. The door is open. She peeks her head in. "Hello?" she calls.

No response. So she steps inside, leaving the door open behind her, just as she found it.

Whatever furniture or appliances used to be here have been scavenged—stolen and sold, maybe, or just stripped for usable parts. Empty plastic bags are crammed into the corners. A gym mat lies on the floor, in the center. There's a candle next to it, but the wick seems burned down.

The floor is covered, just as the hallway was, in cigarette butts and used joints and beer bottles. The only window has a shattered pane, and Kelly spots the culprit on the floor: a rock, with bits of shattered glass around it. The place doesn't smell rotten exactly—just smells the way a wood-shed smells: musty, moist.

Kelly steps into the only other room: a bathroom with a missing door. Water puddles on the ground under a utility sink. Looking up, Kelly sees devastation in the roof, creating a direct line of communication between this apartment and the one right above it. Wind from outside blows in, whistling through the cracks.

And then: the bathtub, which resembles an animal's carcass, cut in two, hollowed out, left victim to nature's decompositional work. The basin has rusted away, dull red chips—almost scabs—lining the bottom of this beast; when Kelly runs her hand along the surface, her fingertips turn the color of brick. She twists the faucet handle, afraid of what will flow from the tap. But nothing comes out. Mom died here, but Kelly can't even make the bathtub fill.

Over the sink hangs a mirror, stained and cloudy, a crack right down the middle. Kelly pushes her face close to it and looks herself over. So much about her seems like Mom—so many features the same. From her pocket, she pulls K.B., unclasps the necklace, and puts it around her neck. Closing her hand around the locket, her palm warms. She looks so much like Mom; Kelly has always known this. But with K.B. around her neck, she can almost envision Mom in this very room, in her last moments—whatever those moments were like.

Then Kelly can't help it: the bathtub pulls her back. And despite the disgusting conditions, Kelly lifts a leg over the side. Before she can stop herself, she is lying in the tub on her back. Overhead, pipes are exposed, and she sees the rusted circuitry of them. Something clear drips onto her hoodie, making the sound of an insect hitting a windshield.

She closes her eyes. Because there's no running water, Kelly has to imagine the miniature ocean collecting around her body, has to imagine her head falling below the rising surface. And what was her mom thinking in those last moments, as she lay in this very spot?

Well, her mom wasn't thinking anything. Mom was passed out. Mom moved into death blindly, unaware of her final escape from what life had done to her.

But then, it wasn't what *life* had done to her. No, that's too abstract. It was Miles Bennett. It was her final escape from what *Miles Bennett* had done to her—that entitled man who took advantage of a college girl, who gave her two children she wasn't prepared to raise, who abandoned them all. Maybe Mom could have done better. But whatever failings she had—and there were failings, of course; failure darkens all human lives—Mom tried. Didn't she try? Yes, maybe she tried in the only way she knew.

Kelly can't imagine what she would have been like if she'd been abandoned with two children when she was twenty-one. She would have been no better. And the way her life is going, how long until she dies alone in a bathtub—or even someplace worse?

Kelly opens her eyes and hears something in the other room—hears the clatter of something running across the floor. She rockets upward in the bathtub, straight-backed, suddenly realizing what a dreadful idea coming here was. A figure darts into the room: Mom's ghost, coming for her daughter, hurtling toward the tub to wrap her hands around her daughter's neck.

But this is no ghost. This is real life.

The old woman stares at Kelly through cataracts, the skin of her face drooping, almost revealing the skull beneath. Her voice comes out as static: "Where's June?"

Kelly forces herself to look at this woman—to fight off the fear and really *see* her. She's so frail, so short, probably not as old as she first looked. She wears a sweater riddled with moth holes, one of its sleeves torn away. Her loose skin is reddened—frostbite maybe. Coming into this barely insulated apartment, shielding herself from the elements in this ramshackle way: this is the best she can do. Yet she survives.

"I'm sorry." Kelly struggles out of the tub. "I'm leaving, I'm leaving."

"June sleeps here. Where's June?"

On her feet now. "I don't know June."

The old woman squints at Kelly. Then all at once, something softens in her face. "Have you been here before?"

Kelly draws in a breath but feels it go right through her, like she no longer has a body to capture the air. Probably this woman doesn't refer to Mom—but for a second, Kelly considers prodding this person into revelations: *Whom do I remind you of? What can you remember about her?* These questions almost slip from Kelly, but no answers would get her closer to Mom. Nor would any answers bring Kelly closer to understanding her own life—or understanding Max's.

What did Mom always tell Kelly to do, in spite of all else?

Look after your brother.

Kelly reaches for K.B. and exhales. Still there.

Man you're a tough critic, huh? You saw zero merit in **Breaking Bad.** **Weerasethakul** *is worthless. You don't like* **Land Without Water.**

I'm not a tough critic, just a correct one.

So what exactly is your problem with my film?

[No response]

What's the matter?

I like you. I don't want to decimate your work.

Oh, please. Roger Ebert gave my film one star. One!

He also gave *Blue Velvet* one star.

Yeah, but **Blue Velvet** *isn't very good.*

Yes! Exactly!

I know Lynch fans aren't supposed to say that but...

It's boring. Trite. Not even that sumptuous visually.

Yeah. And the Hopper stuff is definitely good and Frank Booth is a scary character. But it's still a performance without depth.

You're right. Lynch wants to expose the dark side of small-town America—

—and the dark side of Kyle MacLachlan—

—but the dark side is sort of cartoonish and unimaginative compared with the visceral danger of *Lost Highway* and *Mulholland Drive*.

So you do like antinarrative cinema.

Of course I do.

I thought maybe that was why you didn't like **Weerasethakul**. *Or* **Land Without Water** *for that matter.*

Land Without Water is a well-made film with fine performances and evocative cinematography.

So what's wrong with it?

The problem with *Land Without Water* is that it possesses none of The Sadness.

None of the what?

The Sadness.

It's not sad?

You misunderstand. *The* Sadness.

What does that mean?

M axwell Enright teaches Darren Stanford about The Sadness.
"All great filmmaking beats with the pulse of The Sadness. A director stands on the precipice in anxiety or in misery, his or her life on the verge of ending."

"Huh. That sounds dramatic."

"That director has no choice but to make a film to save his or her own life. Film is a matter of life and death."

"So, Samuel Fuller in *Pierrot*: emotion and all that?"

"No." Max shakes his head and makes a fist. "Absolutely not. It isn't simply a matter of personal expression. The important part is the struggle—the director flailing within the illusion of cinema for his or her own life. That's The Sadness: the struggle. And I'm sorry, but I don't feel that struggle when I watch *Land Without Water*. It possesses none of The Sadness."

"Of course it does. What do you mean? Of course I was struggling."

"But you've given up film. Turned your back. Surrendered in the face of The Sadness."

"How is my abandonment of filmmaking a reflection on *Land Without Water*? It should be taken on its own merits."

"Perhaps I haven't sufficiently explained The Sadness. My apologies."

"No need to be so hard on yourself..."

"Take, for example, Truffaut. His early films—*The 400 Blows, Shoot the Piano Player, Jules and Jim*—are masterworks. One can feel the energy of Truffaut struggling to save his life through cinema. Truffaut was a delinquent, probably destined for prison, or for the morgue. But then he made cinema. His greatest films represent that struggle to live. That's The Sadness."

"But Truffaut made a lot of bad films—really, everything after the ones you're talking about, except *Two English Girls*. Even some much-lauded ones. *Day for Night* and *The Last Metro* aren't very good."

"That's exactly right. Haven't you ever wondered why directors stop being great?"

"But a great director's *always* great, even if the films aren't."

"No. That's the auteur theory. I do not subscribe to the auteur theory. Let me make that clear. There are no great directors. There are great *films*, because the films themselves were made during the director's period of struggle with The Sadness. Bad films come when the director finally wins the struggle. Whenever that happens, they lose their fire."

"So you just fetishize misery and bleakness and all that."

"I do not. The Sadness is redemptive, because at least the director believes in the importance of struggling. But you lack The Sadness. *Land Without Water* is bleak because it presents the world as a horrible place but provides no sense of anything beyond the misery."

"So struggling with misery suggests that there is something at least beyond misery?"

"Yes."

"When do directors who have The Sadness lose it, or win their struggle, or whatever?"

"Usually late in a career—Bergman, for example, or Kurosawa. But it can happen early too. It happened pretty early for Truffaut. *Jules and Jim* was the film through which he won his struggle. After that, all his films are bad. They lack the passion of The Sadness. Even your precious *Two English Girls*."

"That's ludicrous. All directors eventually get bad?"

"No. No. Not all directors. Some never win the struggle."

"Example."

"Buñuel. Cassavetes. Fassbinder. Tarkovsky. They stayed vital until the end of their lives. They were always restless—always struggling through cinema. Hell, even Resnais is still out there, impassioned as ever."

"So let me get this asinine idea straight: you're saying that *Land Without Water*, by definition, can't contain The Sadness, quote-unquote, because I'm never making another film?"

"Or you're never making another film because you don't possess The Sadness."

"So, by your logic, no director who retires can be great."

"Depends."

"On?"

"On whether they won the struggle *before* they retired. But think about it: How many great directors retire?"

"Soderbergh claims retirement. He has his moments."

"Oh please."

Stanford laughs. "Yeah, you're right."

Max smiles.

"But what about Tarantino, who's out there right now saying he'll retire at sixty?"

"Well, he basically agrees with me. The reason he wants to retire is to avoid those late-career calamities that befall a director after losing The Sadness (although he doesn't use my term)—but that isn't how it works, I'm afraid. Anyway, we'll see whether he really retires. I vaguely doubt it, though."

"You're a bizarre human being, you know that?"

"Thanks."

"So you're drawing an arbitrary line between when a director has The Sadness and then loses The Sadness?"

"It's not arbitrary."

"Of course it is. You don't know what was in Truffaut's heart when he was making any of his films. You don't know what was in my heart when I was making *Land Without Water*."

"Except you told me."

"Well, I didn't tell you *everything*."

"You told me enough."

"Okay, fine, forget about me. My point stands, though."

"What point was that?"

"Are you serious? Are you even listening to me?"

"What's your point?"

"Your theory of The Sadness is nonsense. You're drawing an arbitrary line and saying that once a director crosses it, all his or her films become bad."

"Right."

"Has any director lost The Sadness for years and then gotten it back for just one—maybe two—late-career films?"

"That's like asking whether anyone has ever lost one's virginity and then gotten it back for one or two late-life sessions of intercourse."

"Sessions of intercourse? Seriously?"

"When you lose The Sadness, you can't get it back."

"Has anyone ever actually questioned you on this stuff, or do people just tend to assume you know what you're talking about? Because your argument sounds pretty specious."

"Okay, Mr. One-Film. Question me."

"Okay, Mr. Only-Wearing-a-Blanket. You said Kurosawa lost The Sadness. When did he lose The Sadness?"

"After his suicide attempt."

"So then, according to your theory, *Dodes'ka-den* is a bad film?"

"That was *before* the suicide attempt."

"Oh yeah. You're right."

"So that one possesses The Sadness."

"But the other one then... what's it called... *Dersu Uzala*. That's a bad film?"

"Yes."

"*Kagemusha* is a bad film?"

"Yes."

"What?" He says this word like a stepped-on cat.

"*Kagemusha* is a bad film. And so is—"

"Oh no, don't you dare say a bad word about *Ran*."

"Yes. *Ran* too."

"No way, *Ran*? Fucking *Ran* is a bad film?"

"It lacks The Sadness."

"So I bet you think Bergman lost The Sadness after *Cries and Whispers*, thus making *Fanny and Alexander* bad."

"Actually, he lost it after *Scenes from a Marriage*. But otherwise, yes." They stare at each other.

"This is maddening." Stanford shakes his head. "You're deranged."

"Well, you're an *Autumn Sonata* fan, so why should I listen to you?"

"You have one way of looking at the world. That's very dangerous. You can't just try to fit everything into some limited view of how life works."

Max looks around the room. "Are you, of all people, lecturing me?"

"Well, sure, we're both fucked. But at least I know it."

Stanford is wrong. Max knows—most definitely *knows* (but declines to admit it for now).

"So," Stanford says, "what about directors who only made one film, like me?"

"What about them?"

"You claim, because *Land Without Water* is my only film, that I lack The Sadness entirely. Correct?"

"Correct."

"So what about Jean Vigo?"

"He was directing on his deathbed. Literally. And besides, you can't compare yourself to a director who only made one film—well, one *feature* film—because he died. A better example is Klimov, who—"

"No, Klimov made many films. It's just that people only know the one. (Although, he did retire, so I'm curious as to your thoughts about him—but we'll leave that aside for a moment.) A better one-feature-film-only director is my guy, Herk Harvey. Or what about the classic example, Charles Laughton?"

"Are you seriously comparing *Land Without Water* to *Night of the Hunter*?"

"Well... no. But I'm saying—"

A knock rattles the front door. At the sound of this, the filmmaker widens his eyes and sinks into the couch as though shrinking from an attack: "Ford, are you back?" (He went out for sandwiches half an hour ago.)

Max, the protector, stands; with one hand, he clenches the blanket around his body, and with his other hand, he pulls aside the curtain to find (oh, terrific) his worthless sister on the porch, carrying two plastic trash bags stuffed with God knows what. He opens the door a crack.

Kelly, the eternal wuss, shivers and huffs steam like it's something on which she chokes. She stomps her feet. "Lemme in."

"You don't get to come in."

"Seriously."

Max shakes his head.

Darren Stanford resituates himself to identify the visitor. "Your sister again?"

"My apologies."

"The one who used to be friends with Penelope?"

"Best friends," Kelly offers, attempting to circumvent Max's authority—to gain entrance from Stanford himself.

"Let her in. I want to ask her something." The ex-filmmaker stands, straightens his back, becomes a monument.

Max hesitates, refuses for a moment to move. Why would he want her here, his sister? She cares nothing about him, or about Evelyn, or about Mom. She cares only about their wretched father—about his money.

"Let her in," Darren Stanford repeats, his voice stern; Max wonders whether the director formerly used this tone of voice on set. Max sighs and steps out of the way. Kelly breaks in, door swinging (awfully) shut. The click of the latch makes Max feel his sister's violent hand on his face again. He flinches and steps away. Doesn't want to see her. Averts his eyes.

Stanford, on the other hand, grows fearless. He puts his hands on his hips and faces down Kelly. "Do you *really* think it's polite to jabber on and on while somebody's watching a show?"

Kelly frowns and cocks her head. "Is that *really* what you want to ask me?" Like a disrespectful teenager, she mimics the ex-filmmaker's tone of voice.

"No." Stanford takes a deep breath. "Do you know who I am?"

Kelly shrugs.

"Did Penelope tell you where to find me?"

"Frankly, man, I wouldn't care where you are except my brother's here."

"Is Penelope going to keep telling people where I am?"

"How should I know?"

Dismissively, Stanford waves his hand in the air. "I can't believe it. Everyone knows everyone in this goddamned city. I bet you and Penelope knew Evelyn Romanoff too."

Shrugging, Kelly says, "Vaguely. High school. Portland's a small town."

"Can you believe it?" Stanford looks at Max. "Everyone knew her, that poor woman, and I couldn't even find her. Sometimes I hate this fucking world." Stanford hangs his head and touches his cheek as though rubbing stubble (although no stubble—let alone hair—seems to exist on any part of his body). He slumps for a moment, thinking about *Land Without Water* maybe—or thinking about Evelyn and whatever awfulness pulled her beneath the waves.

After a moment, he lifts his eyes. "Hey there, Max's sister—"

"My name is Kel—"

"—what do you think of *Land Without Water*?"

"I don't know. It was kinda weird."

"Kinda weird?"

"Yeah. But I'm not a—"

"What do you think about your brother's whole Sadness notion?"

"The Sadness? I don't know what that means. Max used to say a lot of crazy things. They've all sort of blurred together."

Crazy things? Max sees the redness in his vision and the edges of the room blur—that furious Altman feeling as his temperature flares. Instinctively, his fingers retreat into fist formation. "Do you know how much it hurts my feelings when you say that?"

Kelly's face goes blank. "I was just kidding."

Her tone is soft and conciliatory, but that matters nothing to Max, who shouts, "You've always treated me like shit."

"I'm sorry."

"I've never treated you like this."

"Please, just—"

"Stop talking to me!" The windows rattle on account of Max.

His sister looks to Stanford—maybe for help. But the director just squints at Kelly, apparently not spooked by Max's (admittedly overwrought) outburst. "Max wants to stay with me for a while." Stanford flops onto the couch. "We have an argument to finish."

Kelly looks at her brother. "I know. I'm just bringing his things." She rustles the bags before setting them down. "Do you need anything else? I can run home. Anything you need."

Max doesn't want to turn to her. He's finished talking. So his knees bend. He lands on the couch, next to Stanford. The camera holds his face in tight close-up.

Don't look at her, Max. Don't look.

"Sooo"—Kelly stretches this word, waiting for someone to say something else—"I'm gonna go now."

Nothing.

"Okay. Um. There's stuff here. Make sure I brought everything. I got clothes. Toothbrush. Some ramen. That footage from your film. Let me know what else—"

Christ, no. Max turns to his sister.

So does Stanford. *"His* film?" Then, to Max, he says, "You made a film?"

Kelly raises her eyebrows at Max.

Stanford rubs his hands together. "Oh God, yes. Let me see this." His finger jabs into Max's chest. "I want to see *your* Sadness, my friend."

Max shakes his head, but Kelly goes ahead anyway, removing from one of the bags the old video camera. "My camera's ancient," Max says, his voice spinning like a fan on its highest setting. "I don't know whether you can hook it up to his television."

"Hush. I got it." Kelly plugs the inputs into the television and then stands, blocking the screen, looking at the display on the camera itself.

Max turns to Stanford, who sits on the couch, grinning, a child excited for his birthday. He waits to mock Max. When Darren Stanford sees *The Glazen Shelves* (such a piece of garbage it was), he will discard Max's lessons in The Sadness. Why, after all, would he listen to someone whose own work was so dreadful?

The fan blades in Max's mouth keep turning: "I never finished it, I mean, I ran out of time, I just didn't, uh, I just didn't have time, and I—"

The sound of wind rushing into the room cuts him off, and Kelly steps out of the way, revealing Max's unedited footage from *The Glazen Shelves* on the screen.

Today's date: December 9. Only one month old, this year's winter already feels endless. This year's winter dragged Evelyn into the water, froze her body, spit her out, blue and warped.

But in *The Glazen Shelves*, it's summertime. There's Evelyn on the dock, the sunlight brushing its fingers across her face, the blue of the ocean sparkling behind her, a cape around her shoulders. This isn't the severe black-and-white face of the girl in the newspapers and on missing person posters. This isn't the frozen face in the water. This is Evelyn how she was all those years ago, before the darkness took her.

On screen, she recites the monologue—the one Max made her do again and again:

"I was just a child back then. I realize that now. But I thought my actions would be permanent. Definitive. Can you imagine? I thought I was breaking his heart by not meeting him at the train station. I sat on the bench, feeling like an adult, smoking my cigarette. I was only sixteen. God." A laugh. "I thought my actions were permanent. I thought my life was decided."

"This is it," Stanford says. The hum in him has returned.

"This is what?" Max asks, dreading the answer, what Stanford might say about his film.

"The words she used when she auditioned. This is what she said."

And Max, for just a moment, closes his eyes, and he imagines this scene with a dissolve to the past, Stanford and Hunter sitting with Evelyn as she auditions for *Land Without Water*, the film she never knew was made for her, the camera circling them, circling:

"What a funny thing, to think that, at sixteen, anything of yours, any action, is going to define you. We waste so much time deciding things about ourselves and the people around us, don't we? But that day on the bench, smoking my cigarette, feeling like a goddamned adult—that day, I didn't know how much life I had left to live."

More remains of this monologue (most of which Evelyn constructed from a series of improvisations), but Max stops paying attention to her voice. A million times these words have entered his ear—not only on the Town Landing dock during the months of filming, but also in his bedroom before sleep in the eleven years since losing his actress.

With Evelyn's death fresh in his mind, Max watches this footage without thinking about *The Glazen Shelves*, lamenting its incompleteness; instead, he thinks of Evelyn—tries to imagine what severed her from the glowing version of herself seen on screen and, eventually, pushed her underwater. But he'll never know the solution to that mystery. Darren Stanford was right: Max cannot see into a person's heart just by watching a film.

Evelyn's life wasn't about Max, wasn't about *The Glazen Shelves*.

He turns to Stanford and sees him, captivated by the image of Evelyn, the edges of his face almost seeming softer now (sort of like the edges of a close-up in a silent film). Shaking his head, he says, "I can't believe what I'm looking at. I didn't even know her. Why am I so devastated?"

Should Max answer his question? After all, he knows why Stanford feels so devastated. Here Stanford sits, laying eyes upon Evelyn, upon this young woman whom he built an entire film around. Seeing this footage of Evelyn, Stanford can imagine *Land Without Water*, can imagine the version he always wanted to make. Watching Evelyn on screen has, in this moment, become Stanford's way of watching his own film, of finishing it. So he stares, barely blinking.

Catatonic like this—before a dream flashed on a television screen—Max has passed eleven years of his life, and for nothing. And he knows that Stanford will pass years more, enmeshed in the same futile activity, staring into Evelyn's eyes and selfishly thinking that the ghostly image of them holds some key to the present, or even to the future. But maybe Stanford needs to linger in that place a little longer, as Max lingered there all those years. Max hopes that Stanford moves beyond his memories of Evelyn, but he understands that the ex-filmmaker cannot be forced from the dream—he needs to leave it voluntarily.

But Max knows that he himself can't stay there anymore. He derives no pleasure from gazing upon Evelyn's face. He finds no hope for his own future—however vain (in both meanings of the word)—hiding in her eyes. He sees only the face of a sad young woman who had a life outside of his own—a life beyond *The Glazen Shelves*—that will forever remain mysterious and hidden, like a print of an old film left, through disuse and disregard, to decay, beyond restoration and never to be viewed. Max's work may preserve one moment of her life, but it doesn't encapsulate her.

Maybe it doesn't encapsulate Max either.

Stanford keeps his eyes on the television. If this were a film, he would appear in close-up—maybe would even gaze right into the camera.

What can Maxwell Enright say?

"Keep it."

Stanford breaks from his trance and turns to Max. "What?"

"My film. Keep it."

"Don't you want it? She was your friend. You made this with her."

"No. She wouldn't want me to have it anymore." Max tightens the blanket around him and stands. "I'll come see you again in a couple days."

But Stanford says nothing; already, he's lost again in the film before him.

Kelly stands still, holding those bags, no idea of what has passed here between Maxwell Enright and Darren Stanford. How could she know?

An hour ago, Max would've rather clawed off his own skin than go anywhere with his sister. But now, he notices that necklace around her neck—Mom's old necklace, K.B. He isn't sure what it means to see it on his sister. But it must mean something.

And even if it doesn't, whom else does Max have?

"Take me home," Max says.

"Yeah?" Kelly nods—then, as an afterthought, picks up the plastic bags she brought over. "Do you want to get dressed first?"

"I'll be fine with the blanket." He doubts Stanford will mind lending it to him; besides, Max will return it soon.

As the memory of Evelyn plays on the television, Max will walk away, slow-motion, camera tracking in front of him. Music will swell—but what music? How about the Ennio Morricone score from *Once Upon a Time in the West*, as Claudia Cardinale enters the town, mournful and overwhelming? Or how about the music that ends *8½*—the Nino Rota score, triumphant and bold, to match a man as triumphant and bold as Max? Yes, that's the appropriate music to play as the camera tracks in front of Max, as he passes from the darkness of the house into the light of the outdoors, into the light of whatever is next, yes, yes, as the music reaches closure, as the boy with the flute, the only one left, marches toward the edge of the frame, as the story comes to the end (yes, the real end, the end he couldn't understand eleven years ago, the end he came to understand only today), and the music fades out, and the film cuts to black, and the end titles come up, towering on the screen—

THE
GLAZEN
SHELVES

WRITTEN AND DIRECTED BY

MAXWELL ENRIGHT

(He can dream one last time, can't he?)

There's her brother, eyes gouged by exhaustion, cheeks puffed from Friday's self-mutilation, face drooped like a tragedy mask, body encased in only a blanket out here in the barely-above-freezing temperature—but at least he exited Darren Stanford's house of his own volition. Now, he stares at the sky and squints, even though clouds muffle the sun and make the light dim. He seems better, doesn't he? He seems, if not quite ready to reenter the world, at least ready—as evidenced by his surrender of *The Glazen Shelves* tapes—to try.

Kelly looks around at the bare trees and granite steps. This city block appears old, moneyed. A signpost reminds her of the location: Park Street. It makes her smile, how close Stanford lives to where the Enright siblings grew up—maybe a quarter mile away.

"Where's Mom's car?" Max peers up and down the road.

"It died."

"Died?"

Kelly shrugs. "The engine gave out. We're on foot, I'm afraid."

The siblings start off. With care, they walk along the brick patchwork, watching for frozen streams between the cracks, the salt underfoot scraping the sidewalk. Max keeps his head down, and Kelly examines him. Does he look sad? No, not exactly. He looks like her brother.

"Are you okay?" she asks.

"I don't know," he says—and Kelly believes him.

The list of questions to ask Max scrolls in Kelly's mind, but, like end credits put on fast-forward, she can't make out much—only one question she has been wondering about all morning: "Did you do something to Penelope?"

Max looks at her and swallows. He seems reluctant to answer. But still, his voice mutters, "We were in the water together."

A response—*sort of*, at least.

"In the water? Wasn't it cold?"

Max nods, slouched, knees bent. This time, however, his voice refuses to come.

Kelly guesses that going for a late-night swim in December wasn't Penelope's idea—but she decides now isn't the time to press the issue. "Is that why you took your clothes off? Because they were wet?"

"Yes. We took our clothes off and we sat in the car to get warm. I gave her the blanket from your trunk."

Max and Penelope sitting nude in a car together—who would have been more mortified: Kelly's neurotic brother, or the image-conscious movie star? Maybe each of them simply averted eyes, pretending nothing was happening.

"So she was naked when you dropped her off?"

"I let her keep the blanket."

Kelly tries to imagine the sight of elegant Penelope Hayward entering the ritzy Eastland Park Hotel after dark, shivering, white-faced, a blanket encasing her. How much cash did Ghusson have to slide into the desk clerk's palm to keep that sight secret?

"That sounds fucked up," Kelly says.

"I know."

"I mean, that sounds *really* fucked up. Have you ever thought about talking to somebody? I know it's the sort of thing everybody says but—"

He looks at her sharply. "Yes, it's the exact sort of thing everybody says."

"—but just because it's the sort of thing everybody says doesn't make it wrong."

"Most people are idiots. And I'm working through my problems, I am."

"Most people are idiots, yeah, and you're an idiot too."

"Then so are you."

"Yes. I'm an idiot too. But don't kid yourself. You're not working through shit."

Max keeps his eyes on the sidewalk. Seagulls caw; the siblings are close to the water, to the Casco Bay Bridge. Birds make their music, and a horn blares from the ocean, vibrating the clouds overhead. "I just..." Max shakes his head. He wants to say something. The horn blares again and he looks up, wincing, maybe trying to spot the source of the noise that keeps threatening to gobble up his words. "I have trouble controlling myself sometimes."

"I know you do," Kelly says. "You always did. You used to beat your room up. Used to throw things at the walls. It scared me."

"But I'm getting worse. I can feel myself getting worse."

"Well, I have trouble too sometimes. I have trouble controlling myself too." She considers telling him about earlier—telling him how irrational and frantic the search for Dad made her, how she assaulted a stranger's minivan and uttered that dreadful name, *Girly*—but instead, she bites the inside of her lip, peeling back a layer of skin, letting it sit on the tip of her tongue like a piece of candy whose dissolution she awaits. What she did this afternoon: she'll keep it to herself—will stitch it under her skin and carry it there, unseen, for the rest of her life.

"I have something to tell you," Max says, "but I'm afraid you'll lose your temperature."

"When have you ever been afraid of me losing my temperature?"

"I know where Dad is. I didn't tell you before because I was mad at you. But we can go see him right now. I can take you to him right now."

Kelly's mouth hangs open; she feels the dryness of her lips. "He's close, isn't he?" After Max nods, Kelly asks, "Didn't you ever want to know him?"

"No."

"Why not?"

"Whatever poison he let into Mom's life, I never wanted it in mine. To be with him... to go see him... it would be poison."

Such a simple idea, really: to avoid the things that poison us. Maybe life isn't so much about pursuing happiness but rather minimizing unhappiness. Why not subtract those things that make us miserable? So easy, in theory. Too bad Kelly has never been able to live like that.

Max juts his neck out. Before he says anything, Kelly knows toward what he motions; instinctively, her hand swallows the locket around her neck.

"I never knew you wanted that," Max says. "If I had, I wouldn't have given it away."

"Do you actually remember Mom wearing this?"

Max shakes his head.

"That's funny," Kelly says. "I don't either."

A million memories of Mom often enter Kelly's mind—memories of Mom's absence, memories of her drunken conversations with friends, memories of the phone calls during those last desperate weeks of her life. A million memories whisper a sad story into Kelly's ear.

But today—yes, just for today—she makes a decision for the benefit of her brother, his head hung so morosely as he walks alongside her. Her decision: instead of recalling the wreckage of Mom's life, she will recall something pleasant. Just one little thing. This task is difficult for somebody addicted to—and even comforted by—the feeling of misery (and let's acknowledge the obvious: Kelly certainly fits that description). But at the very least, optimism is something she hasn't failed at yet.

So today, for now, she allows none of the wreckage to enter her mind. Instead, she remembers that one night at dinner, the Thai food steaming on the table, the news on in the background, when Mom, attempting to make fun of the weatherman, said, *Ooh, I'm Joe Cupo and I wish I were made of snow*, holding her hands in the air and fluttering her fingers like spring tree branches holding strong against lashes of wind. They all laughed. It was good. And it wasn't the entire truth of their lives, no— but when does anyone find the entire truth anyway?

They turn the corner. When Kelly sees her old house, she realizes how deeply exhaustion has hooked its claws into her eyelids. Still, she manages to hold on to what Max told her: he knows where Dad is. She can still meet him. Can still do what she came to Portland to do.

The ocean horn bleats again, and then something heavy rattles the street. Kelly knows the sound—the nearby Casco Bay Bridge announcing that it's about to draw upward, allowing a ship to pass underneath.

With this noise coloring the air, Kelly doesn't hear the wheels slowing on the pavement behind her as the police cruiser, by happenstance, pulls up in front of the Salem Street house at the same time Kelly fumbles through her pockets for the key to the front door.

"Kelly Enright?" the officer asks, face hidden behind sunglasses. A second uniformed cop sits in the cruiser's passenger seat, watching the proceedings from the dark.

Kelly turns. "Yes?"

"Did you give this address to the Portland Police Department earlier today?"

"Um, yeah ...?"

"And were you at the residence of Garrett Labrecque on Friday night?"

Not knowing what else to do, Kelly shakes her head.

The cop raises an eyebrow. "You weren't at his residence? Then why haven't you returned our messages?"

Hearing this, Kelly remembers the call she received earlier from a restricted number—but that was right before the crash. When she feels in her pocket now, she realizes for the first time in an hour that her cell phone has gone missing. It must have flown from the car during the accident, or fallen beneath the seat of her pulverized vehicle, or something. "I'm sorry," she says, "but my phone's missing. Broken, I think."

Max looks between her and the officer, flabbergasted.

"Ms. Enright," the officer says, not without kindness, "please come with us."

Kelly takes a look at the back of the police car and its metal grate. Is that where she has to sit? The earth feels liquid under her feet. She tries to balance on a waterbed.

"What's this about?" Max says, his voice steady.

"We'll talk to Ms. Enright about that," the officer says—but of course Kelly knows what it's about. She'd forgotten entirely about Garrett's pledge to contact the police, but it makes an unfortunate kind of sense: she broke their deal. Although it doesn't delight her to take a seat in the back of a police car, a misdemeanor charge—or whatever this will be—feels less severe than what she saw coming earlier today.

"Don't tell them anything," Max says. He sounds firm, almost like a lawyer in a movie, a lifetime of viewing having prepped him to use this sort of authoritative—if pointless—voice. Taking a step toward the officer, her brother says, "Is my sister under arrest?"

The officer rolls his eyes. "Nobody's under arrest. We just need her to come with us."

"I know our rights. You can't take my sister anywhere unless she's under arrest. What's your name, officer? I'll have your badge." Max's protests have become nonsensical—a jumble of lines he has heard actors say in bad films. How close is he to grasping a rock—to beating a face again, either his own or the officer's? If he isn't careful, he might wind up in handcuffs.

"Max." Kelly puts her hand on his arm.

Something in her fingertips seems to calm him. Sure, his eye twitches like he has a speck of dirt stuck there, but he stills himself and takes a breath. He stares at K.B. with the same hazy look he used to reserve for his favorite films.

For just a second, maybe he sees Mom before him.

Kelly remembers Friday, under the Casco Bay Bridge, when she pretended to not know Max. She won't do that again. This is her brother. She knows him.

"It's okay." Kelly squeezes his arm.

"Are you sure?"

"Yes. Just wait here. I'll call you. Can you wait?"

Max nods. Then says, "Do you want to know where Dad is?"

Kelly draws in air, the chill stinging her front teeth. Behind her, she feels the future—whatever it may be—touch her shoulder, preparing to pull her away from where she stands now. And, for once, she feels prepared too.

But first, her brother. His question. Does she want to know?

The flood of bridge noise recedes, and the silence seems to make the air visible, like translucent cloth hanging around them, wrapping the twins together.

Kelly says, "No."

ACKNOWLEDGMENTS

This book was written in Houston (necessarily), Las Vegas (comfortably), Portland (hauntingly), and Tucson (happily).

I share this book with the following people:

Lewis DeJong * Whitney DeVos * Patrick Hanan * Mike Harvkey * Chris Heiser * Liz Marcoux * Ted McLoof * Mark Melnicove * Lynn Moran * Buzz Poverman * Mike Powell * Aurelie Sheehan * Olivia Taylor Smith * Natasha Stagg * Shelton Waldrep * Jonathon Walter

Thank you to the reprobates studying creative writing at the University of Arizona and the University of Southern Maine. Thank you to everyone at Brazos Bookstore.

Thank you to Casco Bay Books, The Movies on Exchange, and Videoport—all now nonexistent.

Of course, above all, I share this book with the McTighes and the Rybecks; and with Bandit, Jen, Milo, Monster, Rex, and Stella—all of whom share the surname "Holland."

PHOTO BY CORBY KELL

ABOUT THE AUTHOR

BENJAMIN RYBECK is marketing director at Brazos Bookstore in Houston, Texas. His writing appears in *Electric Literature, Houston Chronicle, Kirkus Reviews, Ninth Letter, The Rumpus,* and elsewhere. *The Sadness* is his first novel.

PRAISE FOR *THE SADNESS*

"*The Sadness* is a novel with film noir appeal: gritty and absorbing, with just a touch of glamour. Morally ambiguous siblings Kelly and Max, each compelled by their own obsessions and failures, succumb to the pull of home in order to resolve the crippling events of their pasts. With vivid, measured prose, Benjamin Rybeck delivers his characters from the depths of madness toward a quietly optimistic end, in which they discover something far more important than what they thought they were searching for: each other."

— CHRIS CANDER, AUTHOR OF *WHISPER HOLLOW*

"You'll hear among the many declarations of Benjamin Rybeck's single-minded protagonist in *The Sadness*, 'Film is a matter of life and death... the director has no choice but to make a film to save his or her own life.' While this sentiment is shared by others, Maxwell Enright delivers it more as personal manifesto, a possessory truth to which you had better listen. Rybeck has created a razor-sharp blade held with unflinching certainty, the kind only possible within the labyrinthian and door-kicking noisy head of a young artist fighting to find a way out."

— TODD FIELD

"Benjamin Rybeck's *The Sadness* is a book full of wisdom about the fumbling, grasping attempts we all make to fill the emptiness inside us, a book that ultimately leaves the reader feeling less alone in the world."

— JOSHUA FURST, AUTHOR OF *THE SABOTAGE CAFE*

"With this impressive debut, Benjamin Rybeck perfectly captures what it's like to be young and lost, unprepared for adult life, and utterly broken by the past. Rybeck has so much to say— about celebrity, cinema, family, and art as both a weapon and a shield— and he says it all with great intelligence and wit."

— MIKE HARVKEY, AUTHOR OF
IN THE COURSE OF HUMAN EVENTS

"Often humorous, sometimes touching, newcomer Rybeck's tale of youthful woe portrays a generation full of promise as it runs aground."

— PUBLISHERS WEEKLY

"*The Sadness* is a rapturous, absorbing and wholly original novel that announces Rybeck as a surprising and inventive young writer."

— KRISTEN RADTKE

The Unnamed Press
P.O. Box 411272
Los Angeles, CA 90041

Published in North America by The Unnamed Press.

1 3 5 7 9 10 8 6 4 2

ISBN: 978-1-939419-70-5

Library of Congress Control Number:
2016940594

This book is distributed by Publishers Group West
Designed & typeset by Jaya Nicely
Cover art by Matt Molloy

Nick Flynn, excerpts from "Elsewhere, Mon Amour" from *Some Ether*.
Copyright © 2000 by Nick Flynn. Reprinted with the permission
of The Permissions Company, Inc. on behalf of Graywolf Press,
Minneapolis, Minnesota, www.graywolfpress.org.

This book is a work of fiction. Names, characters, places and incidents
are wholly fictional or are used fictitiously. Any resemblance to actual
events or persons, living or dead, is entirely coincidental.